Denis Kehoe was born in Dublin in 1978, where he now lives. He has studied philosophy and European literature and works as a critic, researcher and literacy tutor. *Nights Beneath the Nation* is his first novel.

Praise for *Nights Beneath the Nation*

'Kehoe writes this engaging tale of long-buried secrets with poetic flair' *Gay Times*

'Vivid… a bold and confident debut… This heartfelt tale of love, loss and the possibilities of redemption marks out Denis Kehoe to be a very promising writer indeed' *Attitude*

'This is a remarkable, sharply observed and engaging book which deserves to be well received. Although most of the central characters are gay it is not a gay novel, nor indeed even a book about being gay; it is a book about being alive and being human in Ireland from the 1950s to the present day… the very period is caught in an extraordinary feat of creative memory… Part mystery, part love story, this remarkable first novel has for me echoes of that wonderful Spanish novel *Shadow of the Wind*. I lived through most of the period described in this book and I can attest to its authenticity – that's exactly how it was. Read – and grieve – and celebrate' David Norris, *Irish Independent*

Nights Beneath
the Nation

Denis Kehoe

A complete catalogue record for this book can be obtained from the British Library on request

The right of Denis Kehoe to be identified as the author of this work has been asserted by him in accordance with the Copyright, Designs and Patents Act 1988

First published in this edition in 2009 by Serpent's Tail
First published in 2008 by Serpent's Tail,
an imprint of Profile Books Ltd
3A Exmouth House
Pine Street
London EC1R 0JH
website: www.serpentstail.com

ISBN 978 1 84668 679 5

Designed and typeset in Plantin by Sue Lamble
Printed and bound in Great Britain by
CPI Bookmarque Ltd, Croydon, Surrey

10 9 8 7 6 5 4 3 2 1

Mixed Sources
Product group from well-managed
forests and other controlled sources
www.fsc.org Cert no. TT-COC-002227
© 1996 Forest Stewardship Council

To Paddy, Mary and Paco

Thanks to

Ian O'Rorke, John Williams, Lisa Downing, Andy Davis,
Roisín Maguire, Noëlle Deegan, Darragh O'Grady,
Cathal Kerrigan, Paul McGrath, Kelly-Anne Byrne,
Joseph McCann, Sinéad Hawkins, Charlotte Greig,
Pete Ayrton, Niamh Murray, Ruthie Petrie, Rebecca Gray,
Anna-Marie Fitzgerald, Claire Beaumont, Maureen Neville,
Sue Esterson, Carol McDermott, Mary Maher, John Aboud,
Liz Stein, James Nunn, Aidan Bradley, Olivia O'Flanagan,
David Norris, J. W., D. D., Tom Rabbit, Tonie Walsh,
Regan Hutchins, Keenan Furlong, Brian Finnegan, Tomas,
Aniz Duran, Stephen Place, Rose Marie Tierney,
Matt Stewart, Frances Shackleton, Siobhán Purves,
Max Hafler and most importantly, Maria.

1

September 1997

IT IS A SUNDAY EVENING. I never thought I'd end up here, an American in Dublin, sitting in a silent house that overlooks the sea, at the start of an Irish September. I try not to think, try not to sink, in September. There are pink streaks of promise stretched across the low, grey sky so I suppose it will be a good day tomorrow, but who cares. Days pass. Outside the window people are going home after their day at the sea; moving slowly, lingering in the last light of the day, remembering the sun on their skin and thinking of the summer that could have been but was not. They're hoping they'll get an Indian summer, I guess, a last minute consolation after the cheating months that have passed. I don't believe they get much good weather here. Even days in June can be damp and dull and drive the people close to depression.

There is a group of old folks who go swimming every afternoon down by the tower at the end of the street. They look ridiculous, those wasted creatures with their liver spots and body rot, giggling and chatting like teenagers, their bones creaking with the years as they bend to take off clothes and put on bathing caps. Somebody told me they come here every day of the year, and though I find it hard to believe, I can just imagine it. Those little Irish pensioners wrestling what they can from what is left of their lives, their daily bathes in the bay a battle against time, a battle they are sure to lose. I passed them by on Thursday afternoon as I walked up to Dún Laoghaire. There was an old couple drying themselves after their swim. Their skin was slack and their limbs absurd, brittle and little against the city. They said hello cheerily enough and I nodded a greeting before I walked slowly on, laughing to myself.

Later though, sitting in a café on the main street, I was looking out the window when I caught a reflection of myself in the glass. My coffee turned bitter on my tongue when I saw that seventy was no longer an abstract number, but just a few short years away. I saw seventy staring back at me and I hated those old, wrinkled water rats, hated them because I am just like them.

Why am I writing this, I wonder. What use have I for words? What use are words to anybody? I fell out of love with language a long time ago, with beautiful, quivering emotions lying naked on the page. They only make me feel empty now; all those precious thoughts and suffocating sentences. Once, yes once, a long time ago, I had hopes of becoming a writer. I dreamed of writing novels, plays and poems that would have them reading well into the night, and standing applauding in the aisles and wondering how it was that words could be wound around each other so skilfully. But what does that matter? That was a long time ago, when I believed in truth and tears and stupid little stories. Before I came to control words instead of allowing them to own me. Before I began to use them only to get on, to get exactly what I wanted. But here I am, writing again.

Why am I here anyway? I guess I needed a break, a rest, needed to take things easy. I'm not sick, I'm not dying. Don't you dare think of me as wasting away out here by the sea. I just needed some time away from home, some time out. I've grown tired of New York, or tired of life, or maybe it's the same thing. Listen to me; I never thought I'd say that. I never thought I'd tire of that metropolis, with its movers and shakers, its freaks, flakes and moneymakers, its dazzle and brute ambition. I love that city of indecency and opportunity, of noise and grit and greatness, all manner of human life moving between its great glass palaces.

I made it in New York, where you either have the balls, the willpower and the sheer determination to succeed, or you don't. I did, others didn't, and I don't care anymore if that makes me a good or bad person. I'll leave the moralising to somebody else.

I began my career working for a Jew in a barbershop on the Lower East Side. My customers were mostly immigrants from Russia and Ukraine. When I had saved enough money, I opened up my own shop over in the West Village. I knew the fags over there wouldn't mind splashing out a bit of money on a nice coiffure. This was in the early sixties, before Stonewall and all that jazz, but the area was already crawling with them, everybody knew that. It was the first hip men's hairdresser down that way, all whitewashed walls and the odd geometric pattern. Everything was clear and clean and kept to an absolute minimum and they loved it: the drags, the fags and the little men in suits who came downtown on Friday evening for some furtive pleasure. I suppose it was the fags who made me, who made my business a success. I suppose I should be grateful to them for that.

After a few years I got my hands on another shop in the area and eventually opened a salon, a much more high-class affair, on the Upper East Side. I could smell the money there. A lot of it old money that had been in Manhattan for generations. I could see that these men would have to be pampered and charmed and treated like the royalty they believed they were. They weren't difficult or rude or unfriendly, but as with any customers in business, you had to work out how to work them. And so I indulged them, I listened to them and threw parties for them. I allowed them to wallow for hours in the luxury of the place and they loved it. It was, of course, another hit.

And so on, and so forth. Onwards and upwards and so it goes, my story of success in the city, stretched as it is over the decades. Always bigger, always better, until I owned six 'male grooming salons' in Manhattan, a big apartment on the Upper West Side and a summer house up the coast.

But then a year, maybe two years ago, you can never be sure exactly when these things happen, I began to lose interest in New York. It was all noise and hungry, rapid movement and all I wanted was to sit still some place that was silent. My ambition was spent, my thirst was satiated and my patience was finally strained. I became irritated with the hordes of people that rise and fall like waves along the city's streets. I became anxious about small, unimportant things, indifferent to the business and appalled by all the people I know. In short, I felt used up by the city of my success.

At first I tried not to listen, but slowly I came to the conclusion that it was time to take a break, to get some real time away. I realised I was no longer happy there. No, that's not it. Happiness is an illusion. That's something you realise as you get older. Happiness, and whoever said we had a right to be happy was a fool. That holy grail of the modern age, waved in front of wide-eyed believers. And I'm not saying that my money made me miserable. Money has made my life a lot more comfortable. It's made life bearable. You ask those crazies living underground if they're happy in their subway shantytowns and see what they say. Happiness, no I'm not saying I've lost it and want to get it back. I'm just saying I need a break, that my head is full and I feel empty and tired, that none of it seems to make sense anymore. So I came here to Dublin, to this house in Seapoint, came here to get some time out.

But that isn't the whole truth. There was a little old woman working in the dry cleaner's the other day who asked me what part of America I was from. I looked her straight in the eye and lied to her just as I've been lying to you, to myself. I said I was from from New York. What was the alternative? To admit that I do not come from the States at all, and that I am in fact from Ireland. Not from Dublin, no, but from a town in the southwest. To tell her that once, almost fifty years ago, when I was twenty, I spent a year in Dublin, a year that started in a September much like this one and ended in his death. That I fled this city with bloodied hands and I have never been back since. That I have spent half a century across the Atlantic, trying to forget where I came from, and, thinking I had succeeded, I found, one day, that all I wanted was to come back, come back and write down what happened.

September 1950

YOU NEED A LEVEL HEAD and a steady hand to write about your own life, to look at it objectively, unblinkingly and put everything you see down on paper. I'm not sure I'm doing the right thing, writing about that year I spent in Dublin, but something tells me to go on, that at last it's time to tell my side of the story. Each time I go to start writing though, I find there is more and more to explain, that there are countless events, both big and small, that led me out of Kingsbridge Station and into the city that September morning in 1950. I find myself getting lost amongst the years and stories that are not always my own. I feel as though I'm being pulled this way and that, that there could be any beginning even though the ending will always be the same.

I suppose my childhood would be a logical place to start, if logic can be imposed on something as slippery as a life. A lot has been written about Irish childhoods. Too much, if you ask me. Misery can always be turned into money. I can't say my childhood was miserable. It wasn't interesting enough to be miserable. It was a childhood typical of the place and time in which I grew up, and like that place and time it was, for the most part, uneventful.

I was born in 1930, into a Free State of broken dreams

and bitter grievances. I was the youngest of four children, with two boys and a girl before me. Michael was the eldest and he behaved as the eldest brother normally does; part protector and part tormentor. He tended to keep his distance, acting as if he was superior to myself and the others, until he got bored and came to bother each of us in turn. Next was Kathleen, who was a bit of a tomboy, probably because she grew up in a house full of males. Seán was a year older than me and, being next to one another, there was a lot of rivalry between us. He was a good kid and quiet for the most part, but you didn't want to get on the wrong side of him. He had one of the worst tempers I've ever seen.

Like most brothers and sisters, we enjoyed one another's company some of the time, and the rest we fought like cats and dogs. During the summer holidays especially, the most minor occurrence would turn into a full scale row, which would only be broken up when my mother would threaten that we'd all be sent off to Letterfrack, a real life prison for the boldest boys and girls in Ireland.

My father had taken over the family barbershop when his father died of tuberculosis, or consumption as we called it. It wasn't exactly what he'd had in mind during his days as a young rebel, fighting in the Tans War and the Civil War, but by then he had a young family and they were his priority. At least the shop would provide them with a roof over their heads and enough money to get by on.

The barbershop was on the main street, and Friday evening and Saturday afternoon were the busiest times, when us kids were banished from the place. When it wasn't so busy, or on rainy days when we thought we would die of boredom, my father let us sit in the shop, but only if we were very quiet. It always seemed so warm there, and the air smelled of shampoo, soap and Brylcreem. I became fascinated by the place on those days as I watched my father at work; the rapid movement of his fingers as he snipped at somebody's hair, or the careful manoeuvre of his hand as he ran a deadly razor along a throat that had been tilted back, all the while keeping a conversation going. It all seemed so effortless. Most of the customers we knew, but those we didn't became the heroes and villains of our stories. One was a movie star, one was a murderer, and another was a man with a limp, who had lost three toes in the Boer War.

Our town was medium-sized and in the southwest of the country. The name does not matter. All towns in Ireland are much the same, with more pubs than streets and more gossip than good sense. It wasn't an idyllic or very exciting place, but for many years it was the centre of my world, and there was a great comfort in living somewhere you could know inside out. Life was simple there. There was school, hurling practice, mass on a Sunday and whatever fun was to be had or books were to be read in between. There were the lanes to play in and there was the endless countryside to wander in during the summer break, wondering if the world ever did end or if it went on for ever as we looked out at the rolling hills.

It seemed like the most normal of places, but looking back on it now, some strange events took place there. One of these was the annual open day at the local mental institution, or the asylum, as we called it. As children we were terrified of that ancient red brick building full of crazy people: men who had killed their own mothers, women who thought they were twenty people when they were really only one, and perverted men who did terrible things to other men and who were a danger to young boys.

My father never went to those open days. He said the people of the town only went to make themselves feel normal and superior, and that it was disgusting, how they stared at the inmates as though they were animals in a zoo. To me though, the inmates were much more frightening and dangerous than any animals I had ever seen because some of them looked just like regular people. That was the scary thing. Apart from the ones who drooled, or rocked themselves back and forth, and apart from the special clothes they all had to wear, you couldn't actually tell the crazies from the people of the town. One of those smiling, friendly men might have been a murderer or a pervert and you wouldn't know just by looking at them.

Sometimes, when I got older and my mind began to go funny and play tricks on me, I would think of that place, telling myself I would end up there if I didn't pull myself together. I was careful never to speak to anyone about what went on in my head, in case I was carted off to the asylum by my family. I suppose I was lucky I never did wind up there.

There were also moments of magic in the town though, like the night a travelling theatre company put on *A Midsummer Night's Dream*. That was the night I discovered the theatre and realised that two parallel realities could exist side by side, the world of the town that we knew so well, and that fantastical world that was there before our eyes, close enough to touch. I didn't know how then, but I promised myself that one day, beneath the cover of darkness, I would slip into that other world, into the world of the theatre.

The Ireland of my childhood might have been a peaceful place, but all over Europe conflicts were breaking out. I was just a little kid when the fighting began in Spain in the summer of 1936, and though Franco's rebellion didn't mean much to me in the beginning, I can still remember how that civil war came to our town, our home, that autumn.

We were at mass one Sunday, and I was busy staring up

at the angels on the ceiling, when I noticed that the priest was very angry about something. His voice was booming and, when I looked at him, I saw that his face was very red. I could hardly follow, never mind understand, what he was saying, but I do remember hearing the words Communists and Bolsheviks spat out as if they were poison. I also remember him beaming as he spoke about Irish men who wore blue shirts, saying they were a great credit to the nation, heading off to Spain to fight for Catholicism with a man called General Franco.

When we got home that morning, we had our own drama. I had never known my father to be violent, but on this occasion he looked as though he could kill ten men with his bare hands. As soon as we got through the front door, just barely out of earshot of the neighbours, he exploded in a tirade; cursing a man called O'Duffy, cursing the priest who had said mass, cursing de Valera, cursing the people in the church, the town and even in the whole country. My mother pushed us up the stairs, from the top of which we continued, frightened and amazed, to listen to what was going on, to this man who had recently been our father but was now somebody else. On and on he went until we heard him say he'd had enough of this shit, this hypocrisy, and that he was off to join the International Brigades, that somebody had to fight for justice. He slammed the front door shut behind him.

He never did join the International Brigades, but turned up the next morning, looking tired and smelling of drink. In the years that followed, I would sit with him and listen to events in Spain unfold on the wireless, or listen as he read newspaper articles out loud. His tone would be cheerful or worried, depending on the day, until one afternoon it was finally defeated, and he said there would be no more articles. Franco's troops moved into Madrid soon afterwards.

As soon as this war ended another one began and this, they said, was the big one. This would be the war to end all wars, what became known as World War II, and what we knew as the Emergency. I wondered when the Germans would roll into our town in their tanks, just as they had rolled into a place called Poland, and waited in anticipation for the action to begin, until somebody told me that the Free State was neutral, whatever that meant.

There was a lot of censorship during the war, so we didn't always know what was happening outside, but I do remember the day I heard about the concentration camps. For years afterwards I had nightmares I was a prisoner in one of those extermination camps, waking up just before the gas choked me. When Hitler committed suicide in his bunker in Berlin, de Valera went to offer his condolences at the German Embassy in Dublin. I wondered why he was sorry that Hitler was dead, and if he hated the Jews or just hated Britain. I tried talking about it at school, but most of the teachers were Fianna Fáilers and they didn't want to discuss it.

When I was sixteen, I went to Dublin for the first time. My mother usually went up to the capital every December. She would do her Christmas shopping and visit a sister of hers who was working as a nurse in the Mater Hospital. Normally she went on her own and we were left at home. I suppose it was the only break she had from us for the whole year, and besides, my parents couldn't have afforded the train fare for all of us. This year though, for some reason, she asked me if I wanted to go with her and I jumped at the chance. In those days going to the 'Big Schmoke' for the day was a big adventure.

I will never forget that first trip to Dublin. It was a frosty Saturday morning when we arrived, but even in the misty, crisp white air, the place seemed to be full of life. The trains hissed and screeched in and out of Kingsbridge Station, and from the tram I saw smoke billowing from the enormous Guinness plant, and then the splendour of Christchurch Cathedral, both on the other side of the River Liffey. A minute later, on our left, was the Four Courts, which had burned for days during the Civil War. Meanwhile shoppers were crossing the Ha'penny Bridge that arched over the river, passing from north to south and back again.

We went to all the big department stores that day, huge places like Clerys and Arnotts, where the best looking girls I had ever seen stood invitingly behind the make-up counters. We had lunch at Woolworths on Henry Street. On Grafton Street there were glamorous women and men smoking American cigarettes, and I couldn't help feeling like a little bumpkin next to them, try as I might to imagine myself a sophisticated hero in a smart Hollywood film. Dublin seemed a whole world away from our town, where the seasons came, the seasons went, people grew old and died, and nobody was ever any the wiser.

From the time I returned home, I had one great ambition; to get out of my town and go and live in Dublin. I suppose I had been growing bored and frustrated with provincial life for some time, and that trip to the city cemented those feelings of discontent. I realised I was different. No, perhaps that isn't true. I realised I wanted something different, and that little town life didn't satisfy me. I looked at my future there and it wasn't enough, wasn't what I wanted. It wasn't that I was aloof and put a great distance between the other people and myself. That wasn't it. I did well at school, at sports, and I was well liked. I had a gang of friends I would hang around with after school and at weekends. It wasn't that I was so different, more that I saw myself doing something else entirely, living a life that was full and exciting up in Dublin. And while they might settle for one of the local country girls, I was deter-mined to take out one, or perhaps more, of those foxy ladies I had seen behind the make-up counters up in Dublin that Saturday.

I grew to hate my town, with its whispering walls of twitching curtains, with its cheer and its false smiles, with its gossip and good humour, and with its explosions of violence every weekend, when the drink left all the lads either angry or in agony. I became irritable and critical, and began to argue more and more with my parents. I suppose I was terrified I would end up like them; compromised and conformed, emo-tionally deformed. I wanted out.

It was after I came back from Dublin that I met John. John was about the same age as me, and lived in an enormous house outside the town. His family were Anglican, and while the 'locals' were never outrightly hostile to them, they always looked upon them with suspicion, always had something to say about them, and always kept their distance. We met when I was out for a walk one Sunday afternoon. He asked me for a light, we had a smoke together, and spoke about how much we hated where we came from.

I started spending a lot of time with John. He was different to the other friends I had. He was the first person I could talk about things, really talk about things, with. He was clever and rebellious, and he didn't care if the toothless townsfolk despised him. I wanted to be just like him. We planned to move to Dublin together. He was going to study at Trinity, and I would get a job in the Civil Service. We'd share a flat, throw wild parties, and have classy girls stay the night.

I was all set to apply for the Civil Service, not long after I had finished the Leaving Certificate, when my father was diagnosed with tuberculosis and the doctor sent him to a sanatorium in Wicklow for the best part of a year. There was no question of me going to Dublin now. As Michael, my eldest brother, said, 'The family has to pull together in times like these.' He was right, of course. He had been running the shop with my father for a while, and there was no way he could manage on his own. I had picked up some tips over the years, had even managed a few haircuts on the customers when they were stuck, and with Seán in England, that left me as sole and natural candidate for the job of assistant barber in my father's shop.

I felt terrible about my father. Tuberculosis was a serious disease in Ireland back then. At the same time though, selfish as I was, I went into a black mood, thinking I would be stuck there for at least another year. By that time I thought I would suffocate if I had to spend another week in the town, and suddenly the weeks had multiplied and spread out before me like a never-ending purgatory. But my father was sick, and helping him and my family mattered above everything else. John left for Trinity just as I began working in the shop, and though I would see him again when he was back for the holidays, our friendship was never the same.

Winter came early that year, and ate into the spring of the following one. I got on well enough with Michael. He had grown up, and as an adult he was good to me. I learned a lot during my time working with him, skills I could put to use and turn into money, so much money, in New York. But the incessant chatter of the local men who came in drove me insane, with their talk of animals and crops, of hurling and football. They might have grumbled about their wives, but to me they were worse than gossiping old women, with their petty grievances and endless complaints. I wondered if they too had once been young men who had dreamed of escape, only to find themselves trapped; watching, disbelieving, as their lives slipped away and they became the fathers they had once defined themselves against.

On more than one occasion, when I had lathered their faces and they were ready for a shave, I thought about slipping that sharp blade into the the fat, pink flesh of their necks, if only to shut them up. I would see myself laughing as their eyes filled with shock and the warm blood spurted out of them. Instead, and with a steady hand, I did an expert shave on each and every one of them, before dusting them off and saying goodbye.

Eventually my father came home, a veteran of the worst war he had ever fought; his personal war against a bitter disease. He still wasn't in full health, so I stayed working in the shop until he was strong enough to come back full-time. It was good to have him home, even though I had come to resent him for being a hero who had hung up his boots and settled for a life of mediocrity. During those months before I left there were a few moments, all too few, of real communication between us, but one or other of us always pulled away; the awkwardness of the Irish male.

Around this time, I applied for a job as a clerk in the Department of Education and though the competition was fierce, I did the exam, went to the interview, and not long afterwards received a letter saying that I had been successful. I had made it. I was off to live in Dublin.

It was a sunny morning when I left. Bright with golden September sunlight, as if nature had put on its best coat to wish me on my way. There was a sadness that morning, and a feeling of panic in my stomach. Okay, I was only off to Dublin, but that was a big deal in those days. People didn't move around like they do now. Once you went to live somewhere, it was generally for life. My mother was tearful as another of her sons left. She gave me a silk tie and embraced me more warmly than she ever had before. I felt a mother's love and I could not speak.

My father gave me a barber's kit that must have cost him a small fortune. There were scissors in different sizes, a comb, a razor and a brush for lathering the soap. 'This is so you can make a bit of extra money if you need to,' he said. Then he handed me something else, a long, slim velvet box that looked as though it had seen better days. It creaked as I opened it. Inside was a razor blade with a carved ivory handle. It was my father's razor, said to have been picked up in the south of Spain by an adventurer of an ancestor, and passed down through the generations. I took it out and ran my finger along its edge. There was a drop of blood. 'Ouch.' I grimaced. 'Be careful with it,' he warned, 'it's very sharp.' I smiled. 'That it is.' 'Good luck, son,' he said, and put his arms around me, something an Irishman never did at the time. There was an awkward silence, but Michael broke it with a joke as he shook my hand. I took Kathleen in my arms. I knew I'd miss her, but by then she was married to the son of a local grocer and had started a new life of her own anyway.

The five of us went to the station and there was one last goodbye before I stepped up into the train. And then I was off, off to start a new life in Dublin, capital of the Republic of Ireland, declared just a year before. Off to begin a new life, another life in the new nation.

I've been crying as I write this. I know, sometimes I even surprise myself. It's just that thinking about my father, my mother and those raw, tender emotions that morning still hurts. You think that memories fade with time, but it's not true. You might go through decades without thinking about it and then one September morning, when the sun shines a certain way, or the air smells the way it can only in that month, you find yourself back in that town, barely twenty years old but full of plans and hopes for the future. Only you're not. You're a man who is almost seventy, a man who once, on a morning in September, felt loved as he left his family for a new life. Fight against it as I might, that gets me even now. Damn these melancholy Irish Septembers!

2

October 1997

HALLOWEEN NIGHT IS HERE. For weeks fire-crackers have been exploding and fluorescent colours have been lighting up the night sky. It's become more and more like the States on this island. The amount of Halloween trash in the shops is unreal: banners and plastic pumpkins, synthetic costumes and candles in the shape of skulls. Witches' broomsticks hang from hall doors and I have seen rows of cardboard skeletons stretched across windows in homes around the city. I guess the kids all want candy or hard cash now. The days of any apples or nuts are long gone. I imagine they'd throw the fruit right back at you if that was all you dared hand them.

I'm not superstitious, and I don't buy most of that New Age bullshit that is becoming more and more popular, but there is something in the air here at this time of year, something I haven't felt in decades. Something, dare I say it, spiritual. Perhaps it's just the changing of the seasons, or the sharp taste of these sunny, autumn days, or the thick fog that rolls in from the sea. Or maybe it's just the fact that I am suddenly surrounded by nature after so many years in New York City. Oh, I probably just have too much time on my hands, and that is what happens when you're not working and you spend your days alone. You begin to walk, to watch, to listen, in between bouts of driving yourself demented.

I didn't want to be at home on my own tonight, this Halloween night, so I came into town. I came in to get some air and to be amongst people, instead of sitting thinking of my dead. My dead are gone, my dead are buried, my dead they are no more. But here I am, sitting in Bewley's on Grafton Street, and it's hard not to think of them.

I come here sometimes when I'm in town. It's one of the only places I can recognise on this street that has changed so much. I can sit here for hours, watching what is going on. As darkness falls crowds of people pass through the big open doors at the front. Some stop to buy packets of tea and sticky buns off the women behind the great glass counters filled with cakes and breads. Others take the stairs to the small restaurant above, whilst a cluster of people enter the tiny, creaking lift that will take them to the theatre upstairs. I always walk into the main room of the café, following the dim yellow light coming from the dusty chandelier.

In the past they had waitresses here and in all the other cafés, women who would come to your table, smile good-naturedly and take your order. It's all self-service now, but there is an attractive army of energetic young men and women from all the countries of Europe marching about the place and looking incredibly busy. The girls are dressed like Edwardian maids and the guys like minstrels. They move about the enormous café at a fantastic speed, collecting crockery and crumbs from the tables, reminding me of tiny insects scuttling around and picking up things here and there.

The place is always busy at this hour. Everywhere there is movement and sound; chips sizzling in fat, the clanking of plates and cutlery, bejewelled hands reaching out for creamy cakes, the hissing of steam from the coffee urns, and an endless line of customers moving with their trays of food.

Later on, when the clamber and clutter of dinner hour has subsided, the artists, intellectuals and misfits descend on the café. They are a funny, eclectic lot: the two men dressed in Victorian clothes, the old hippie who will not accept that peace and love are the talismans of a lost age, and the young poet who steals off to the toilet to shoot junk into his veins when he thinks nobody is looking. The café might look a bit different, but in other ways it is much the same. It is still a haven for oddballs.

I'm sitting by the fire in the corner now, where I always sit if I can. Here on this burgundy velvet couch that is now torn and faded, that has seen and heard so much. Here beneath the stained glass window. There is a momentary lull, all the noise around me suddenly disappears, and it's October 1950. I look up and I see the most amazing creature walk into the café. I've seen her here before. She's wearing stilettos, a black coat, and on her head is a small hat, tilted at an angle. Her dark hair has been pulled back and not a strand of it is astray. Her face is frozen, unmoving, and the lips are painted scarlet. I feel a surge of desire, a strange kind of desire, as I look at her. Her eyes fall on me, pick me apart, and leave me an embarrassed, red-faced mess, looking anywhere but at her.

A few seconds later I glance back up at her, just to get another look, and I see that she is staring at me, that her eyes are eating me up hungrily, that she's walking towards me. She walks up to me, her head thrown back. 'Would you mind if I joined you?' she asks, and before I can give her an answer she is sitting beside me on the couch, lighting a cigarette. She puts the long black cigarette holder up to her lips, inhales deeply, and slowly, slowly, exhales.

It is fully dark now, and I can hear the fireworks in the distance. I can't stop thinking of her. Thinking of Maeve and that first night we spoke, when she came and sat down beside me. Thinking that if she hadn't come up to me, sat by my side, and casually lit her cigarette, then what would happen might never have been. My life could have been so different, if I hadn't met Maeve, if I hadn't gone to that Halloween party in her house, if she hadn't introduced me to Anthony and Fitzer, to García Lorca and his *Blood Wedding*. His blood might not have spilled, spilled and stained me for half a century.

Maeve died earlier this year. I had to know, had to know if she was dead or alive, so I went to the births and deaths registrar. She died of a cancer that had been eating away at her for years. I hope she was at peace, that she knew she had given all she could to life and that it was finally time to let go, to draw her last breath. Maeve, so vital and full of ideas, so sensual and strong, a woman before her time. Maeve, and maybe it's with her that my story really begins, that night I met her and that Halloween night that followed all those years ago.

October 1950

YOU CAN NEVER RELIVE your first experience of living in a new city. That sense of excitement and liberation, of discovery and possibility, of dreamlike dislocation. Suddenly you find yourself in a place where nobody knows your name and you are free to be what you want to be, to begin your life again. Streets of potential stretch out before you, and each house and face tells a different and vital story. Everything in this new city is immediate and unreal. Sometimes you stop and ask yourself if this world has come to life just for you, a pop-up storybook that only came into existence as soon as you began to experience it. You ask yourself if all this could have been: these people passers-by, these nuns moving like a wall of black cloth down Sean McDermott Street, and all of this grey city suspended beneath the evening sky, with its traffic, its trains and Trinity College, while you were somewhere else, starved and strangled by time in a small country town. You ask yourself how such different worlds can exist simultaneously.

I spent my first weeks in Dublin exploring; cycling and walking its streets, straddling Our Lady River Liffey and moving out to sea. The leaves were beginning to change colour as I cycled up a hill in the Phoenix Park, and stopped to sit on a bench and look out over the city. There below me was the Royal Military Hospital in Kilmainham, the clock tower at Kingsbridge Station, the brown spire of John's Lane Church on Thomas Street, and the green dome of the Four Courts; the whole city nestled beneath the Dublin Mountains while the River Liffey snaked its way down to the docks. The sun was shining that Saturday afternoon in early October when I cycled out to the Forty Foot and dived into the sea for my last swim of the year. And the weather was fresh and brisk as I walked around Merrion Square, looking up at the house where they said Oscar Wilde had lived, before going into the National Gallery, where I stood for hours, staring at the paintings.

Those early days, when I wandered along crooked, cobbled streets, looking up at decayed houses and abandoned buildings, when I peered into the windows of strangers' homes, wondering what kind of lives were lived there. Those bright, light mornings and those darkening evenings when I discovered the city by the glow of the gas lamps, going home only when they had been extinguished after midnight.

They say that Dublin is split in two, north side and south, with nothing in between, but to me the city will always be a thousand small scenes, strong smells and startling sensations, and no matter how many nets of words I throw around it, I know I'll never truly capture it.

I moved into a bed-sitting room on Victoria Street about a fortnight after I arrived in Dublin. I had been staying with my mother's sister and her husband in Drumcondra and, grateful as I was for a bed and a roof over my head, I knew I hadn't come to Dublin to while away my evenings talking about the family back home, the weather in general and the price of cabbage in particular, with these relations I hardly knew. I marked a few ads in the *Evening Standard*, and the room on Victoria Street was the first I saw. While it wasn't exactly the Ritz, it was pretty much what I was looking for. It was a small, clean room, with a little kitchen off it, and a big window that looked out over the street and the church on the corner. The house even had an inside toilet, something which wasn't all that common back then, and I shared it with the other tenants: a young married couple who had the flat downstairs and who were saving up for a house of their own, and another young civil servant, whose room was next to mine.

The landlord was Jewish and his parents, like most of the Jews who had come to Dublin from Eastern Europe at the turn of the century, had settled in this area. Being young, thinking I was incredibly ordinary, and being drawn to anything that was different, I loved those streets with their Jewish bakeries and businesses, with the synagogue on Adelaide Road and the Zion School at the bottom of Bloomfield Avenue. And the names of those shops on Clanbrassil Street were so unusual and exotic to my ears that had only ever heard of O'Reillys, O'Briens and O'MalleyLynch-MurtaghMcEvoyscouldn'tgiveashitMcPaddy. Here were shops like Rubenstein's the butchers, Aronovitch's the grocers and Cristol's the photographers.

I worked in the Department of Education on Marlborough Street. My job, like most jobs in the Civil Service, wasn't the most exciting position in the world, but that didn't really matter to me. It gave me a steady wage and I looked at it more as a means to an end rather than an end in itself. It afforded me the opportunity to live in Dublin, and for that, if for nothing else, I was grateful. I worked in a big, uninspiring room with more than thirty other people, carrying out the usual clerical duties that are the lot of lowly civil servants in every country.

Most of my colleagues were men and women from all the

provinces of the Republic, with accents ranging from Cork singsong speak to the loose, messy vowels of Dundalk. Many of them were middle-aged men who had turned grey from the years of dreary paperwork, but some of the younger workers, just like me, saw this job up in Dublin as their chance at escape, and made full use of it. I had two good friends there: Paddy was from Clontarf and he wanted to be an actor and Eileen was from Wexford and caused a scandal every now and then when she turned up at work in trousers, instead of the regulation skirt.

I liked working on Marlborough Street, mainly because it was smack bang in the middle of town. Every morning I cycled over O'Connell Bridge with all the other cyclists making their way to work. The city's main street still had a certain dignity about it back then, with its fancy hotels, its picture houses and its ballrooms, its ice-cream parlours and smart office workers. During my dinner hour, I would often wander the length of the street and back again, gazing up at Nelson's Pillar soaring into the sky, a cluster of flower sellers at its base. Or I would stop to stare into the street's shop windows, into Clerys, Eason's, Tyler's or Lemon's Sweets. From the statue of Parnell at one end to the figure of Daniel O'Connell at the other, I would dream my dreams of Dublin, moving with the heartbeat of the city.

As well as being next to the picture houses on O'Connell Street, I was near some of Dublin's greatest theatres. There was the Abbey down on Abbey Street, and I would always look at the posters when I passed this way, to see what was on there. There was also the Gate Theatre, beside the Rotunda Hospital. Micheál MacLíammóir and Hilton Edwards were the big names there at the time, and it was widely believed that they lived together as man and wife. I saw Micheál MacLíammóir during my first week in Dublin and, having no idea who he was, I stood staring open-mouthed at this man who was wearing full make-up on Henry Street in the middle of the afternoon. He caught me looking at him and gave me a quick wink and a smile before he continued on his way, leaving me standing there, mortified. It was only a few weeks later, when I told Paddy the story, that I found out who he was. Paddy burst out laughing and said I was trying to get onto the stage through the back door. 'You fuck off,' I responded, 'I'm no queer.'

Sometimes, on my way home from work, if I hadn't had a big meal at dinner hour or if I wasn't in the mood for cooking anything on the tiny stove back in the bedsit, I would go to one of the cafés on Grafton Street: to Fuller's, to the Monument Creamery, or to Robert Roberts where a trio played the music of Ivor Novello every afternoon. Within a few weeks I had been to every café on the street, where I would watch the customers as I had my tea, making up stories about so many strangers I would never know.

My favourite café was Bewley's. It was the smell of the coffee being roasted in the window that drew me in time and again. That and the fact that of all the cafés on Grafton Street, Bewley's seemed to attract the most colourful mix of customers. There were writers who came there to write and homeless men who came there to keep warm, nursing a pot of tea for hours. It was a place where everybody was welcome and everybody was equal, from lauded poets to loud and proud street traders. It seemed so cosmopolitan to me, and I never felt out of place there. On those odd occasions when I did feel like Little Boy Lost in the big city, I would head straight for Bewley's, sure that I would find a little comfort and company amidst the familiar cacophony of faces, noises and smells.

So many evenings I whiled away in Bewley's, over

sausages and chips, or fish, vegetables and mashed potatoes, or white pudding and a fried egg. There were cakes there to beat the band: Battenberg and iced fancies, almond buns, cherry buns and London buns, chocolate cake and custard slices, pound cake and Black Forest Gateau. When my pocket could afford the stretch, I'd have a cake and a coffee myself, thinking wouldn't the family say I was living the high life if they could see me now.

Bewley's was a place of drowsy teas and lazy afternoons, of chance meetings, crazy characters and surreal encounters. It was where I first met Maeve.

Of all the faces I came to recognise in Bewley's hers was, without doubt, the one that fascinated me most. I will never forget the first time I saw her, when she strode into the café, all dressed in an expensive brown suit, the small veil of a neat hat down over her face and a crocodile skin purse under her arm. I both loved and hated her in that instant. I tried not to stare and concentrate on my newspaper, but it was of no use. My eyes were drawn back to her again and again, so much so that the Korean War and Maeve will always be linked in my mind, as if she were a bomb dropped on that café, her presence an explosion that would come to change the course of my life forever.

I watched her from behind my newspaper that evening, as if I were a spy sent to track her every move, and I must have made one cup of coffee last a couple of hours. Soon after she arrived, a handsome man walked up to her table and sat down opposite her. The two looked as though they were deep in conversation, when all of a sudden the man got up and left. Not long afterwards, another man came and sat at the table. He said goodbye after about half an hour and a few minutes later she was joined by yet another man. This time she took his hand and gently caressed it as they spoke, looking into his eyes. When he left she sat there for a while, looking into space, before she got up, arranged her hat, and left as commandingly as she had entered.

I spent the rest of the night, both in the café and at home, wondering who and what she was. Putting everything together in my mind – the stylish suit, the made-up face and the three gentlemen who had come to her table – I decided that she was a high-class prostitute. 'Yes, that's the only explanation,' I thought to myself, 'she's one of those ladies of the night I was warned about. Those were her clients, and they were arranging assignations in some of the city's more discreet hotels.' I felt both aroused and disappointed.

I saw her a number of times in the café after that evening. The same thing always happened; she would walk in, looking proud and indifferent to what was going on, and take a seat before she was joined by a string of male companions. I always tried to be discreet and not paw her too much with my eyes, but my curiosity always got the better of me and I would wind up gawking at her and her ever-changing clients until she had left. She was always well-dressed, undoubtedly the most stylish woman in the whole café. 'She must be making a good bit of money on the game if she can afford that kind of get-up,' I remember thinking to myself. Never, not once, did she so much as glance at me, not until that night in October when I was sitting by the fire and she walked straight up to me, sat down beside me and lit a cigarette.

'What are you reading?' she asked. Feeling intimidated by her presence and uncomfortable with the way she was staring at me and saying nothing, I had opened my book, pretending to read even though I couldn't concentrate on the print before me. I turned to look at her. 'It's called *The Great Gatsby*,' I replied, trying to remain as calm and collected as possible. 'It's about a man, Gatsby, who—' 'Yes, I know what it's about, dear,' she cut me short. 'Dear Gatsby! I wouldn't have minded being a guest at one of his parties, wouldn't have minded at all.' 'Have you read it?' I asked. 'Read it?' She was incredulous. 'I adore *The Great Gatsby*, it's one of my favourite novels. But I still haven't forgiven Mr Scott Fitzgerald for dying so young. We were robbed of a great talent.' She looked away and back again. 'You must be quite the young romantic, reading *The Great Gatsby*,' she ventured. Her eyes were probing me and I could see she was waiting for a reply. 'Oh, I don't know,' I responded, 'I just found it in a shop.' My face was burning and I didn't know what else to say. 'That Gatsby sounds like a wild man,' I eventually managed, feeling like a clumsy, country fool who can't quite get the hang of words. 'Indeed!' was all she said and ordered tea with lemon from the waitress.

'So what has you here all on your own, reading a book on a Friday evening?' she wondered out loud after a very long time, a smirk on her face. 'Don't you have a girlfriend to take to the pictures or to go window-shopping with?' I asked myself if she was making a pass at me and shifted uncomfortably in my seat. 'No, she's actually working late this evening,' I lied, looking her straight in the eye. 'So you're all alone, poor little thing,' she said in a voice shot through with a sarcastic kind of saccharine. She had the look of a cat toying with a mouse before tearing it to pieces, and whatever game she was playing I didn't like it. 'Yes, I am all alone,' I shot back at her, 'and I was actually enjoying it until quite recently.' 'Okay, dear,' she seemed startled, her voice sounding more real now, 'I was just having a bit of fun. Please don't be offended.' 'Don't worry, I'm not,' I replied firmly, trying to keep my voice steady.

Just then a man about ten years older than me came up to the table. I supposed he was a client of this woman's, but I had never seen him before and didn't feel all that enthusiastic about the stares aimed in my direction. Not sure if he was about to lunge across the table and punch me on the nose for talking to his gal, I made an excuse to leave and stood up. 'Charlie, be a darling and give us a moment,' she requested of the man, and with one last, lingering look at me, he went and sat at another table.

She was pleasant now. 'You haven't told me your name,' she said. 'Yes, and you haven't told me yours,' I responded. 'Oh, how rude of me!' she exclaimed. 'I'm Maeve, Maeve O'Donnell.' She held out a hand that ended in carefully painted nails and I shook it. 'My name is Daniel,' I said, 'Daniel Ryan.' 'Well, Daniel Ryan, it was nice talking to you. Promise me you'll come back and see me again.' She was still holding my hand and, caught in her grip and the glare of her eyes, I promised I would return. She smiled and I couldn't help smiling back at her. 'Nice to meet you, Maeve,' I bid her farewell and turned away.

'Daniel,' I heard her call from behind me, and turned around to see her leaning back on the couch. 'Yes?' I answered. 'You're one of us, aren't you?' she half asked, half stated, but before I could ask her what she meant she had waved me away. 'Come and see me soon,' she said, 'I'm often here in the evenings.' I walked out of the café and into the dark evening on Grafton Street, where reality had shifted slightly.

On my way home, I asked myself what she had meant when she said I was one of them. 'Does she see me as a potential customer?' I wondered. 'Or maybe she's just from my part of the country and that's all she meant.' I doubted it though. In my mind she was definitely from a city, from Dublin or even from London, not from the back of beyond like me. 'Perhaps she isn't a prostitute at all – she could be from the theatre and think that I too am an actor?' I ran this thought over in my head before I got home, looked at myself in the mirror – my safe grey suit, my shirt and tie – and accepted this was wishful thinking. 'What if, what if she and her friends are aliens who have come to Earth to abduct me?' I began to think about the question half seriously as I lay in bed, unable to sleep, remembering those stories about UFOs that were coming out of America. 'Or what if they are something more terrifying than aliens?' I asked myself. 'What if they are Communists?' I felt slightly uneasy, but also a secret thrill, that perhaps I was about to be initiated into a secret political sect.

Over the days that followed, my suppositions grew more and more outlandish until I decided enough was enough, I would go back and see Maeve and ask her what she'd meant, even if she did make me feel a bit uncomfortable, even if I wasn't sure I liked her. In the end though, I never did ask. Perhaps I was afraid of what she'd tell me.

That first evening I returned to see her, we spoke about different things: about books, about Dublin, about the theatre, but mostly about myself. Even though she had only met me once, she seemed to know almost everything about me. She guessed that I was from a country town, supposed that I was a civil servant, divined that I was from a good family, and speculated that I had come to the capital to escape the monotony of life at home. I was really put out by the fact that she could place me so easily, that I was that predictable and boring to her, but far from dismissing me as a bland country lad, she actually seemed interested in my story, and asked me question after question about myself. I was both confused and flattered by the attention, and perhaps it was this flattery that brought me back to her again and again, when I would sit with her in the café for about half an hour, before she would say she was expecting somebody, and that it had been nice to see me again, whereupon I would be replaced by another rival for her affections.

I may have told Maeve a lot about myself during those early conversations, but I found out very little about her. There was never any point in probing her about her life. She would close up and look off in another direction if your questions got too personal. It soon became apparent that she wasn't a prostitute. Of course she wasn't. My imagination had proved to be over-active again and when she guessed what I'd thought she laughed out loud for a very long time, while I sat there feeling like an idiot. 'Oh, you are naïve,' she said through tears of mirth. 'If only you knew.'

But I didn't know, I couldn't understand why all those men came to see her, and I was sure there wouldn't be any easy answers. In those first few weeks, all I discovered about Maeve was that she had trained as an actress, that she was involved in the theatre, and that she lived somewhere on the other side of the river. Even her age was a mystery. One evening she could look the same age as me, only to turn up the next looking old enough to be my mother, albeit a glamorous, sultry kind of mother. Eventually I put her down as being in her late thirties.

Towards the end of October, Maeve invited me to a Halloween fancy dress party in her house. I felt privileged to be asked, but I wasn't about to parade around in a silly costume in front of strangers, so I told her I was busy. She insisted though, and eventually I gave in. When I asked Eileen at work if she would like to go to the party with me, she accepted on the spot, saying it sounded terribly decadent and bohemian, a costumed ball in an eccentric lady's house. I wasn't so sure, but in any case I found myself in Ging's on Dame Street the following lunchtime, being prodded and poked by Eileen as she forced me into various costumes, all of which looked equally ridiculous on me. Eventually, and only because we were already late back for work, I gave in and said I would go as a gangster. Eileen, being much more adventurous than I could ever be, had already decided she was going as Cleopatra, Queen of the Nile, even if I refused to be her Mark Antony.

That Saturday evening was mild. I had picked Eileen up at the flat she shared with three girls on Lower Rathmines Road, and we had taken the bus to O'Connell Street, from where we would walk the rest of the way to Maeve's house on Mountjoy Square. I felt like such an ass, traipsing through town dressed as a poor man's Al Capone. For her part, Eileen was relishing her new role, gliding along with supreme confidence, the fringe of her black wig dead straight and her eyes carefully made up with thick black kohl. On Parnell Street the pubs were full of men and we heard one wife threatening her husband, 'Yi'd better be home for your bleedin' dinner or ye won't be sharin' me bed tonight.'

We turned and walked up North Great George's Street, up that steep hill where most of the old houses had been carved up into tenements. I could hear those buildings and their tenants gasping for air as we passed. We continued on up to Mountjoy Square, that ragged lady who had lost her money and slipped into decay. Yellow light streamed out from the windows of the houses that stood all around the square.

The door to Maeve's house was opened by a young woman wearing a black tuxedo and a bow tie. Her dark hair had been slicked back and her face was carefully made up. Myself and Eileen smiled and said hello, but instead of responding she just stood there, hands in her pockets, looking at us both in a provocative manner, before she waved us into a room to her right.

My costume seemed pathetic as I looked at all the

colourful creatures there. Various vampires, both male and female, moved about the place with a casual menace, while a deathly pale woman, wearing a long Victorian dress and with a trickle of blood coming from her lips, eagerly eyed up a male victim. Two women who were dressed as 1920s flappers were dancing together in the middle of the floor, and an amorous Ophelia, with flowers twisted about her hair, was sitting on a man's knee in the corner, apparently drowning in lust beneath her flimsy shift. Meanwhile a stocky cowboy chased a half-naked squaw around the room. Just then there was a knock at the door and a figure in a black, floor-length cape came in. The pianist struck up a tune and in an instant the cape was off, revealing a young woman dressed in not much more than a corset and feathers, who began to kick up her legs as if she were performing in the Moulin Rouge.

Somebody put a drink in our hands, and I was still staring at everything that was going on, not knowing whether the party was wonderful or downright freakish, when I saw a louche Marlene Dietrich sitting by the piano. She must have sensed me looking at her because she turned toward me and smiled, but only after I'd returned her smile did I realise Dietrich was actually a man in women's clothes. My face burned with embarrassment and shame and I looked away quickly, only to find another man, wearing earrings and a silk scarf, dancing with a soldier. I felt my stomach lurch. I turned to Eileen to tell her we were leaving but I felt somebody touch my elbow. 'Daniel, darling, how good of you to make it!' It was Maeve, her green eyes glistening like a cat's from behind the black mask she was holding up to her face.

We spoke to Maeve for a few minutes, before she went to welcome another guest. There was no way we could leave now that she had seen us and besides, none of what was going on seemed to faze Eileen, in fact just the opposite. 'Isn't this the most wonderful party you've ever been to!' she exclaimed, before she went off to dance with a Dracula who'd been giving her the eye.

Left alone, wishing I was invisible, and praying that nobody would try and talk to me, I sat in a corner, downing one whiskey after another, cursing Maeve, but also cursing myself, for believing this celebration could have been anything but the freak show it had turned out to be. I sat there drinking and hating the lot of them, especially those queers, wearing their mothers' jewellery and their sisters' make-up. I had come to Dublin to get away from the banality of country life, for excitement and stimulation, but this party, full of people proudly displaying their perversions and not caring a damn what anybody thought of them, wasn't exactly what I'd had in mind. 'The lot of them are sick, sick bastards,' I said to myself.

The hours crawled by and the whiskey kept flowing, but instead of trying to look away from everything that was going on, I found myself staring at the other people in the room, staring as if from a burnt-out crater. I couldn't take my eyes off them. Marlene Dietrich was singing 'Falling in Love Again' in a mock German accent, two sailors were kissing in the shadows and Maeve was laughing and smiling with her friends, a glass of champagne in her hand. All of a sudden, I felt myself begin to sway and when the two flappers became four, I knew something wasn't right. Slowly, and as carefully as I could, I got up out of my chair and staggered out of the room, wanting only to get sick, to vomit up the whole night, to get the party out of my system and those smiling queers from my mind. The next thing I knew, I had fallen flat on my face, and a man in a suit was helping me up. 'You're all right,' he said. I flopped into his arms like a puppet, unable to hold myself up. 'Are you going to be sick?' he asked. I nodded my head, unable to speak.

He helped me upstairs to the bathroom, and over to the toilet. I collapsed on the floor, my head hanging over the bowl. As I began to vomit, I felt his hand gently rubbing my back and I began to cry, massive wet tears that wouldn't stop. 'It's okay,' he said, 'it's okay,' but that only made it worse. I just sat there, bawling and vomiting while I hugged the toilet. 'Thanks, thank you,' I managed to say, and he ran a hand through my hair. 'Don't worry,' he replied, and it was then, without thinking, without asking myself why, I stood up and put my arms around him, put my arms around him and kissed him.

I woke up the next morning in one of the rooms at the top of Maeve's house. I was alone and beneath the covers I was still wearing my costume. As I lifted myself up on my elbows, my head began to throb, and slowly images from the party the night before began to stretch themselves across my mind. I could remember a woman in a tuxedo, a man wearing earrings, everybody dancing, people singing and then getting sick in the bathroom. 'Wait, there was somebody with me,' I thought to myself. 'Somebody helped me to the bathroom. A man, a man brought me there.' Suddenly I remembered his hand on my back and I saw myself kissing him. My mind twisted about itself, I began to shake and, thinking I would be sick again, right there and then, I ran out of the room and down the stairs, pulling back the enormous front door with a strength I didn't know I had. I fled from the house and into the chilly morning outside, running away from the place, not once looking back.

Perhaps I should have kept running. Perhaps I never should have gone back to that house on the square and to that room, that room where it all happened, where I was condemned by his blood. Perhaps, but what use is perhaps? We're both still standing, that house and me, both still crumbling and confronting the past.

3
November 1997

I MADE MY FIRST REAL EXPLORATION of Dublin's gay nightlife last weekend. There are a number of places for gays here now. Gay, God I hate that word! What's gay about us miserable, bitching, selfish bastards? People here now call themselves gays, lesbians, bisexuals, trisexuals, transsexuals and polysexuals, using more and more bizarre classifications to say what they are. As if a label could make them more interesting!

When I lived in Dublin, there were no gay bars that pronounced their presence so openly, though there were bars, of course there were bars. Funny how some people believe there were no gays in Ireland back then, and that they are a modern invention of suspiciously foreign origin. That's bullshit, of course. Men had sex with men: in parks, in public toilets, behind hall and hotel doors. And there were even long-lasting relationships between men, but such relationships, such acts, were hidden much more than they are today. We existed and yet we did not; a people without a nation, without any objective notion of ourselves.

Downtown there are a handful of pubs, often packed to the gills with unbelievably confident young men, dressed in the latest fads of fashion and forever fumbling on their cell phones. It's all pink pounds and pounds of pink flesh pro-pelling itself out of the past here now.

I don't quite know where I fit into this whole scene. I hadn't expected this, couldn't have imagined that the Pied Piper of progress would lead the children from the narrow streets and into this plastic, fantastic future. I was amongst a people who were somehow lost, and now I have returned I find that I am lost again, this time in the open air, in the bright lights, in the loud music and furious movements of the bars and clubs. Alone in a city that does not recognise me as much as I do not recognise it, a city of out and proud youth, with their Pride parade, forever getting laid. And here I am, nothing more than a relic of an unimaginable age.

The pub I went to is called The George. It's a showy, tacky place, almost aggressively announcing its presence on George's Street. It's really two bars, the bigger part a poor excuse for a nightclub, even by Irish standards, and a smaller, more traditional bar. The young fags call this Jurassic Park, and it's where the old gays go before they die, a scrapyard of sagging asses and shrivelled cocks. Maybe I belong there, okay I probably do, but I'll be damned if I'll let those little queens drive me into hiding. I'll be damned if I'll let them push me towards the grave.

I walked into the bigger part, and though I haven't done it in years, I found myself looking over my shoulder on the way in, just in case anybody was watching me.

And then I'm sitting in the bar with a beer before me. How many times I've done this through the years, going to bars alone and seeking out strangers to spend my solitary nights with. I can size up a place in minutes, selecting the best-looking candidate for the job: the blow job, the hand job, the fuck (always them and never me. I haven't been fucked since… Well, since I lived in Dublin as it happens, since…) I'd chat them up, buy them a drink, maybe bring them someplace else and then take them home.

We'd fuck, maybe fall asleep and I'd always take them out for breakfast the next morning. Anything to get them out of the apartment, anything to stop them from insinuating themselves into my life. I didn't want companionship, I didn't want a boyfriend. If I hadn't needed the sex, I wouldn't have gone to the bars in the first place. I would have done without all of it: the small talk, the little flirtations, turning on the charm and then trying not to look into their eyes the next morning, in case they wanted something more, knowing I had got all I wanted, that I didn't want a relationship, all I wanted was a fuck.

From Christopher Street Pier to the bars down in the Village, to the bathhouses and sex parties, I slept my way through New York City. I fucked my way through the decades. Through riots and raids, through plagues and parades, I was always picking up and getting off. Fucking furiously somewhere else when the drag queens marched up to the cops, as friends and acquaintances dropped like flies from AIDS, as others took to the streets in their ACT UP T-shirts.

But somehow that doesn't matter here. I'm just a rotting body with a receding hairline, an anachronism, defunct, decayed and despised. These little provincial pounders with their crop tops and streaked hair, their pasty skin and drunken babble. Most of them don't even notice me, and those that do don't even try and hide their looks of amazement and derision at this intruder, this interloper in their territory. God, I wish I was back in New York, where age is nothing more than an arbitrary number. Where women over a hundred still go, carefully made-up, to the Russian Tea Room. Where I am not just one of the few. Where there are thousands of men like me, who've been there, seen that and fucked him, who still know where and when they can find a bit of sex on a Saturday night.

But Dublin, I still haven't got the hang of it. I still don't quite know how to work the bars, how to get what I want. And do I want it at all? Do I want anything from this bitching, preening, backward freak show they dare to call a scene?

So, I'm sitting at the bar, thinking about all this and watching everything that is going on. I'm on my second beer, it's about half past midnight, the music is pumping, everybody is moving and pushing one another along, and then he sees me and smiles. Instinctively I smile back at him, this good-looking blond guy in his mid-twenties. He looks as though he's drunk, but his eyes are studying me, trying to place me or figure me out. I take a good look at him. He's cute all right, but there's something I don't like about the way he's looking at me, something that makes me feel uncomfortable, exposed. I look away, but too late. He's at my side, leaning drunkenly against the bar. 'So, Babycakes, can I buy you a drink?' he asks, swaying a little and smirking to himself.

'No, I'll get it,' I say. I reach for my wallet. 'What will it be, a beer, a vodka?' But he's insistent. 'No,' he refuses, 'I'm paying. I'm not looking for Daddy. Not any more at least.' His hand is on my arm and I sink back into the chair. 'Let me get a mineral water,' I surrender, not wanting to get drunk, determined to stay in control of the situation.

'So, what's a pretty thing like you doing in a dump like this?' he asks, sounding like a detective in an old film noir. I laugh to myself. I like him, I like something about him, even if I don't exactly trust him. 'I'm just sitting here, looking at a pretty thing like you, and wondering why you're all alone,' I reply. 'I'm not alone,' he contradicts me. 'I have the voices in my head. Haven't you met my friends yet? They're dying to meet you.' He laughs out loud and I laugh with him, because his eyes light up and he looks alive.

'What's your name?' I inquire. 'Gerard,' he responds, 'and you?' I'm not sure exactly why, but instinctively I lie. 'Anthony,' I reply. We shake hands. 'Nice to meet you, Anthony,' he says. 'Where are you from?' 'New York,' I tell him without blinking. 'That's a shame.' He sounds disappointed. 'I don't think you'll be any use to me.' 'What do you mean?' I ask, a little puzzled. 'Well, I'm trying to interview gay men who were around Dublin years ago, in the forties and fifties. It's for a— ' 'Well, I wouldn't be able to help you anyway,' I interrupt him, 'I've only just turned thirty.' 'Really,' he says in mock amazement, 'I thought everybody was here tonight for your twenty-first.' He's a bit bleary eyed from the alcohol as he looks at me and smiles, rubbing my shoulder as if we were old friends. I move slightly away.

'What do you want to interview all these old people for anyway?' I ask. 'Well, it's like this, Anthony,' he says, 'I'm working as a waiter at the moment, but I'm also writing a book, and I need some help with the research.' 'A book?' I ask incredulously. 'You're writing a book?' I almost burst out laughing. This was the last thing I had expected from this drunken, sassy kid. This was the last thing I thought he'd come out with. 'Yeah, a book, Daddyo! Didn't they have them back in your day?' His face contorts for a moment with hurt and aggression and I know I've said the wrong thing, know I've put my foot in it again. At the same time I want to tell this little smart ass to get out of my face, but I swallow the urge. 'Sorry,' I apologise, 'it's just not something you hear in a gay bar every day.' 'Well, maybe I'm not an everyday kind of guy,' he shoots back.

It's then I feel a pang of envy, a savage kind of envy, for this drunk but determined young man who is setting out to do what I once dreamed of doing. For a moment I think of tearing his dreams to pieces with my cynicism, with my realism, but I don't. I can't. 'So, tell me about your book,' is all I say to him.

'Well, it's a novel, but it's based on the life of a real person,' he begins. 'It's about a New Yorker who came to live in Ireland. Apparently he was an orphan and as a teenager he knocked around the theatres off Broadway and later became an actor. He went to fight in Spain when the civil war started there, and when the war ended for some reason he decided to move to Ireland. He worked as an actor and lived in Ranelagh for years. But the really interesting thing is that he was gay and was with his partner for more than forty years. Everybody knew they were gay. Can you imagine living as an out gay man in Ireland back then?' There is an incredulous look on Gerard's face.

'So that's why I'm interviewing the Old School,' he goes on, 'to try and find out what Dublin was like in the decades when Fitzer first lived here.' In that instant everything goes silent, I feel my heart slow down, and I catch my reflection in the mirror. 'What did you say his name was?' I ask, not sure if I've heard him correctly. 'Fitzer,' he says. 'Well, that wasn't his real name but everybody in Ireland knew him as Fitzer. Why, have you heard of him?' 'No, I've never heard of him,' I lie, unable to take my eyes away from the mirror.

After some time, I look back at this stranger beside me, trying to see if he's playing some kind of game with me, asking myself if he knows all about me, all about that summer night, that night of blood, that night Fitzer was there. He only looks confused though. 'Sorry, I can't help you,' I tell him firmly and I get off my stool. He looks even more confused now. 'Oh, you're leaving?' he asks. 'Yeah, I've better things to do than sit here talking about the 1950s with somebody who wouldn't know anything about it,' I say, surprised at how aggressively I turn on him. 'Why do you want to dissect this guy anyway?' I demand. 'Why don't you just leave him alone, write something about people your own age?' He looks as though he's lost for words, but not for long. 'And why don't you just fuck off back to New York?' he says very calmly and turns away from me.

Trying to look as casual as possible, but wanting only to get out of the place as quickly as I can, I walk away from him. I walk away from Gerard. When I'm at the top of the stairs I look back down at him. I know I shouldn't, but I do. Already he has his tongue stuck down some guy's throat. 'Fuck him,' I mutter to myself, as I push against the tide of youth and leave the bar.

November 1950

THE STREETS WERE STILL THE SAME that morning I ran from Maeve's house. My world, and everything I'd thought I was certain of, had just turned upside down, but the streets hadn't changed. They were just a bit quieter, that was all. It was a Sunday morning, a bright, benevolent morning, but inside I felt black and I couldn't understand why the sun was shining on this day of all days. There were families dressed up and heading to Mass all over the city. To Gardiner Street Church, to the Pro-Cathedral, to Saint Teresa's Church off Grafton Street. They looked so respectable, so normal, and there I was; a freak, an invert, a pervert, walking amongst them. 'Did they know, did they know how I had changed, even though I still looked the same? Could they somehow sense it?' I wondered.

'I was drunk. We didn't do anything. I just kissed him. I'm not a queer. He just helped me to bed. That's all. He didn't try anything on with me. It was just a kiss.' I rattled these defences off again and again in my head, but just as I would convince myself I wasn't a queer, I would see myself lifting my mouth up to the stranger's. I looked at those safe, sane families walking to Mass, and all I wanted was to be like them, to go back home to my family and be normal again.

But even as I fought with all the mental energy I had to erase that kiss from my mind, to wipe it out and pretend it had never happened, there was another part of me that brought it back again and again, that wanted to relive it, watching myself reach up and kiss this man who seemed a bit shocked that I was being so forward. When I thought about that moment, I felt a great sense of release; my head felt lighter, clearer, and reality changed in a small way that only I could see. Somehow it didn't feel wrong to me, it felt right, felt like I'd found something I'd been looking for. I felt alive and I wanted to stop all those normal people and shout in their faces that there was nothing wrong with me.

'But it wasn't right. It wasn't normal. It's disgusting,' I agonised to myself as I walked around Stephen's Green and up Harcourt Street. 'You're one sick fucker. You're sick in the head. You might as well sign yourself into an asylum now.' I lowered my eyes because I didn't want anyone to see me, and because I kept looking at men who passed, looking straight into their eyes, challenging them to see if they were like me.

My stomach was in knots, and as soon as I got back to the house I ran to the toilet, as if I wanted to shit the whole night out of myself. I sat there with my head in my hands, willing my brain to stop working, trying to halt all the crazy thoughts running around in my head. I took the razor my father had given me and ran it along my wrists, thinking I could end it all now, that if my life was over then I'd be free, free from this madness, this battle with myself. But after a while I put the razor down. Whatever else I was unsure of, I knew I wasn't ready to die.

I ran a bath. I felt grimy and sweaty from the alcohol, from what had happened, from the whole freak show of a party. I took off my shirt, my shoes, my socks and underpants. I didn't look down at myself, I couldn't look down at myself. I felt betrayed by my cock, even though nothing had really happened. I didn't feel like a real man. I didn't feel like I deserved a cock. I'd made a laugh of it. But as I stepped into the bath I could feel it moving with the knowledge of my naked body, as if I'd discovered it for the first time. 'You fucking queer,' I said out loud, before I submerged myself in the water, closed my eyes, and managed to push everything out of my head.

And laying there in the hot water, naked, not thinking of anything, I see his face before me. I undress him furiously, tearing at his shirt, pulling at his flies, pulling down his trousers and pushing him onto the bed. I don't kiss him. Why would I kiss him? I'm not like that after all! No, I'm just going to fuck him because there isn't a woman around. I reach for myself in the bath and I hear the water begin to splash. Standing over the bed, I pull the stranger towards me. His arse is naked. It's a woman's, it's a man's, it's just an arse. I pull it towards me, put myself inside and begin to fuck this man/woman/freak. Harder and harder. I'm not abnormal. It's just physical. Just two men having a bit of fun.

I have a good rhythm now, my hips slapping against his arse. I wet my hand and grip him tightly. That's it, yeah. Faster and faster. Yeah, yeah! I'm fucking this man. Yeah! It's just a bit of fun. Yeah, I'm deep inside him now. He's going to get off, I'm going to get off. Yeah, but then he turns his head around and his face is intense with pleasure. Without thinking, I kiss him. I put my lips to his, put my tongue in, push inside him one last time, move my hand up and down, quickly, quickly, and then we explode, me inside him, he on the bed and me in the bath, all three at exactly the same time. I feel free.

I keep my eyes closed for a very long time and when I open them there is a school of slippery fish floating in the water, the proof of my sin. Exhausted and unwilling to think about everything that has happened, I get out of the bath, dry myself, crawl to my room and into bed.

I fell asleep almost immediately, but it wasn't a comfortable sleep. I had crazy, horrible dreams. I saw myself walking up to a stranger in a forest. He was staring at me and fondling himself, and I began to do the same. Then I was standing in front of him and, without saying anything, he put his hands on my shoulders and pushed me down so that I'd suck him off. I put my mouth around him and began to move my head backwards and forwards. At the same time he was pushing himself into me, more and more aggressively, and I felt myself choke. Suddenly he let out a terrifying howl of pain and then my mouth was full of blood. I stood up and, touching myself, I began to kiss him, but his face was full of hatred. Then he had a knife in his hand and he was stabbing me again and again. I was bleeding to death in this forest but I couldn't believe it. This wasn't me, this wasn't my death. I laughed and then he was cutting my balls and dick off, hacking away at them. There was blood everywhere and I was terrified, but I couldn't stop laughing.

Then it ended in a flash and I was sitting across from my father. Without saying anything, he got out of his chair, walked over to me and hugged me, hugged me for no reason. Later I was found walking through the town in my mother's dress and everybody was laughing at me, laughing and laughing until I felt something hit me, a stone, and then another one, until they began to stone me to death. And somewhere in my dreams I was with John, and it was the morning he was leaving for Dublin. We were in his room, lying on his bed, and we were both sad and nervous. I leaned over and looked at him. He looked back at me, then closed his eyes. I kissed him, I took his mouth in mine, and then we just lay there, holding each other and he didn't have to go away.

When I woke up the next morning I vowed I would wipe the memory of Maeve's party from my mind. If I didn't acknowledge it, if I didn't think about it, then it wouldn't exist, it wouldn't be real. It shouldn't have been that difficult because by that time in my life I was an expert at forgetting things, at pretending things hadn't happened. This may have been the first time I had done anything about it, but for years I'd had mad, disgusting thoughts about other guys, about friends from school, about John, about some of the men who came into the shop. Sometimes at night, when it was dark and my desire was invisible, I'd masturbate thinking about them and as I wiped away the mess, I'd wipe the incident from my mind. I wasn't queer. This was just something in my head, just my imagination, just a part of growing up, and it wasn't like I'd ever done anything with these people. Besides, I masturbated thinking about girls as much, if not more, as I did when thinking about guys, and if I was turned on by girls then there was nothing wrong with me, I was normal.

Through the years, until that night, my perverse thoughts had been a kind of secret I'd managed to keep from myself. But now I had gone further and actually kissed another man, and this time I was doomed. 'But no, if I just don't think about it, it will go away,' I told myself as I left for work. Of course I could have forgotten about what had happened, of course I could, but there was a small part of me that didn't want to, that didn't want to forget anything about that night.

It's only from the distance of years that I can put the weeks that followed into perspective. Life carried on as normal, as it does, at least on the outside. I got up every morning, went to work, came back in the evening and went home one weekend. If you'd seen me, you probably would have said I was fine, that I was just a young civil servant up from the country, living the life you would have expected of such a person, but inside I was a mess. It was a turbulent and terrifying period for me.

But it was also a beautiful, vital time, when new doors opened before me. Life became something I lived, instead of something I watched from the sidelines. I'm not saying I'd want to go through the madness, the uncertainty, the despair and the sheer terror of those weeks again, but when I look back on that time now I can't help but feel a certain nostalgia for it. There are so few times in life when the world takes on completely new dimensions, when everything changes, and for me this was one of them. In Dublin I discovered my desire, I discovered myself, and this city and that discovery can never be separated in my mind. Perhaps that's why I had to come back, because so much of me is here, stretched across these streets.

I dreaded facing Eileen at work, petrified that she might know what had happened at the party. 'Did that man go downstairs and tell everyone that I'd just kissed him, that the gangster in a drunken coma upstairs was a queer just like them, was one of their little gang?' I asked myself as I cycled past Woolworths on George's Street. I was grateful he hadn't taken advantage of the situation, but I still hated him, hated him because I had kissed him and shared my secret with him.

I saw myself grabbing him by the throat and warning him that if he told anybody what had just happened, I'd smash his face in. I hadn't done that though. I was a stupid bastard who'd fallen asleep, and now this man knew something about me, something that nobody else knew. He had my whole life in his hands. 'He could blackmail me, or have me fired from my job, or send an anonymous letter to my parents. He could ruin my life,' I thought to myself. 'Don't be stupid. He's a queer and he wouldn't put himself at risk like that. Anyway, he didn't seem like that kind of person, even if he is an abnormal. He probably didn't say a word,' I persuaded myself. 'Eileen probably doesn't know anything about it.'

As luck would have it, Eileen was the first person I met in the office that morning. I smiled at her and she smiled back at me. 'Great night, wasn't it!' she said. There was a bit of mischief in her eye and for a moment I felt my heart sink and I began to panic. 'No, she doesn't know anything, she can't,' I reassured myself. 'Sorry for leaving you,' I apologised, 'I was slaughtered. Did you get home all right?' 'I did indeed,' she replied, and her eyes lit up again. 'It was a blessing in disguise, you getting so drunk. I was walked to my door by Clark Gable. He's taking me to the pictures tomorrow night.' 'Good for you, Scarlett,' I chuckled and went to sit at my desk.

For the next couple of weeks I avoided Maeve and I stopped going to Bewley's. In the end, if the blame for that night rested with anyone, I decided it was with her. She was the one who had accosted me in Bewley's, who had tried to get me involved in her underworld, who had invited me to her ginger beer party. I came to see her as dangerous and destructive, a woman who made no bones about messing other people's lives up. I began to despise her for being a sick ringmaster who collected freaks to add to her private circus. More than anything though, I hated her because she had seen something in me that she had seen in those other men, in her deviant little friends. 'That was what she meant when she said I was one of them.' The truth of the situation finally dawned on me. And so I avoided her, I avoided her because I was shit scared she'd force me to see whatever it was she had noticed in me.

I spent a long time looking at myself in mirrors during that time. I would study my face, my body, my gestures for hours, puzzling over exactly what it was Maeve had identified in me. I would spend whole days convincing myself she'd been mistaken, that she was crazy and I was nothing like her faggot friends. There were moments though, nervous, exciting moments, when I would look straight into my own eyes and recognise my desire for what it was. There was truth in those moments, a truth that couldn't be defeated, a truth that just was, and which existed whether I accepted it or not. I could spend a long time looking at this new self, this unknown self, this hidden self, and only when this new me and the world outside came into collision did I turn away from the mirror or lift my fist to smash it, good sense stopping me only at the last minute.

Trying to avoid Maeve and her world didn't succeed. The more I focused on cursing them and keeping away from them, the more I became obsessed with them, with this secret sect I had stumbled upon, this weird world that everybody else seemed oblivious to. I found myself back in the café, spying on Maeve and her friends from a safe distance, where I knew I wouldn't be seen. With the newfound knowledge that most of these 'clients' were actually abnormals, I wanted to see what made them different, what made them queer. I looked carefully at how they walked, how they drank their tea, how they smoked and how they sat, searching for clues that would betray them as inverts, as untouchables. I was searching desperately for characteristics I did not have so that I could confirm my status as a healthy, normal young man. I wanted these men to be mincing, preening Nancy boys who wore make-up, men who I was nothing like.

There were one or two of them who were more feminine than the average male, and others who held a cup in a certain way, or looked around the café in a very specific manner, thus giving the game away, but more often than not I couldn't tell these homosexuals from ordinary men. Besides the odd, idiosyncratic difference, I wouldn't have been able to pick out one of these queers in a police line-up. I wouldn't have been able to pinpoint any of these faggots, and that both disturbed and fascinated me. There was only a hair's breadth of difference between two people, but their desires could be so different.

Whatever their desires, I managed to convince myself most of the time that they weren't mine. Around this time I began a concerted campaign of taking girls out, in order to prove my normality. I took out a couple of great-looking girls that any straight man would have given their hind teeth to go out with. I went to the theatre with the first and an early evening picture with the second. I fancied both of them. Honestly, I fancied them in a way, and did get a bit hot and bothered with both of them even though we didn't have sex. That didn't matter though. If I fancied them, enjoyed kissing them, and could get an erection with them, then I wasn't queer, and because I was with these girls the entire world would know it. The evening of the second date though, a foggy night in late November, something got inside me, and after I had left the girl to her bus, I turned around and went straight to Bewley's.

Maeve was there, of course, speaking to a good-looking man I had seen once or twice before. They couldn't see me, but when this man got up to leave I did the same, suddenly feeling brave, feeling alive, not asking myself too many questions about exactly what I was doing, but determined to follow this stranger to wherever he was going, to wherever these people went after dark.

When I got outside the fog had thickened, and it took me a moment to make out the figure of the stranger. Without thinking, I left the lights of the café window and followed him, my heart racing. He walked up Grafton Street, then crossed the road and turned left at South Anne Street. I could just about make out the facade of Saint Ann's Church on Dawson Street. He walked towards it, then turned right. I wondered then if he was heading for Stephen's Green, if it was in this park these men met, exploring their forbidden desires in the dark. He wasn't going there though. Near the top of the street he turned into a doorway. For a moment I thought he knew I was trailing him, and that he had stepped aside so that I'd pass him by, but when I got to the doorway I saw there was actually a narrow staircase that led down from the street. At the end of it was another door.

My heart was pounding as I stood at the top of the stairs, asking myself what I should do, if I should go home and forget about the whole evening, or follow this man downstairs. In a split second I made my decision. I'd followed the stranger this far, I had put myself out this much, and there was no way I could walk away now. With my heart about to explode and the blood rushing to my head, I took a look over my shoulder and began to descend the stairs.

I don't quite know what I had expected to find behind that door. I suppose I thought I'd stumble into a den of male flesh, with scores of naked men all writhing in different states of passion. It came as something of a shock then to find what was behind that door was just a pub, a pub like any other. Sure it was tiny, maybe the smallest pub I'd ever been in, but it was still just a pub. There were men drinking at the bar, men sitting at the tables drinking, just men drinking together, as they did in every pub across the country, on almost every night of the year.

I felt relieved but also strangely disappointed. I took a look around, and was about to leave when I saw the stranger looking directly at me. He looked at me for a long time and then he smiled as if he knew me. I froze for a moment and didn't know whether I should run or wait and see what happened. I decided I would leave, but too late. 'What are you having?' the barman asked me. I felt my face turn red. 'I'll have a bottle of stout,' I said. I took my drink and sat in the corner, avoiding eye contact with Maeve's friend.

Nothing happened in the bar that night, and nobody tried to touch me up, which I'd half expected. I began to wonder if the other men there were like me at all. 'Maybe they aren't,' I thought to myself. 'Maybe they're all normal and I'm the oddball.' But still, there was something different about the place, the way people looked at each other as if they were seeing one another for the first time, and the relaxed, easy-going atmosphere, the fun in the air. These men, or some of them, were like me. I knew it, knew it instinctively. And if they weren't perverts, if they were just normal-looking guys that wanted something different, that liked something most others didn't, then perhaps I wasn't a pervert either, perhaps none of us were. For the first time in weeks, no, in years, perhaps for the first time in my life, I felt okay about who I was and what I wanted.

As the barman called last orders I saw the stranger leave. I wondered if I should follow him to wherever he was going. After all, I had seen him look at me a few times throughout the night. I wouldn't go after him though. I might have followed him to the pub, but I didn't want to get that mixed up with him. At the end of the day we both knew Maeve, and I didn't want him to have any more evidence he might share with her. I saw him look at me as he left, but instead of going after him I went up to the bar and ordered another bottle of stout.

As the pub closed up I was putting on my coat, about to leave, when a man came up to me. 'If you fancy another drink, myself and the lads are heading out to a bona fide,' he said, nodding in the direction of a couple of men. I must have looked a bit uneasy. 'Don't worry,' he reassured me, 'we're just going for a drink. We're driving out and we'll drop you back later.' He looked honest enough and I had a thirst on me for another drink, so I decided I'd go with them. 'Thanks, if you're sure you don't mind me coming along.' 'The more the merrier,' he said warmly.

The four of us bundled into a car parked outside. Not long afterwards we had left the city behind and were driving through a dense fog along deserted country roads. 'Where are we going?' I asked, wondering if this was a good idea, but also enjoying the adventure. 'To The Stepaside Inn,' replied the man I'd spoken to in the pub. 'It's not far out.' After a while the car stopped at the foothills of the Dublin Mountains. We all got out, and the darkness of the countryside swallowed us up.

One of the men, I don't remember his name, knocked at the door of a pub that looked as though it had shut up for the night. There was no response for a few minutes, when all of a sudden it was opened by a heavy woman in an army shirt. I stood there staring at her. 'Come in, lads, before I catch my death,' she commanded, and pulled back the door to let us in.

Again the place seemed like a normal pub, with ordinary-looking men in it. There were no chintz curtains, no cross-dressers, no wild-eyed sex freaks around me. I got talking to a man that night, an artist who was a few years older than me. I liked him. He was good-looking, intelligent and interesting, a million miles away from the bumpkins I'd grown up with, whose stupid talk and clumsy walks had killed me slowly. 'If he asks me, I'll go home with him. I'll go home with him,' I vowed to myself as I sat there talking to him. I wanted to be naked with him, to touch him, and that felt all right, that felt right.

'So, do you want to spend the night with me?' I asked as the pub closed up; feeling brave, feeling wild, feeling if I didn't take this opportunity, I would never do it again and the moment would be lost forever. 'I thought you'd never ask,' he said. 'Let's go to my flat if that's okay with you. I have the car outside.' 'Sounds perfect,' I agreed, smiling, and as we walked out of the pub I felt as though I was making a declaration of life, as if I wasn't entering hell but finally leaving it. 'If this is a sin,' I remember thinking to myself as we got into the car, 'then it's my sin and I'm going to make damn sure I enjoy it.' He turned the key in the ignition and we drove back towards the city.

4

December 1997

CHRISTMAS DAY YESTERDAY and I spent it on my own. Not for the first time, not for the last. It isn't that important to me anyway. We only stop work for one day in the States. Not like here where it seems to start right after Halloween and go on into January. Thanksgiving is the big one over there. Anyway, who gives a shit? They're all holidays for people pretending to be happy families and not for old faggots like me. So I spent another 25th of December alone. So what! And don't start pretending to be all caring and humane because an old man was home alone on Christmas Day. The Irish! Mother Teresa for a day and snakes in the grass for the rest of the year. I ate like a pig, drank like a lush, took the last of the cocaine I bought last week, when drugs were the only thing that could get me to stay here, and danced around to some sixties CD. An old man off his face, all by himself on Christmas Day. How tragic! Who cares! Old men can have fun too, and I've always had the best fun on my own.

I went for a walk this morning. It was a damp, grey morning, a hangover after the Yuletide cheer, a bang of reality after the pretences of the Christmas colours and the blind optimism of the manic Christmas shoppers. I had just passed the tower when I stopped to look at the swimmers. A man with long dark hair and a wetsuit dived into the water, and a woman in her late fifties wearing her hair short, in a swimsuit, strode bravely down the steps towards the slight waves that lapped against the concrete. There were others already in the sea, moving slowly through the water.

A man maybe a decade older than me came and stood beside me, looking for a chat. 'Fuck, this is the last thing I need,' I thought, my head pounding from the night before. 'Why can't they just leave you alone here?' I asked myself. 'Why can't you be alone for ten minutes without somebody striking up a conversation, without somebody whining in your ear? Does it worry the people in this country so much to see somebody alone? Or are they just afraid of being alone themselves?'

'Not a bad morning, is it?' he said. 'No, not bad at all,' I answered, even though I could feel the damp seeping through my bones. 'Are you not going in for a dip yourself?' he asked, not looking at me but out at the winter swimmers. 'I wouldn't get in there for a million bucks,' I replied. 'These guys are lunatics.' I laughed. 'How about you? Aren't you gonna get in?' 'Nah, the awl heart wouldn't allow that.' He shook his head, still looking at the sea, his face expressionless. 'I took a stroke a couple of years ago and the doctor said the cold water would be too much of a shock to the system. Told me I had to give up the swimming.' His face was blank. 'Little fecker, what would he know? But still, better to be safe than to be sorry.'

'Maybe it's for the best then,' I suggested, not knowing what else to say. 'Maybe it is,' he said, 'but I was used to swimming every day of the year.' 'Did you swim here?' I asked. 'Ah, we used to swim up in the Forty Foot years ago. We'd swim in the nip and then the wind would dry us around the back of the wall as we did our exercises. That was when I was working up in Guinness's.'

I saw him for a moment as he must have been years before: young, strong, naked, doing his scissor splits and squats in the breeze down at the back of the Forty Foot. A young, working-class man with all the time in the world, and now he was this stooped figure, slowly losing his grasp on life.

'I started coming down here a few years ago though,' he went on, 'when the current got too strong for me up at the Forty Foot. I'd meet the gang every afternoon and we'd have a swim and a bit of a chat. We always had a bit of laugh down here,' he reminisced. 'Do you still come down and see your friends?' I asked. 'Ah, I come down some days but it's not the same when you can't get in yourself. It's not the same at all.'

I looked at him then. There were tears coming down his cheeks, great snotty tears. I don't know. It could have just been the strong wind making his eyes smart, who knows, but he stood there crying by the shore as the woman in her fifties made her way up the steps. I wanted to leave him alone. I felt embarrassed and uncomfortable, but more than that I didn't want to invade his grief. I knew there was nothing I could do, nothing I could say, to make it better. I knew despite the chat, the cheer, we are all alone in the end, always all alone.

'Ah, life can be a bitch sometimes,' he finally said and smiled. 'Good luck.' He shook my hand and walked up towards the bus stop.

Life can be a bitch, as he put it, especially to the body. My own ain't what it used to be, that's for sure. I don't feel sixty-seven, whatever that is supposed to feel like. My brain is still the same, it's all still working up there, but my body keeps reminding me of all the years I've lived. Sometimes I don't recognise myself: the grey hair, the grey pubes, the slack muscles and wrinkled eyes. Sometimes I think life is playing a joke on me, reflecting a man who is not really me, a man who has no connection to who I am in my head. But then life is playing a joke on all of us. You don't grow old, that's the thing, you don't grow into old age. You just live your life as best you can and time does the rest for you, time takes care of the body. And you don't wake up one morning feeling forty, fifty, sixty or sixty-seven. Feeling and being never were the same thing, not really. Some days my twenties seem like yesterday and other days I feel as though I've lived forever and I could sleep for an eternity. A life isn't linear, it's circles, ellipses, moving in time.

When I was younger, back in the day, I thought that people gave up the ghost of sexual desire when they got older. The image of an old man spilling his seed seemed pathetic, his orgasm closer to a death spasm, more a premonition of the final death rattle, than anything else. Their fat, sweaty bodies, their half-hard, half-limp cocks, their drooping balls and their heavy, heart-attack breathing all seemed so ridiculous to me back then. Oh, it's not as if I didn't have my share of old guys coming on to me and trying to get me into bed, both in Dublin and in New York. It's not as if I didn't know that dinosaurs haunt every gay scene in the world, still holding out some hope that somebody will sleep with them, still lying to themselves that they haven't lost it yet. It's just I didn't take them seriously. I brushed them away or laughed them off without a second thought when they got too close for comfort. They didn't matter to me. Why would they? I was too busy getting my own rocks off to think about a few old dudes trying to get laid. And if I did think about them, if I did look at them for more than a moment, then it was with disgust at worst and mild sympathy at best. 'Poor fuckers. They should really give it up, go home, have a hot chocolate and go to bed,' I'd think. 'Get on with the business of getting old.' What I never, never thought was that I'd end up like them. I still don't, I still can't … believe that I am. Funny how things turn out, isn't it?

I went to a sauna downtown last week. I'd been sitting at home having a drink, bored and horny as hell. I knew beating the meat wouldn't do it. I wanted a hard, hot body. I wanted to touch someone, to fuck someone. I needed that release. So I turned off the porn and took a taxi downtown. I jumped out on Dame Street, went down the laneway where the sauna is and pushed open the door. I paid my admission to some English guy behind the glass who had that depraved, wasted look of people who've worked too long and too close to sex, who've seen the barrel of humanity being scraped too often to have any faith in people left. He barely looked at me, just passed me a key on a piece of plastic and buzzed the door open.

The place was busy for a Thursday night, but then it was the week before Christmas. There would be guys who'd wind up there after their company Christmas parties, and executives who'd come to shoot their spunk on some stranger they strangely both loved and despised, before going home and cosying up to their wives who were knee deep in Christmas preparations. And then there would be the ones who went there all the time, the regulars who would see the chance of a cheap coupling with some new hot guy who was part of the Christmas rush.

Oh, I've been in enough saunas over the years to know what to expect, to know exactly who I'd see there. I could have listed off all the types on my fingers before going in: the Drunk Fag, the Married Fag, the Old Fag, the Sauna Fag, the Drag Fag, the College Fag, the Bi-curious Fag, the Misfit Fag, beautiful but half mad, the Tourist Fag who'd found the sauna on a map, and the Puke-bag Fag who might, just might, get lucky in the dark room. There would be the Oriental fags looking for Daddy and the Daddy fags looking for son … 'That's it, good lad.' And worst of all the Looking for a Relationship Fag, thinking something beautiful could begin amongst the steam and damp towels, the poppers, pills and pink pricks of the place. Give me a break, for Christ's sake. You're in a goddamned sauna!

And what kind of a Mr Man was I? Mr Get Your Threads Off, Get What You Want and Get The Hell Out of There. Mr Let's Get to It, Let's Do It, Let's *Not* Fall in Love. Mr No Conversation Necessary.

Walking towards the changing room, I put my chest out and held my head up, with a slight swagger and that look of arrogance and indifference I've perfected over the years. All right, so I didn't feel half as confident as I pretended but that's all part of the act, all part of the gay game, the gay ritual. I found my locker, slipped the key into it and took out a towel, a couple of condoms and two little sachets of lube. There were a few guys there, one I'd think about fucking, the rest I wouldn't touch with a bargepole. I undressed quickly, threw the Calvins into the locker, wrapped the towel around my waist, trying not to focus on the flab, and went upstairs, attempting not to walk as an old man should.

I'd been to this sauna a handful of times since I'd come back to Dublin and I knew the place well enough by now to find my way around. There were the actual saunas: the small wooden one, a bigger one that never had that many people in it for some reason, and then another one where guys sat in a row along a concrete bench and eyed each other up. There were the showers on two floors. There was the jacuzzi, always with some fat queen with frosted hair in it. There was the porn room at the top, with two TVs showing films from the States and from Europe, with guys lounging around the plastic-leather couches, maybe touching themselves under their towels and looking up at every other guy who came into the room. Then there was the dark room behind this, where you went when you weren't going to make it with anybody, when you refused to leave empty-handed and wound up with a handful of some stranger's scrotum or a mouth full of some stranger's cock. And then there were the small cubicles on three floors, where guys who had hooked up could go to get each other off, rows and rows of them sometimes, those black padded cells of sex.

I had a route planned out in my head. A shower, ten minutes in the sauna, a cruise around the cubicles upstairs, a quick look into the porn room to see who was there, and then down the back staircase to start the search again. I knew it might take some time to hook up with someone. I was used to the towelled treadmill of saunas. I'd spent the best years of my life there. Well, years anyway. And even if the number of possibilities had dwindled and decreased over time, I knew I could still get with someone. I knew who to approach and who not to approach, who was trouble and who wasn't worth the effort. I knew who would waste my time, who wouldn't come near me in a million years, and who I could have a little fun with.

I had a shower, where I eyed up some toned guy in his late thirties. He looked as if he might go for it, then changed his mind at the last minute and walked away. I spent ten minutes in the sauna, sweating and silent as a guy older than me stared at me, hoping to see the realisation of his hopes reflected in my face. I left him hoping and stepped back into the shower for a minute.

Walking upstairs to the next floor, I passed a cute young guy I thought I recognised. He made me feel horny so I looked back down at him, and at the same moment he turned his head. I hadn't thought he'd be salivating over me exactly but still, I hadn't expected him to be looking at me the way he was. His face was hard and his eyes were cold. He was swaying slightly from whatever alcohol he'd drunk but there was a sneer on his face. No, more than a sneer. I threw him a dirty look but he continued staring at me. It was then I saw there was something more to his expression, something wild, something savage, something dangerous. At that moment I knew exactly who he was. He was the guy I'd met in The George a few weeks earlier, Gerard. The guy writing the book about Fitzer, the guy sniffing around my past.

It was sweltering in the sauna, but even so I began to shiver. I felt the blood drain out of my face as I turned to walk away, as he turned away at the same time. 'What the fuck is he doing here?' I asked myself. 'Did he follow me here? Does he know more than he let on? Does he want to corner me at my lowest, an old man in a sauna looking for a fuck?' I felt my heart thumping and told myself to relax, that it was just another coincidence, him being here, but something didn't sit right with me. Sure this city is small, but some guy coming up to you in a bar, saying he's writing a book on someone you knew in another life, someone who was there that night, and then turning up again a couple of weeks later, staring at you in a sauna! It was all just a bit too coincidental. Somebody was out to get me, out to strangle me with my past. I just knew it.

I wanted to get out of there as quickly as I could. I felt dizzy, I felt sick, nearly fifty years after the fact. I stumbled into the porn room where somebody sniggered at me. I stayed there for a moment, trying to catch my breath before I turned to leave. I only wanted to get out, to get away. I wished then I'd never come to the sauna, never come to Dublin, never come to this vindictive island.

I've been trying not to think about it ever since, telling myself I overreacted, that he was just there for the sex like the rest of us, that he knows nothing about me. But something doesn't seem right about him being there. He doesn't belong there. And even if what he was doing there has nothing to do with me, I still want to know why. Why he was there, what brought him there. He frightens me a bit, that little faggot, that much I know. But more than that he fascinates me. I made a promise to myself that night, a promise I'd find out exactly who he was.

December 1950

AND SO I'D TAKEN the big leap. Slept with my first real flesh and blood man that foggy night in November. I was nervous as hell when we got back to his flat in town, of course I was. This was one of the most important things I'd done, something I knew would change my life. And even if I tried not to focus on the weight of the event, I was still nervous. Excited as well, and not just sexually, though I did think I'd come, release all those years of stored up lust, of denied desire, as soon as he touched me. I was animated and happy in an edgy, manic, half blind kind of way because I knew I had taken up a challenge life had thrown at me. I was no longer a prisoner to a disgusting, maddening, repulsive desire. I was now a healthy, horny young man in control of that very desire. Still, I don't want to make out that all my fears and my anger and self-loathing, all that paralysing fear and confusion, disappeared in that one night, in that one brief encounter. That would be a lie. But something began to change for me that night and suddenly everything seemed possible. I don't know if you can understand exactly what it feels like, to experience something as powerful as that possibility, that hope, that life I felt that night.

As I sat there in the car, his hand casually on my knee,

saying to myself 'I'm going to sleep with a man, I'm going to sleep with a man,' I felt a great weight being lifted off my shoulders. There was such a sense of release and from that moment everything would begin to change: how I walked, how I looked at myself in the mirror, how I saw, how I ate dinner. Not that it changed physically, not that I began mincing around and drinking my tea from china cups with my pinkie in the air. That ain't what I'm saying. I'm just saying that fear is a terrible weapon and sexuality can be a terrifying thing, and when you put the two together the concoction can be lethal. I've seen enough people take their lives with that cocktail to know what I'm talking about. That fear, that terror, that constant anxiety and almost always repressed desire can infect everything you do: how you think, what you say, how you look at people (not too long, not too intensely), how you sit (not too girly), how you smoke (try to smoke like a man with cigarette between thumb and forefinger), how you eat, sleep and shit. And most of the time you manage to keep the fear at a certain level, so that it's just a constant buzz in the back of your head, but then there are the mornings when you can't get out of bed, can't imagine how you can go on, hoping, praying, willing to do anything to get this desire to go away, willing to sell a kidney to be normal again.

And then one night you feel brave, you feel strong, you put all the madness to one side and you walk straight back into your own life, you intervene in your own existence and you change its course. You throw down your dice, put your money on the table, whatever gambling metaphor you want to use for this game of life, it doesn't matter. The point is that I turned everything upside down that night, I turned my life around. I changed the way I saw everything, I began to change the way I lived. And you, if you've never experienced that, then just be happy for me, happy because I was young and for a moment I was winning.

So the sex wasn't the greatest that night. I'd have much better over the years to come. I was awkward, I was hesitant, I didn't know exactly what to do, even though I'd imagined it often enough, before filing it away under 'TOXIC THOUGHTS: DON'T GO THERE AGAIN.' The guy was nice. His name was Edward and he was from England. He was an artist and his first floor flat on Baggot Street doubled as a studio. As I walked around the place, staring at his paintings, picking up random, stray objects and looking out the window onto the silent street below, I could feel my relationship with the world changing. The world outside was bright and full of new things, new experiences. It wasn't a dark, shady place whose reality I had to navigate carefully every day, where there was space after space cordoned off to me because I was a freak, a queer, an aberration. No, now anything seemed possible in the world outside that window, because I had made my way to that room, because I had walked down the stairs of that bar, and got into that car that took me to The Stepaside Inn, and asked this chap, asked him straight out, straight up, if he wanted to sleep with me.

So the sex wasn't great, so what! So I came not long after I'd put myself inside him the first time, and didn't even make it that far the second, pearls of too-rushed lust trailing along one of the cheeks of his arse and down the back of his hairy legs. I can still see him lying there, a naked man, with his hair all tousled and his body trusting, beautiful, laid out on the bed. Here was the real thing, the beauty of a naked man, of two naked men together, and it was every bit as erotic, every bit as breath-taking, as heart-racing, as I'd dared to imagine it. Two naked men together, and if that wasn't thrilling enough, and the kissing, the spilling, the holding, the warmth, the breath, the heartbeat, the hard, eager cocks and malleable, responsive bodies, then what was was the doors that night opened, the everything it changed. Whatever we shared that night, it was nothing compared to what I took away from it for myself, what I've kept through all of these years, what was mine and mine alone, what nobody, no matter what else they've taken, could ever, ever wrestle from me; my first time with a man. And for all of its imperfections and awkward movements, there was something so powerful, so astonishing, about that experience. I was a young man on the brink of life. So there!

I never slept with Edward again. He did ask me out and though I said I'd call up and see him sometime, I never did. I saw him in pubs and at parties over the months that followed, and we always said hello to one another and had a friendly chat. It wasn't that I didn't like him, that I hadn't enjoyed my short time with him. I had, I did, but the thought of having an ongoing something with another man didn't cross my mind for a moment during that period. And the thought of two men having a relationship seemed ludicrous, ridiculous, impossible. Two men settling down together; that was absurd. And however far I'd come in those weeks after Maeve's party and that night I spent with Edward, the idea of two men going out together like man and woman, or setting up home together like husband and wife, still made me feel uncomfortable. No, it was more than that, it terrified me.

Besides, now I'd slept with one man, jumped that fence, crossed that hurdle, made that leap of faith, I saw no reason to stop there. Why would I? There were other men: handsome, beautiful, funny, smart, talented men out there. I don't want you to think I was a whore, slutting myself around Dublin at that time, though a whore I have been since. I wasn't, but I'd had a taste of something so seductive, so goddamned beautiful, it was only natural that I'd want more. So many years I'd hidden who I was, locked myself away and tied myself up in knots. And now there was a taste of liberty in my head, and the touch of a man's lips on my mouth, and his weight under me and the taste of his skin on my hands. I wanted more, I was ready for more, of this madness, call it badness, this brave, bold beauty, this impossible moment that existed in so many rooms across the city, this coupling that shouldn't have been, that couldn't have been, that they said never was. This lovemaking against all the odds, this slash on the face of a commonly agreed upon reality, this chink in their truth, the plain cold fact of two men together.

I left a braver, bolder young man the next morning. I walked out of the flat, along Baggot Street and over to work. And as I walked around by Trinity, the hands of the clock were moving with life, and as I strolled over O'Connell Bridge the seagulls that swooped in from the sea, and the dockers, and the barges and the bridges, and the bright white light of that winter's morning, shouted life, life, life at last.

I started going to certain pubs around that time. Sometimes I went to The Dawson Lounge, that tiny pub I'd gone to that first night. It was always so warm and smoky in there, on those winter nights. It was a friendly place and we had some great evenings there. Though it might have been a minute place, it was always full of possibilities. I met a few fellas in there at that time. One was a young solicitor and one worked for Radio Éireann, doing some kind of research. They were nice guys, and I had great fun with both of them, even though I can't remember their names.

I also began going to Davy Byrnes on Duke Street. Now this place wasn't an out and out gay bar, but mind you none of the bars really were back then. Not like now with their fucking Pride flags, and their over-priced drinks and queens screaming for attention. Back then there were no gay bars in the way we think of them now. There were just certain bars, like Davy Byrnes and The Dawson Lounge, where 'Friends of Dorothy' hung out, bars that those in the know knew about. We didn't make a fuss about ourselves. We didn't have this great burning need for the rest of the world to know we existed, to recognise us, to define us, confine us, and constantly remind us of what we were. We left that to the gay liberationists who would come later, with their whistles and their coming out. What a fucking joke! I wish half of them would stay in.

We weren't forcing ourselves on the world. We had it much better than that. We had two worlds, we moved between two worlds: the everyday world of everyday folks, and then our own private world, our world that was secret, discreet, classy, with an elegance, a dignity, a warmth and humanity you won't find in those cesspits of fags you find in every city in the western world today. We had our spaces, our ways, our days and our great nights. We, all of us, existed back then, almost fifty years ago, and don't let them tell you otherwise.

And Davy Byrnes was such a fascinating place for a twenty-year-old from the country to find himself. You can't imagine, unless you've moved from some godforsaken hole in the Appalachian Mountains or Rednecksville, Alabama to New York City, or from Hull to London, or from some village in Spain to Madrid. Here I was, a kid from the back of beyond, sitting with writers, artists and intellectuals, some of them homosexuals, some of them not, but all having a drink, having a chat and having a laugh, or having the craic as they say over here. And the writers might have whined about the place, and how the city had declined and how all the great men of letters had left or were dead, and how the government was strangling them with its stupid censorship, but to me these living, breathing writers were stars, these boho, hard-drinking guys.

Davy Byrnes, with its writers publishing stories in *The Bell*, and sending off pieces to *Points* magazine in Paris. Davy Byrnes, with its banned books brought back from abroad. Davy Byrnes, with its rapid wit and its clever conversations. With its novelists falling out its doors. With its fair share of guys like me on any given night. I left that place with more than one man. I left with a couple of hopeful writers, a sculptor, a sales assistant in a fancy department store, and a guy who was a dray man with Guinness's. There were others I wanted to sleep with but who weren't interested in me, and others who wanted to be with me that I had no desire for. But none of that mattered. I loved each and every one of those men in Davy Byrnes, in The Dawson Lounge, in the bona fides out at Stepaside and Goatstown, in Bewley's, and at the parties and all the places we met. Each and every one of them had his own story and each and every one of them spoke to me of life, of life against the odds, of lives and loves and intimacies that should not have been but were. There was something magic in that.

At first I couldn't believe how many of us there were. Like most, I'd thought I was alone, or virtually alone, condemned to keep quiet, to conform, to reform, to run away. But here I was, and there were hundreds like me, and they were mostly friendly and warm, and funny, and some of them were good-looking and some of them weren't. And it wasn't just the sex that mattered, though of course that did and of course that was great fun. But it wasn't just that. It was to live alone with an unnameable desire, a lust, a love, a fundamental need for two decades, and then realise, accept, understand, that there were others, so many others, like you. It was living alone and only letting the rat out of its cage on the odd night, only to enter a pub, a party, a café, and see that there were others who were the same as you. It was beginning to let go of a furious need to strangle that deathly desire, to begin to find a language for all that you had never been able to say to yourself. To realise you weren't alone. We were the resurrected, the buried come to life again.

And to feel that new life, that new love, both for myself and those other men, as the Christmas lights were strung along the streets, as the Christmas trees were put up on O'Connell Street and at St Stephen's Green. To have that moment as the Christmas cheer wrapped up the city in its warmth and its decorated windows is something I cannot forget. That sense of the new, that hope, as I cycled to work on mornings sharp with frost, and as the festive lights flickered in the evening darkness and I made my way to one of the bars where already I knew many of the faces. And the thought that I might meet someone that night, some beautiful new body, some new face, new story, new life. That's something that's been with me every Christmas since, no matter where I've been.

I began going to see Maeve in Bewley's again. We never spoke about what I was going through, about my new life, my new love of life, of men, my new self as a man. We didn't have to. She understood, understood much more than I did. I can see that now. She acted as though I'd never been absent, never stopped coming to see her, never really started hating her. I suppose she'd seen enough young men like me in her time. I suppose she'd seen them them pass through all the phases of self-loathing, to hating her, to beginning to learn how to live a different kind of life. I felt bad that I'd cursed her so much, that I'd thought of her as a ringmaster, as a busybody, as a cruel bitch. She'd wanted to help me, that was all, I could see that now. She'd seen something in me I wouldn't accept, couldn't accept, and she'd opened a door for me, opened up a world for me. I was lucky, lucky to know her. I hadn't had to find that world on my own. She'd helped me cut short my years of hating, of wasting away, before I found a place where I could belong.

Who knows what would have happened if she hadn't come into my life. I might have married, had kids, might have buried myself in a stranger's life, in a life I thought should have been mine but never was. Maybe I'd have started sneaking off to the saunas, the parks, the public toilets, to get my fix, my dicks, my pricks. Had my wife at home and my men on the side. But she had made something else possible, she had altered the course of my life. Whatever else came after: the death, the guilt, the running away, the hiding, the fear, and all the years tainted by that terrible night, whatever came later, Maeve gave something to me then. For a few moments, a few months, she made everything possible.

'Maeve, what's the matter? What's happened?' It was an evening in December and Maeve was sitting in the café, sitting very still, with tears streaming down her face and looking out into the distance. 'Oh, Daniel,' she apologised, 'I'm sorry. I didn't see you come in. Sit down.' She took a tortoiseshell compact and a handkerchief from her bag, and very carefully began to wipe around her eyes, looking like a small bird studying its own reflection in the water. Somehow she hadn't managed to smudge her make-up, even though her eyes were red and I could tell she'd been crying a lot. 'Look at the state of me!' she said with a soft chuckle as she studied herself in the small mirror.

I sat there wondering what was going on. It was the first time I'd seen Maeve crack, the first time I'd seen her lose control, the first time I'd seen her emotions get the better of her. Maeve was a lot older than me. She was an intelligent, beautiful woman, a grown-up to my twenty-year-old eyes, and somehow I'd never expected to see her like this. She was strong and smart, dominant and in charge. She was kind and friendly in her way, but also somebody you wouldn't want to mess with. I'd already seen her tear somebody to pieces with her tongue, and I had both admired her and feared her a little for that. She commanded respect as well as turning heads wherever she went. Always in control of her image, sure of what she was projecting and what people thought of her, so confident and self-assured. I never thought I'd see her look so vulnerable, so inconsolable. But there she was before me, putting herself together after she'd broken down.

'I'm sorry, Daniel,' she apologised again. 'It's just Fitzer was here and he brought it all back.' 'Who's Fitzer?' I demanded, not knowing what was going on. 'What did he say to you? What did he do to you?' 'Oh, he didn't do anything, Daniel. It's just every time I see him, he makes me think about him. They were together, together in Spain, you know.' She was looking off in another direction. 'Maeve, I don't know what you're talking about,' I pleaded, looking at her, bewildered. 'Who's Fitzer? Who was together in Spain? What's happened?' Maeve being a lady of the theatre, I began to wonder if this was all some kind of elaborate act, preparation for a role or something, I don't know. She gave a deep sigh then and looked at me. 'Oh, Daniel, I don't expect you to understand all this. How could you? But if you don't mind listening to a miserable old wretch talking about her past, I'll tell you why I was crying. I'll tell you the whole tragic story.' She smiled at the self-conscious drama of her words. I smiled back at her. 'I'm on for it if you are,' I said. 'Okay, let's go to Jammet's for a bite to eat,' she proposed, brightening a little. 'My treat, for having such a handsome young dinner companion.'

I blushed a little, laughed, and told her she was the most beautiful woman in the world. She laughed at that but I meant it. She even looked beautiful when she was crying. As we got up from the table, I held out my arm for her to link as we walked. What an odd couple we must have looked!

'I was married, Daniel, did you know that?' Maeve stated more than asked as we sat at a table in the plush surroundings of Jammet's, a fancy restaurant on Nassau Street I'd passed often but had never been to. 'Yes, I had wondered, to be honest, if there was a husband in the picture,' I replied. 'Oh, there was, Daniel. His name was James. James!' She looked straight into my eyes as she began to tell her story. 'We met when I was quite young, through the theatre. It was back in the thirties. We were trying to do something different, trying to put on work that would speak to the people. He was from a wealthy family and worked as a doctor, but really he was interested in theatre, in theatre and politics. We were putting on a piece by Brecht the first time I met him. When he walked into that rehearsal space he took my breath away, took it right away.' Maeve smiled to herself as she remembered the moment.

'I fell in love with him there and then,' she continued. 'I know that sounds terribly romantic and unrealistic, but it's true, Daniel. I knew I'd marry him there and then, knew he was the one. Has anything like that ever happened to you? Have you ever felt such an incredible, immeasurable love for somebody you have never once spoken to?' 'I, I don't think I have,' I said, fumbling for words and feeling a bit uncomfortable with this older woman spilling out her heart to me. But then I hadn't experienced that jolt of love by then. Little did I know how soon I would.

'I fell in love with him, Daniel, and I suppose he fell in love with me in a way.' 'What do you mean, in a way?' I wondered, noting her sentence was loaded and wondering exactly what she meant. 'Well, he wasn't like other men, not exactly. I could see that when I got to know him better. Oh, he was strong and handsome and intelligent and wonderful, but I knew there was something different about him. I knew he needed something other than me. I knew he loved me, was in love with me, I never questioned that, but I also knew there was something I couldn't give him, something he could only find for himself.' I must have been looking pretty dopey and confused because Maeve looked at me hard and said, 'Oh, I'm talking in circles, aren't I. What I'm trying to say, what I want to say, and please try to understand, please try not to judge James or me— God, why do I still find this hard to say? What I'm trying to say is that my husband loved me, but he also loved men. My husband loved men.'

'What do you mean your husband loved men?' I asked. 'How could your husband love men?' I was completely baffled by what she was saying. At the same time though, while what she was saying sounded completely bizarre and impossible, nothing anybody said to me could have surprised me that much after what I'd been through myself in the previous weeks. 'I can't dress it up, Daniel. I mean exactly what I've just said. My husband loved men.' 'But why did he marry you? Why did he get married if he knew he liked men?' I probed, trying to figure out exactly how they had ended up together. 'Like I say, we were in love. It wasn't that he wasn't interested in women and was using me as a smokescreen to hide another life. It wasn't like that. He was completely open with me from the start. We talked about it for a long time before we decided to continue with the relationship and get married.'

'And how did you feel when he told you? Didn't you want to break off the relationship?' I asked. 'Well, I must admit I was very upset at first and decided not to see him for a few weeks. It wasn't that I was angry with him for what he'd told me. He was what he was and there was no way I could change that. I don't even know if I wanted to. I just needed some time to see if I could accept it, if it was something I could live with. It takes such a lot of strength to share somebody you love with others.'

'But in the end you decided it was worth it?' I ventured. 'Yes, I did rather. I'd never met anyone like James. He was so intelligent, so kind, so different, so handsome. And we made some couple, Daniel. Everybody said it about us. Said we were the perfect couple, that we looked as though we absolutely belonged together.' I was so used to seeing Maeve on her own, so used to thinking about her as the arch individual, it was strange for me to think of her as part of a couple, but when I imagined her sitting in a restaurant with her husband, or dancing at a party, or just laughing with him, I felt happy, happy for Maeve.

'But wasn't it hard for you, knowing your husband had other lovers, and male lovers?' I asked, knowing that it must have been tough on her. 'It was difficult sometimes, of course it was, but we had certain rules. Of course he slept with other men and got involved with one or two of them, but ours was the most important relationship, and he never did anything to jeopardise that.' 'You must have really loved him,' I said. 'Yes, I did, very much. And that meant not trying to change him, not trying to own him, not trying to make him into something he wasn't. And don't think I didn't have my own fun. I've never been the kind of woman to stay at home pining for her husband.' There was a smile on Maeve's lips. She looked so sensual, so sexual, delicious! I smiled and blushed a little as she scooped a cherry from her cocktail glass and bit into it.

'What, what happened to James?' I asked, finally working up the courage to ask what had happened to her husband. 'No, Daniel, he didn't run off with a man if that's what you're thinking,' said Maeve, maybe guessing what was going on in my mind. 'He ran off to fight for Spain.' 'He went to fight with the Blueshirts?' I blundered. 'The Blueshirts,' Maeve spat the words out. 'What do you think he was? The Blueshirts! My word, no. Not in a million years. He went to fight with the International Brigades. Joined up and went to defend the Republic, the democratically elected Republic! He'd turn in his grave if he thought anybody could believe he'd fought for those fascist bastards.' Maeve was angry now, so angry I thought her emotion would fill up the whole of the restaurant. 'Bastards,' she said, loud enough for a man at the table next to ours to turn around.

Maeve was sad now as well as angry. There was a slight crack in her voice and something broken about her. 'He died there, didn't he?' I said softly. 'Yes, Daniel, he died there. Died by a fascist bullet outside Madrid in 1937. Died for what he believed in, died trying to help those poor people. It was Fitzer who got the news to me, Fitzer who sent me the letter. Fitzer was there when he died. Said he'd told him that he loved me more than anything, that he was sorry, so sorry to leave me.'

Her eyes were watering. 'That's why you found me like you did earlier, Daniel. Because Fitzer had come to see me. Because every time I see him, I think of James dying in Spain, dying for Spain, Spain that we'd loved and travelled around before the war. I still can't believe he's gone, Daniel, I can't believe he's gone.' Two enormous tears sailed slowly down her cheeks and she looked at me from a lonely, lonely place.

'You haven't met Fitzer or Paul, have you?' she asked after she'd wiped the tears from her face. 'No, I haven't,' I replied. 'I'll have to introduce you to them,' she said. 'The most wonderful couple in Dublin. Everybody knows them.'

'So Fitzer came and saw you after the war?' I half stated, still trying to piece together Fitzer's story and how he had come to be living in Dublin eleven years after the war had ended. 'Yes, he came to see me. He managed to get here when the International Brigades were disbanded, when the Irish came home. James had asked him to come and see me and he did. I think he pretended he was Irish, or something like that. Who knows, maybe his heritage is Irish. He's always been so sketchy about his past. I'm not even sure he's from the States. Anyway, he came to see me. He wrote to me and said he was coming.

'I was there at Westland Row to meet him that evening,' she continued. 'There were only a few of us there: wives and mothers and friends who'd come to welcome the men home, who thanked God that Spain hadn't taken their men. I still somehow thought that James would be with them, still had a vague kind of hope that it had all been a mistake, a misunderstanding, that he was really okay.' Her face lit up a little, maybe because she was remembering that hope that still connected her to James, that tiniest possibility of life as she stood there on the platform at Westland Row station.

'He didn't get off that train, of course he didn't,' she went on. 'Fitzer did though, I knew it was him the moment I saw him. I knew it was him right away. I liked him from the moment we met, even though there was something deep inside me that hated him because he had survived and James hadn't. But when all was said and done, I couldn't blame Fitzer for James going to the war, for getting killed. At the end of the day, I liked Fitzer, and I would come to like him even more. He's become such an important part of my life, Daniel. Fitzer means the world to me.' 'So, he stayed here?' I asked, knowing the answer to my question already. 'Yes, he stayed here. Fell in love with an actor soon after he arrived and decided to stay here. He's become more Irish than you or me, Daniel. You'd hardly know he wasn't from Ireland to talk to him now.'

'Maeve, can I ask you something?' I said a few moments

later, finally plucking up the courage to ask her a question that had been running around inside my head. 'Of course,' she responded, 'go ahead.' 'Were James and Fitzer lovers in Spain?' I asked, feeling a bit nasty and blunt for asking the question but wanting to know the answer more than anything. 'Oh, lovers, Daniel, what does that mean anyway? No, they weren't lovers, not in the physical sense. But did they love each other? I suppose they did, but more like friends or brothers. I know they took care of each other after they met. I know they meant a lot to each other. I know whatever they shared is their own, it belongs to them and that time and place. And I suppose that's part of the reason I love Fitzer so much, because James loved him, because I can still feel James through him.'

Maeve looked around the restaurant. There were people at only a couple of tables. 'Shall we go for a night-cap?' she asked. 'I'd love to,' I said. 'Thank you for listening, Daniel,' she said, taking my hand in hers. 'I don't speak to a lot of people about those times. Thank you.' 'No, thank you,' I murmured, taking her hand between mine and caressing it.

It was a couple of weeks after this that I met Anthony. I was at a Christmas cocktail party at an ambassador's house, somewhere on the south side of town. I'd been invited by a man I'd met the night before. In truth, I wasn't all that keen on him, even though he'd spent most of the night looking at me with Bambi eyes. Still, when he asked me to go the party, I said I would, thinking it wouldn't be any harm, and so used to the cycle of Christmas parties by now a night in would have been unthinkable. So I went with this man, who was okay I suppose, but a bit too eager to impress me. I borrowed a tuxedo from Paddy at work, slicked my hair back carefully, and was picked up by him at half eight.

Even though I'd only been speaking the love that dare not

speak its name for over a month, already I'd become an expert at spotting people like me in a room, and this party had more than its fair share of them, sprinkled in amongst all the posh husbands and wives. There were one or two couples I'd seen around town. There were middle-aged diplomats dripping in youth, smiling like the cats who'd got the cream. And there was a small group of good-looking men over to one side, and by their near constant laughter, their polished appearances and the incessant glances around the room, looking for potential mates, I could tell they were from my club. I suppose that often made it easier to go new places and try new things, the thought that there would be some of your kind there, the knowledge that you wouldn't be alone. There's security in that. What can I say, I'm not standing on my soap box and preaching about the Gay Community (Capital G and capital C), I've never gone in that much for community, always felt pretty much outside whatever community I was supposed to belong to. It's not that. It's just that sometimes it made life a lot easier, it made life a lot more fun.

I was having a drink, listening to some witty repartee, or whatever we called shooting the shit back then, a little bored by the man I was with, feeling a bit like a poor relation to such high-class people, a little bumpkin in such a sophisticated place, when the door opened and he walked in. He was blond, he had blue eyes and a good body, and though he was young, just a little older than me, his face had a sexy, experienced kind of look, kind of world-weary, kind of been there, done that. He was about my height but the tuxedo he was wearing made him look taller, made him look sophisticated, entirely confident and, what can I say, beautiful. He looked a bit drunk, a bit wild, a bit dangerous. He looked a little bit like trouble and I liked him more than any man I'd ever seen.

I watched him as he quickly took a glass off a tray a waiter was carrying, downed it in one, grabbed another and went to change the record. He put on some jazz, Dizzy Gillespie or some other American musician who was all the rage at the time. He turned around and began to click his fingers, moving his hips as he half-walked, half-danced his way into the centre of the room. I stood staring at him as others did. He moved slowly to the beat, lost in the music, lost in his own world. But then he stopped for a moment, as if he could sense somebody looking at him, as if he knew I was staring at him. He stopped for a moment, looked right at me, looked at me for a long time, and smiled. He smiled a broad, beautiful smile and his eyes lit up. He looked like the most extraordinary man I'd ever seen and I saw there and then the possibility we might be together. No, I knew there and then that we'd be together, that we'd spend that night in bed together. I felt a slight panic for a moment but then I smiled, smiled back at him; as surely, as confidently, as knowingly as I could. I grinned back at him and without words, with only our eyes, we made a silent contract that we would spend the night together. And there it was, Anthony and I, two bees drowning in honey.

'Hi, how's it going?' he broke the ice. It hadn't taken us long to make our way towards one another. In fact that had become our sole aim of the night, and I'd left my date blathering on about American economics and waved goodbye to him in my head. 'All right,' I replied, smiling. 'How about you?' 'Good, thanks,' he said. 'I'm Anthony. What's your name?' He held out a hand, which I took and shook, holding onto it for longer than I should have, wanting him to know, if he hadn't already guessed, that I was interested, very interested. 'I'm Daniel,' I responded.

'Where are you from? Who are you with? What do you do? Where do you live?' he asked, I answered, I asked, both of us knowing all of these preliminaries were just the polite formalities before the act that we both knew the night would end in. Everything was a kind of foreplay: the movement of my hand along his sleeve, the low whispering in my ear about some sworn enemy of his that was at the party, his eyes on me as I went to get a drink, my eyes on the golden hairs of his chest when he took his bow tie off in rebellion, and my sideways glances at his crotch as he swayed to the music. There were our hands touching, and hands resting on lower backs for a moment. There was our sweet breath as we moved into each other and spoke about who knows what. There was the surge in my trousers and his, with the sensuality, the potential of one another's body and all the night we'd spend together, all the time our eyes meeting, our smiles meeting, and whatever bond had begun growing stronger by the minute, our instincts drawing us further into one another. There might have been a hundred or more people at the party that night, but as soon as we found one another across that room, there was only Anthony and me, would only ever be Anthony and me.

Anthony was from Wicklow, he was studying French and Spanish at University College Dublin, and from what I could tell he was from a rich family. He wasn't very enamoured of the guests at the party. 'What a pack of fucking idiots,' he said, looking around the room at the middle-aged men smoking cigars and drinking whiskey, their evening-gowned wives ever at their sides, the fags tittering in a corner, and so many people trying to be somebody. It wasn't the most exciting party I'd ever been to, but Anthony's reaction towards it shocked me a little. Shocked and thrilled me. It made me like him even more. He didn't give a fuck what people thought about him, wasn't buying into any of the clever chitchat, barely concealed bragging, and notch-on-the-bedpost sexual machinations that the room was full of. To him it was all bullshit and he made no apologies for thinking that, made no pretences otherwise. There I'd been a couple of hours earlier, thinking it was a privilege to be there, and he'd suddenly turned my whole perception of the place on its head, shown how empty and hollow and absurd the whole scene was. And if he was against this world, then I was right at his side. Anthony and me, and our first evening against the world.

'Do you want to go somewhere else?' he asked invitingly. 'I've got some drink back at my flat and we can put on some records.' Of course I wanted to, of course I did. It was what I'd been waiting for all night, the only conclusion to that moment our eyes had met and we'd smiled at one another. And yet something made me stop and think for a moment, something made me stop and think, instead of following my primal, animal instincts, as I'd been doing all night. I guess somewhere at the back of my drunken mind, I knew whatever was about to happen with Anthony would be more than a one night event. He wasn't somebody I'd spend the night with and wave goodbye to in the morning, no regrets. This was something else, something more, something so removed from what I'd experienced before that it would change everything. And I guess I knew that somehow as I stood there, staring into nothing, wondering if I wanted to get into this. Anthony snapped me out of it. 'Are you coming?' he half-demanded, and I could see there was a hint of disappointment on his face, a flicker of a terrible sadness. 'Yeah,' I replied, 'of course I'm coming. Wouldn't miss it for the world.' We left the party without saying goodbye to a single, solitary person.

We walked back to his flat, just off Leeson Street in the Mespil Estate. As soon as we got into the lobby, we began to kiss, began to run our hands along each other's bodies. We wanted each other so desperately that first night, falling in the door of his flat, falling to the floor, before we dragged ourselves, now completely naked, to his bed. We were so drunk and mad for one another and nothing could have dragged us away from the sweet, wild, miraculous taste, that hard, wet weight of our combined bodies.

Our lovemaking was a wild, crazy dance of flesh; tumbling, falling, sucking, kissing, caressing, pushing, opening, grasping, gasping, tearing, trembling beauty, wild and wonderful. We both wanted to, no, had to, possess the other as completely as we could. We reached and wrestled until I gave myself to him, gave myself to a man for the first time in a way I'd never believed I would. I let Anthony put himself inside me.

The pain was vicious at first, but slowly I began to enjoy it, the wildness, the freedom of it. I moved my body to the rhythm of him hard inside me. And soon we were flying, flying off somewhere beyond ourselves, beyond that room, beyond that little city below us. Off. Off and it was magic, unbearable, exquisite, unbelievable magic and we kept our eyes closed, flying away until there was no end it to but that violent release. Anthony! We collapsed into one another, fell asleep, woke up and made that mad love again, and again, and again and again, until there was nothing left of us but whatever we'd shared.

And it was that night I'd think about two days later as I sat at my mother's dinner table, and my father sliced into the turkey on Christmas Day. That night and his flesh, his body and the two of us kissing and flying and falling, the two of us making love against that freezing December night.

Anthony! Jesus, how I loved you. Jesus, how we loved. Can it have been so long ago, Anthony? So long since we shared all that, since it all began?

5
January 1998

I'VE LEFT IRELAND. Driven away again!

I walked into a travel agent's in Dún Laoghaire last Wednesday, the wettest Wednesday I have ever known, and asked them to send me somewhere with some sunshine. I haven't left Ireland for good. It isn't time, I'm not finished there yet. There's still more, so much more, to remember, to write down. But I did need a bit of sunshine to shake off these winter blues. I did need a break from that place that was beginning to suffocate me again. Oh, okay, and I needed some time away from my past. It was either hit the Prozac or take a package holiday. I chose the holiday. What can I say?

They sent me here to the Canary Islands. Spain! Not the mainland, no, not Granada. I still don't know if I could bear to go to that city. But Spain anyway and who knows, perhaps I'm getting closer to that place, perhaps one day I'll make it there, feel strong enough to visit that city of dead men, that place we'd planned to visit together. But enough about that. I'm tired of thinking about the past, of thinking about him, of those days and that night. I want a break. I want it to stop. Oh, I know it's my own fault. It was me who went digging up the past when even the worms had given up on his corpse. Maybe I should have left well enough alone. I've lived long enough with what happened, with what I did or didn't do. Maybe I should have left it for somebody else to tell the truth, when I am no longer here. Oh fuck it! I didn't come here to think about all that.

So, Gran Canaria. Not exactly Martha's Vineyard, but still, when needs must. I'm not above slumming it, if only once in a while. There are tourists from all over Europe here: English, Irish, German, Dutch, French, Spanish. All here for the same thing; to get laid, get a tan and get drunk. Nobody has any pretensions towards anything else. You don't come to the Canaries for the culture or the museums. At least it's honest. Sun and sex, not a bad way to spend the end of January.

I'm staying in a small complex close to the gay beach. I walk down there early every morning when there's hardly anybody around. I swim, swim out as far as I can, and maybe it's only then, against the vastness of the ocean, that I can begin to forget the vastness of my past. I spend the day soaking up the sun and watching the eye candy on the beach. There are dark, cute Spanish guys, some sexy French guys, and a few good-looking Germans. There's a couple of cute ones amongst the Brits and the Irish, but most of them aren't anything to look at really.

Lots of guys go naked here. Big German guys with their big German cocks hanging out. The Dutch are the same. Walking around bare assed as if it were second nature to them. The Irish stare at the naked queers as if they were aliens, tittering like little girls. 'Oh my God, I can't believe these people are naked!' And all the time so uncomfortable with their own bodies, so unsure of themselves, so fucking repressed. I don't normally go naked myself though. My days of baring the flesh are long gone. It somehow doesn't seem right, me letting my bits hang out at this stage in my life.

It's like watching a hundred guys play ping-pong with their eyes, lying on this beach. Faggots crack me up. Always out for the kill, always ready for a bit of action. And their faces become so intense when they're cruising, their eyes so full of a need for a certain guy. Until they spot a hotter one that is, and then they're off, faster than you can say fellatio. Sometimes guys hook up on the beach, eyeball each other and get together for a chat, maybe a kiss, but everybody knows the real action isn't on the beach but in the dunes that stretch along behind it. I've been there a couple of times. I'm not above, and certainly not too old for, a bit of a cruise myself. I've hooked up with a few guys there. One young guy, another in his forties, and even one just a few years younger than me. French, German and Dutch. Nothing major, nothing life changing or earth-shattering. Just some good old gay fun. Just a break from whatever book I'm reading on the beach, *The English Patient*, *Flesh and Blood*, *L.A. Confidential*.

I mostly stay in at night, after I've had something to eat. Read a bit or write a bit, which I've got so used to doing I can't seem to stop, even if I am just describing what I see around me every day. Or sometimes I just lie on my bed as the ceiling fan whirs slowly around above me and let it all recede into the distance, this story of my life, this life I'm involved in living. I close my eyes and let it all drift away.

One night I went to the Yumbo Centre, one of the weirdest places I've ever been. I mean I've lived in the country that invented the mall for more than forty years, but this place takes the biscuit. An actual mall full of fag bars and clubs. Bars with tacky British drag queens, tackier British fags and a few breeders who've wandered in to see the show. A leather bar with more than a score of men who look like they've walked straight out of a Tom of Finland book. A bar pumping out music with shirtless buffed boys enjoying the sight of their own carefully constructed bodies. A bar with an older crowd. Bars with dark rooms, bars decorated with balloons.

I didn't particularly like the place and still it fascinated me in a way. I wandered around it a couple of times, wondering if it was real, if it was for real. Finally I went for a drink in one of the bars, a place that wasn't too full of drunken queens. Maybe I drank too much and that's why I began thinking about him. Not about Anthony, not exactly. About Gerard.

I saw him before I came here. I'd spent a couple of weeks looking for him, trying to find him, to find out what he was up to. I went to bar after bar, night after night, but he wasn't among the die-hard January drinkers. I went to different restaurants where I thought he might work, and probably put on ten pounds in the process. He wasn't in any of them. I went to a club and left feeling old and mortified and depressed. He wasn't there. I even went back to the sauna, not to be with anyone, just to see if he was there again. He wasn't.

I began thinking about him at strange times, wondering what he was doing, if he was trying to find me, if he was watching me when I didn't know it. I started to try to place him, to piece together his life in my head and understand how he'd got involved in all of this. Whatever I imagined though: where he was from, where he lived, who he loved and what he was doing right then, the fact was I still didn't know anything about him. He, and exactly why he was interested in the past, if he genuinely was, why he'd walked up to me in the bar, and why he'd been in the sauna that night, remained a mystery to me. And it wasn't so much that I was scared of him anymore, though I have to admit I still was a bit. It was more that he interested me, he interested me a lot.

And then I saw him just before I came here. Saw him one

morning where I'd least expected to find him. I found him in the National Library. It was a freezing winter's morning, but bright with a strong, undefeated sun. A morning full of hope that was a surprise, a gift, in the middle of days full of the same old misery, days full of darkness. It was a day of clear thoughts and new insights, when I could face anything, when I could see that night objectively, clearly, from the distance of these years.

I went to the library to look at the newspapers from all those years ago, to see exactly what they'd said, to face the official version of my past, the nation's version of that night. I got my visitor's ticket, just like the fat American couples who waddled around the library looking for ancestors who'd fled to the States during the Famine. I left my coat on the rack and walked upstairs to the reading room. It was so silent, so silent and sunny in there. Even that early in the morning, there were already people working at the old wooden desks, their heads bent as they pored over their work and made their way through books. I stopped at the door, stopped to look at the place: the domed ceiling, the old wooden counter, the shelves of books, the readers.

I had a moment then, a kind of deja vu as I stood there. I could remember it so clearly, feel it so vividly. Going to the library once to meet Anthony when he was studying for his final exams. Standing there as the late May sun spilled into the room. It was such a warm, benevolent day, a day when nothing bad could happen. Anthony was there at a desk on the back row, his blond hair falling over the hand his head was resting in. Looking at him there, looking golden, looking focused, looking strong and beautiful, I thought he'd make it. I thought he'd make it through.

I snapped out of it and went to the counter where you request books. There was a good-looking guy behind the desk.

I scanned his face, his gestures, for the mark of Sodom but found none. I told him what newspapers I was looking for. He said they were on microfilm and asked me to write down exactly what I wanted. I put the information on the card slowly and carefully: the names of the newspapers, the month and the year. I felt so calm, like a journalist researching a story or a scientist conducting an experiment. It didn't seem like my own life I was investigating. I passed the card to the librarian, looking him straight in the eye. He took it and said somebody would drop them down to me shortly. I went to a room at the back, sat at a desk, turned on the machine for the microfilms and waited in the glow of its lamp. A few minutes later, two small cardboard boxes of film were dropped on the table. The story of a life, of two lives, reduced to two little cardboard boxes, two little cardboard coffins.

I put the film in place and began to flick through the pages. Slowly at first, then quicker and quicker. Wars, political events and cinema and theatre pages from the time zipped past me. The fate of Julius and Ethel Rosenberg in the States, the continuing war in Korea, news about Israel, a photo from *Sunset Boulevard*, pictures from a hurling match, an article about ladies' fashion, ads for Bird's Custard and Royal Baking Powder. As I came towards the date I was looking for, I slowed down again. Slowly, slowly, closer and closer, until I saw the first mention of it, the evening after it had happened.

There it was, in black and white, the headline I'd been looking for and the story of what had happened that night, or the newspaper's version of it anyway, or the nation's.

I scanned the rest of the page. There was a shot of the destroyed Abbey Theatre that had burnt down the same night he died. In the next day's paper there were more articles about his death and a photo of Maeve's house. Over the days that followed there were insinuations that the party that had taken place in Maeve's house that night had been decadent and immoral, and that the house was renowned for its 'unconventional' celebrations. There was an interview with somebody who'd been to one of Maeve's parties, a guy who described what went on there as disgusting and perverted. He was the same married guy who'd tried to get me in the sack once. There were photos of Maeve, looking harassed, looking hounded. There were pictures of actors, artists, and a doctor who was said to have frequented the house.

There were no photos of me and though they didn't print my name, I knew who they were talking about when they mentioned a young man who'd run from the house, who'd been taken in for questioning. I knew how they relished his death and all the allusions to our intimacy. I knew they saw us as filth, as perverts, knew how they rolled around like fat pigs in the dirt they imagined of our lives. I knew how they enjoyed every minute of their judgement. I was the faceless, nameless enemy that had made the nation shudder. I was the link between our kind and his death. I was the one they were terrified of.

'Hypocrites and parasites the lot of them,' I said out loud, surprised at the rage I still felt after all these years. I turned off the machine, and put the film back into its box. I couldn't look any more at what they'd made of our lives, at how they'd confined and condemned us in print. I was so angry all I wanted to do was get out of that fucking library.

I left the room and was walking towards the counter to return the film when I saw him. At first I wasn't sure it was him, thought I'd been mistaken, but when I took a closer look, I could see it was him right enough. It was Gerard. He was sitting there quietly, peacefully, working away.

I began to suspect he'd followed me, but I knew that wasn't true. The streets had been deathly quiet that morning and I would have noticed if somebody was on my trail. That's what I told myself anyway, as I stood there watching him, pretending I was looking up something on the computer. I stood staring at him in his black sweater and jeans, completely involved in his book, save for the odd glance about the room. 'Maybe he is actually writing a book, maybe that much is true,' I thought to myself, feeling a bit relieved. I wondered if the book he was reading at that moment spoke about the productions Fitzer and Maeve had been involved in. I wondered if the book mentioned me, spoke about that night. Suddenly the thought of him wading around in what some stranger had said about my life, about that night, made me feel furious. I wanted to storm up to him, snatch the book out of his hands and snap it shut. I wanted to tell him to get the hell out of our lives, our past, our history. I wanted to tell him that words were dangerous, that they didn't have anything to do with the truth, that nobody except me could know what had really happened that night.

I couldn't though. I just couldn't do it. He looked so interested in something, such a part of something, and I began to see that he belonged there amongst those books. Okay, he could have been just acting, but at that moment I doubted it. His face wasn't flirtatious like I'd seen it when he was so bright and breezy in the bar, or so full of hate like it was in the sauna. It was full of life and stories and thoughts that were his own, only his own. I felt something stir inside me then: happiness, hope, sadness, regret. I saw Anthony sitting there and suddenly I couldn't tell who I was looking at. I saw scenes from my life, scenes from my past, and I felt like I was about to cry, about to start balling like some drama queen there and then. The tears were coming, my head began buzzing, and it was all too much. I dropped the films and got out of the place as quickly as I could, cursing him and cursing Anthony as I left, hating them both a bit.

First thing the next morning I booked this holiday. Maybe you can't escape your past, but who says you can't take a holiday from it.

January 1951

SO THERE IT WAS BETWEEN US, our first night together, Anthony and I. The first night of our story. I couldn't stop thinking about him all through that Christmas with my family. I couldn't wait to see him again, to kiss him, to hold him, to lie with him again and let the world rot away for all we cared. My head was full of Anthony, only of Anthony, that Christmas. I was due to go back to Dublin on the 27th, and we'd planned to meet that evening for a meal. 'That can be our Christmas dinner,' Anthony had joked the morning I'd left him, the morning after the night our lives were brought together.

It was nice at home, warm and cosy, and I was treated like a prince, the son up in the capital back in the bosom of the family. Still though, I couldn't wait to get back to Dublin, which was my home now, my city now, the only place I'd ever felt I belonged. Nice to see the family, yes, but country-town life wasn't me anymore, not after the new existence I'd begun for myself, the life I was dying to get back to. And there was also a slight gnawing feeling in my stomach, a feeling that I wanted to escape, needed to escape again, that my new world wouldn't survive against this reality, the reality of a country town. I suppose there was a certain amount of fear in the background, a fear that I'd never find my way back to what I'd started up in Dublin. I tried not to think about it too much.

Then on St Stephen's night I went to the local pub with my brothers, like we always did. The place was full and everybody was in great form, full of the Christmas spirit. We stood at the bar. A couple of my brothers' friends joined us and then a couple of guys I'd palled around with in school. There was a lot of laughter and joking and slagging. They were all drunk and happy. The talk turned to girls and they all stood around talking about who they were screwing, who they wanted to screw and who they would never screw. That exaggerated, macho, stupid talk straight men do so well when they get together. I began to feel uncomfortable, like I didn't belong there, like I just wanted to get out of there. The chat went on and on and I stood there in silence. What could I say to their talk of getting a feel of a tit or a leg over on a Saturday night? That I'd been fucked for the first time a few nights before, by a guy I'd fucked too? That we'd fucked all night long? And what could I say to the ones who had married, who had settled down, who spoke about their new solid, respectable lives? That I really felt something for this fella I'd spent the night with, something I'd never felt before? That maybe we had a future?

I should have left, made my excuses and got out of there right then, but I didn't. I was too scared that they'd know something was up, that they already knew what I'd been up to, that there was a queer, a ginger beer, a nancy boy amongst them. I stood there in a paranoid panic. I could feel my hands sweating and my heart thumping. I drank more and more quickly, unable to snap out of whatever I was thinking until I became paralysed by my fear and was unable to move. I couldn't even go to the toilet because I thought somebody would come in and beat me up for being a queer. Or somebody would say I'd been looking at them at the urinal, or that I belonged in the Ladies, or in the asylum.

I started thinking about everything that I'd seen and been and lived in Dublin, and my new life began to seem strange, to seem sick and strange and revolting. It began to feel a million miles away from the normality of that pub, the normality of that night. I wasn't strong enough, or wise enough, or brave enough, to stand my ground, if only in my head. My two worlds, my two lives, my past and my present, had come into collision, and I left the pub that night drunker and more depressed than I'd been in a while. My hopes that anything special could happen between Anthony and me were defeated. Defeated by them, by me, defeated. I swore to myself I wouldn't go and meet him the following night.

I took the train early the next afternoon, not really wanting to go back to Dublin, but at the same time dying to get away from the town. I was hungover and exhausted. I'd hardly slept at all the night before, thinking about everything, trying to find a way out of my life. I'd tried fantasising about girls, tried imagining myself going out with girls again, maybe getting married, but of course I knew it was stupid. There was no point in lying to myself. I knew what I was and I wasn't about to go back to that old life of self-delusion.

But still, these feelings I had for Anthony were too much for me to handle. I knew what I felt for him was more than sexual, knew that it hadn't just been a one night encounter, knew that I wanted to see him again, couldn't wait to see him again, and that scared the shit out of me. You have to understand, I might have finally accepted the fact that I was into men, that I slept with men. Accepted it in a way, even though I tried not to think about it. But now suddenly there was the possibility of something I'd never thought about, the possibility of something I couldn't yet conceive, the idea that two men could love one another, that I could be in love with a man. This was more than going to bed with someone, this was the real thing. This was something completely different from having sex with somebody you met one night and might or might not see again. This could have been love. This could have meant a future. Oh, of course I'd only just met Anthony, and sure we barely knew each other, but I knew there was something special there, and the thought that I could have a life with him suddenly made me want to run a mile.

I tried to get him out of my head all through that journey back to Dublin. Of course I couldn't, and ended up thinking about him for the whole of the trip. It was no use attempting to put him outside my head, like an empty milk bottle you put out on the doorstep. When I got back to the bedsit, I went straight to bed, wanting to forget I'd ever met him. I dreamed of him looking for me in different pubs in the city, looking for me at my flat, at my parents' home in the country. I woke up suddenly, sitting straight up in the bed. I turned the lamp on. At first I thought it was the next morning, that I'd stood him up and it was all over and I'd never see him again, but when I looked at the clock I saw that it was only a quarter past seven. We'd arranged to meet at eight at the gates of Trinity College. 'I can still make it, I can still make it,' I remember thinking to myself. 'If I get ready quickly, I can make it there by eight.' I grabbed a towel and headed for the bathroom, but on my way all my doubts from the night before, from that morning, came back to me and knocked me over like a wave. I couldn't go, I wouldn't go. I sat down on the stairs, knowing I wouldn't go.

The bells of the church chimed eight o'clock, the newscaster on the radio said eight o'clock, my heart, my head, told me it was eight o'clock, as I sat in my room, sure that he would be waiting for me. He'd still be thinking I was going to turn up, walk around the corner any minute. He'd still be expecting me. At five past he might look at his watch and say to himself I'd just been delayed. At ten past he might begin to wonder, but not too seriously, whether I was going to appear, but tell himself it was probably just the buses or a puncture in my bike. At a quarter past he'd begin to think seriously that I might not be coming at all. At twenty past he'd give up any hope of seeing me that night and walk away. He'd curse me and call me a bastard, but by midnight he wouldn't care anymore. And by the next morning he'd have forgotten he'd ever met me.

I told myself it was for the best and still... I sat there on my own, sat staring into space, when I could have been with him. All I wanted, in spite of everything I told myself, was to be with him. I felt so empty, so alone, that whole night.

If I thought Anthony would wake up the next morning with me wiped out of his memory, then I also fell asleep half believing that I wouldn't even give him a second thought after that night. I was wrong, of course I was. I woke up feeling guilty and feeling sick at the thought that I might never even see him again. I told myself I'd done the right thing, told myself to snap out of it, to get real. I began to get ready to get back into my own life. I promised myself I'd go to the canal and drown my fledgling emotions like a bag of unwanted kittens. Only instead I found myself wondering if I'd bump into him. I found myself wandering slowly past the gates of Trinity College, thinking that somehow he'd still be there, waiting for me, unwilling to leave the spot until I arrived. God, I was so self-absorbed. But what can I say? I was young, I was in love with a guy I'd met once. What can you do?

I spent the next few evenings going to the cinema, going to pubs I thought Anthony wouldn't be in. Anything to get my mind off him. I still wanted to see him, to see what would happen, could happen, between us, but I told myself I was being stupid, foolish, romantic. I got on with life and I supposed, wherever he was, he was doing the same.

I'd planned to go to a dinner dance with Eileen on New Year's Eve, and though I wasn't really in the mood for it, there was no way I'd try and get out of it at the last minute. Besides, we always had a good time when we went to dances together. We moved well as a couple, even though we both knew we'd never be one, and we knew the dance halls well: The Metropole on O'Connell Street, The Crystal Ballroom off Grafton Street, and The Ierne and National Ballrooms on Parnell Square, where the country crowd went. The ballroom at the top of Clerys, the department store on O'Connell Street, was one of our favourites, and it was there we'd decided to spend New Year's Eve. We'd booked the tickets for the dance back in November, and by this stage Eileen, who always marked an occasion with great energy, was very excited about the evening.

I picked her up at her flat, and if there were ever any moments when a girl could have turned me heterosexual, that was surely one of them. She looked so beautiful, so elegant, so sexy in her black evening gown, with a white mink she'd borrowed from a rich relation around her bare shoulders and faux diamonds around her neck. She'd had her dark hair cut short and set in soft curls. 'Daniel, you look so handsome,' she exclaimed and kissed me on the cheek. 'You too, Princess,' I said, twirling her around and then standing back to look at her as she stood with her hands on her hips, always ready to strike a pose. She went over to the gramophone player, took the record off, picked up her handbag and skipped over to me in her stilettos. 'Shall we to the ball?' I joked as she took my arm and the two of us left the flat. Eileen had put me in good spirits already and I was beginning to look forward to the dance.

We laughed our way through the meal and when the music began, we took to the dance floor. Man, we took that dance floor! We danced for the whole evening: the Foxtrot, the Quickstep, the Jitterbug, and then the more exotic dances: the Rumba and the Mambo. Eileen was a sure-footed and sexy mover, her body came alive and her face lit up when she danced, especially if it was to a Latin beat. When another man wanted to cut in and Eileen didn't think he looked too bad, I would go back to our table and have a cigarette and a drink of the champagne we'd splashed out on for the occasion. Watching her glide across the floor with some stranger who'd already fallen for her charms, I regretted that I couldn't love Eileen the way a man loves a woman. I regretted we never would make it as a couple. But still, I was happy for her out there on the floor, happy and hopeful for her. I knew she was gold dust and whoever she ended up with would be a very lucky man.

Late in the evening the dance floor was full and before I knew it, it was a quarter to midnight, then ten minutes to midnight, then five minutes to midnight, then sixty seconds to midnight, then everybody was counting, ten, nine, eight, seven, six, five, four, three, two, one, 'Happy New Year!' And the place erupted; balloons and streamers poured from the ceiling, there were cheers and whoops and claps of celebration, the band began playing 'Auld Lang Syne', and every couple began to kiss. All of those happy men and women who looked like they were so much in love, even if they weren't. Even Eileen was with somebody she'd met earlier. And standing there, I felt so alone, so out of place. I felt so miserable all of a sudden.

But then I turned and there he was, walking towards me through all those courting couples. There he was, Anthony, and his blond hair was slicked back, and he wore a black tuxedo, and he looked so handsome, so distinguished, so fucking beautiful. I didn't think, I didn't wait, I didn't weigh things up. I began walking towards him; automatically, hypnotically, as if it had only ever been this way, could only ever be this way. Our eyes were only on one another and all of those couples receded into the background. And then, in the middle of that dance floor, beneath the chandelier and in the middle of all those guys and girls, we kissed. Two young men on a dance floor in Dublin, New Year's Eve 1950, two young men in love, and we kissed and we held each other for a few long moments, and if anybody batted an eyelid, we didn't notice, we didn't care.

New Year's Day 1951, and I woke up into a new life, into a new way of life. When I opened my eyes, our limbs were twisted around one another's like branches in a storm. We were both hard and while Anthony was still sleeping, I took him in my mouth. He stirred a little and there were a few small moans of pleasure before his eyes slowly flickered open and he began to run his hands through my hair. 'Good morning, beautiful,' he said in a voice that was low and hoarse after the night before. 'Good morning, handsome,' I said and pulled myself along the length of his body to kiss him, to take those pink lips in mine and his tongue in my mouth, to bite him a little, then kiss him again. Before I turned him gently over and kissed him on the nape of his neck, then kissed him along the length of his spine. I kissed his arse before I entered him; swiftly, hungrily. I pulled him into me, onto me and held him as closely as I could, held him and kissed him uncontrollably as we found our rhythm. I never wanted to let him go. Our bodies belonged together. Already it felt as though we'd always been together.

'What do you want to do today?' Anthony asked as I came

back from the bathroom. He was sitting up in bed, smoking a cigarette. 'I don't know,' I said, putting his fingers to my lips and taking a drag, 'I thought you'd be going out to see your parents.' 'No, I couldn't bear to see them today,' he moaned. 'Do you not get on with them?' I asked. Of course I was thrilled I'd get to spend the day with him, but at the same time I wondered why he wasn't spending the holiday with his parents. 'We don't exactly see eye to eye, to put it mildly,' he said. 'Why?' I asked.' 'Oh, I just despise them, that's all,' he replied, his tone heavy with sarcasm. I laughed, unsure how serious he was. 'Won't they be expecting you though?' I pressed. 'If they think I'm going out there to play happy families with them, then they're even more deluded than I thought,' he responded. 'But why don't you get on with them?' I pushed, too stupid to know when to shut up. 'Daniel, can we just forget about them?' he half-snapped, half-pleaded. 'I've let them destroy enough days in my life without them taking this one.' 'Okay,' I apologised, 'sorry.' 'Don't worry,' he said, 'it's not your fault.' He smiled and kissed me. 'Let's go for a walk.'

Before we left the flat we took a bath together, washed every inch of one another with soap, with water, with our tongues. We washed one another's hair. We put on our underpants and began to put on our trousers, then pulled them off again. We were so hot for one another, so taken over by the sight of one another's bodies, we couldn't bear to see them hidden away.

Eventually we made it out of the flat, dragged ourselves away from one another for long enough to get out of the building and into the world outside. It was a freezing afternoon, but we had the warmth of each other, the warmth of the night before, the warmth of that morning, and the warmth of all our days and nights to come. We walked along the canal, where two swans glided along the water. We rambled down Harcourt Street, full of tall, silent houses. We strolled around St Stephen's Green as the light began to fade. All the while we stole glances at one another. We felt our stomachs jolt with the magnitude of what had begun, and every so often our eyes met and one nervous, tongue-tied smile was reflected in the other's face. God, we must have looked like two love-sick puppies!

We had dinner in the Shelbourne Hotel, with its smart, spruced clientèle, not too showy, but full of class. Anthony moved with ease amongst them, but I felt a bit more self-conscious, a bit more like an intruder. At the same time though, I was somehow at ease there with him. Like we could do anything, go anywhere, together.

'What do you do when you're not working, Daniel?' Anthony asked as we sat waiting for our main course. 'Oh, my life isn't very interesting,' I said, sure that his was much more fascinating. 'I go to the cinema sometimes, go to the theatre, go to the pub.' 'You're interested in the theatre?' Anthony brightened. 'Well, I go the odd time,' I replied, not wanting him to think I was some kind of aficionado on an art form I knew very little about. 'Have you seen anything good lately?' he asked. 'Hmm,' I thought, 'I saw *The Goldfish in the Sun* at the Abbey a while ago. Have you seen it?' 'No,' he answered, 'I don't really go in for Irish plays.' I felt a little foolish. 'I've heard good things about it, though. Did you enjoy it?' he asked politely. I thought for a moment. 'Yeah, I did,' I said with conviction. I might not have known that much about the theatre, but I knew what I liked and I wasn't about to sell my own opinion short. 'You should go and see it.'

'The last play I saw was *No Exit* by Sartre,' he continued. 'Where was that on?' I asked, thinking I hadn't seen it listed in the paper. 'Oh, I saw it in Paris a few weeks ago,' he replied.

I looked for traces of self-consciousness, wondered if he was showing off, presenting himself too eagerly as a sophisticated cosmopolitan, but couldn't find any. Anthony wasn't a show off about these things, not really. Travelling to different European cities was no big deal for him, just part of life. I guess it was equivalent to me going to Limerick or Cork for the day. Jesus, what a pair we made, the Prince and the Bumpkin.

'What's the play about?' I asked. 'It's about three characters who are trapped in hell, and you only find out after a while why each of them is there,' he explained. 'It sounds a bit intense,' I said. 'Yeah, it is. Amazing, though. It reminded me of being stuck here in Ireland, trapped in hell.' We laughed and he spoke about a new movement that was taking place in Paris. Existentialism, he called it. Man taking his fate into his own hands, living his life with responsibility and dignity, choosing, choosing every day. 'That sounds good to me,' I said when he'd told me all about it, 'but do you really think we can have that much control over our lives?' 'I think so, I hope so,' he responded. 'It has to be possible, has to be. We have to be able to choose our own fate, to make our own lives.'

We spoke about many other things that night. Talking, talking, as if no silence could come between us, the exciting tension between two people when their lives come together, the intoxicating effect of our presence together keeping us rambling on and on. We went to my house, collected my clothes for work the next day, went back to Anthony's flat and fell into bed again.

There are so many things I remember from those first days together, so many images I couldn't forget, wouldn't forget. They're mine, they're ours. What do I see when I think of those days? I see the sole shadow of the two of us reflected on the wall of his flat as the strong winter sunlight streamed through the window one Sunday morning. I see frost on the roofs and a cat warming itself beneath a car as Anthony walked me to work before turning around and heading to his lectures. I see myself walking through the gradually brightening evenings to meet him at the library. I see us getting drunk in the pubs around Grafton Street, celebrating our love. I see us shivering and diving beneath the covers in my bedsit. I see us getting back to his flat one night when we were soaked to the skin from the rain, undressing one another and making a slow kind of love that lasted all night. I see the golden hairs of his thighs against the fresh white cotton of his underpants. I see him smile, I hear him laugh. I see us lying there, naked. I see us dancing. I see life, two lives, life.

And what can I say about Anthony? What did I know of him in those first few weeks? Only that he was so handsome I could have looked at him forever. That he was very clever and did well at university, even though he hated the professors and everything that was old and staid about the institution. That he drove them crazy because he was always arguing with them. That he was drawn to what was new, what was radical, what was happening. That he didn't give a fuck about history and tradition. That he was fascinated by Europe and America, and wanted to get out of the backwater that was Dublin.

I'd never met anybody like Anthony before. He was such an original spirit, drunk on his own thoughts. And he didn't give a fuck what anybody else thought about him, about us, or so it seemed. He was so full of life, of the wild, mad, heart-pounding energy of life; with his drinks and his parties, with his ideas that he was so passionate about. He was uneven, edgy, brilliant. What can I say? He changed my world instantly. He was like a drug and I couldn't get enough of him.

And everything seemed to happen so quickly. So surely, so

definitely. Our love moved at a furious pace and carried us along with it. We didn't think about it, couldn't think about it, couldn't put into words or clear thoughts exactly what was happening. We hurtled along with it, afraid to stop, unable to stop, moving, moving.

We knew we belonged together and yet we were different in so many ways. He was worldly wise and I was a bit naive. He was a student and I couldn't afford to study. He loved to hold court, to be the centre of attention, and I was more reserved, quieter. He was from money and I was from dirt poor folk. Well, not really, but you understand what I mean. He was blond, I was dark. He was a city guy and I was a country boy. He spoke three European languages, I spoke only English and Irish. He ate fancy food and I ate potatoes nearly every day. He hated Dublin and I loved it. And still, for all our differences, for everything that we hadn't got in common, we fitted together, fitted together perfectly: physically, mentally and, dare I say it, spiritually. Besides, we both loved books and the cinema. And we both loved the theatre. The theatre! Perhaps that was our downfall.

I joined the drama group in work that January. There were so many amateur drama groups in Dublin back then. Every big firm had one. Okay, so they weren't all exactly the RSC, but what can you do? Some of them put on great shows: serious plays, musicals, pantomimes. And then there was the other stuff! I'd been thinking about joining the drama group ever since I'd started working in the Department of Education. Eileen and Paddy were already members and they'd asked me to join loads of times, but I'd felt too intimidated, too unsure of myself, to sign up. Yes, I loved the theatre, and the thrill of seeing actors on stage right before you, telling a story like that, but the thought of getting up there myself terrified me. Well, terrified and thrilled me. It was something

I would have loved to do, but didn't have the confidence to. If I'm honest with myself though, I have to admit that even though I was frightened of the stage, I still thought, somewhere in my head, that I would be great on it, diva that I was.

Anthony encouraged me to join up. He was involved with the drama society at the university. He'd acted in *Candide* and a new French play I'd never heard of. He'd even directed *The Cherry Orchard* by Chekhov, which seemed really grown up to me. 'I've been thinking about joining the drama group inside,' I said to him one evening in late January. We were having a drink in Davy Byrnes. 'That sounds great,' he replied. 'I'm always telling you you'd be wonderful on the stage.' And it's true, he was. He had none of that bitchiness, that insecurity, that actors often have when they sense a rival in their midst. At least he didn't with me. At least not then. 'Oh, I don't know. Do you really think I'd be any good?' I asked, looking for support and probably fishing for compliments. 'Of course you would,' he insisted. 'You got the looks. You got the talent. Kid, we're gonna make you a star!' he joked, sounding like a Hollywood studio mogul. 'Give over,' I laughed. 'No, seriously, Daniel, you'd be great,' he encouraged me. 'You'll be the next Montgomery Clift.' He looked at me with eyes full of confidence, full of pride and love. 'Some chance,' I muttered.

At dinner hour the next day, I went to the head of the drama group and said I wanted to join up. I'd seen the man around and Eileen had told me a few hilarious stories about him. I knew he was like me, like Anthony, like all the other men we knew, but I also knew he lived with his mother and would never do anything about his desires. He was about forty (which was ancient to me back then), skinny as a rake, wore bottle-lensed glasses, and had a high-pitched, rasping voice. In spite of all of this, I suspect he thought he was Judy

Garland and when it came to the theatre group, *his* theatre group, he had all the attitude and ambition of Joan Crawford.

'Mr O'Malley, could I have a word with you?' I requested, as he dashed from his desk to a lunchtime meeting of the drama group. 'Can't stop, the troops are waiting for me,' he replied in a voice full of self-importance, not even condescending to look at me. I wondered if I wanted to join the group at all, but I remembered Eileen had told me not to take any notice of him. 'It will only take a minute,' I insisted, taking hold of his arm as he tried to mince away. He turned around, a shocked look on his face, but after a moment I could tell he liked what he saw, even if he'd never admit it to himself. I knew if I'd been an overweight, ugly creature, Norma Desmond here would have waltzed out that door. 'Well, if you insist,' he said, sounding like he was doing me a great favour. He brushed at his shirtsleeve where my hand had been and plonked himself dramatically down on his chair.

'How can I help you?' he asked, with self-conscious patience. 'Well, it's about the drama group,' I replied in a confident voice. 'I want to join.' He studied me with beady eyes through his jam jar lenses. 'I see,' he said. 'And may I ask if you have any experience in the theatre?' 'Well, no,' I began, 'but I go to the theatre sometimes. And I've always wanted to try my hand at acting.' 'I see,' he repeated. 'But you do know this is a very reputable drama group, and we're not in the business of taking in anybody who wants to be an actor on a whim.' 'Oh, I know, Mr O'Malley,' I said with mock diffidence. 'I promise you I'm really serious about this.' 'Well, at least that's something,' he sighed.

'And exactly what do you think you can add to our theatre group, Mr…?' 'Ryan,' I stated, 'Daniel Ryan.' I was beginning to feel like I was being interrogated by the KGB and I didn't know whether to laugh or punch him on the nose. 'Well, Mr

O'Malley,' I said, 'I have a genuine interest in the theatre, I don't have a bad singing voice, and I think I could give the acting a good try.' (And I've got a great pair of legs, I thought about saying, just for the laugh, but resisted the urge.) I started to smile to myself, thinking of his face if I'd thrown that in, and my smile seemed to take him aback, made him lose whatever control he'd thought he had over the situation for a moment. 'Well, Mr Ryan,' he bid me farewell, standing up and putting his hand out to shake mine, 'we'll be in touch. I suppose we can find you with the other clerks?' He couldn't resist that last dig, that reference to my lowly status in the Civil Service. 'You certainly can,' I shot back, playing up the situation. 'I'll be the dark, good-looking one.'

And so I joined the drama group. Sang a song, recited a monologue Mr O'Malley had given me to learn, and I was in. I met the drama group that Friday lunchtime. If I'd been expecting all the glamour of Hollywood from the twenty or so people in that room, then I would have been sorely disappointed. Thankfully, I wasn't. Eileen was, as I'd expected, the most glamorous of the lot of them. Around her were a load of dull-looking young women, with one or two exceptions, and about five or six men, of different ages, one of whom I suspected was gay.

Everybody introduced themselves, as I did, and they told me about their last production, which had been a musical they'd put on before Christmas. Mr O'Malley had taken the lead male role, of course. I'd wanted to go and see it at the time, but I'd been too busy enjoying myself in the pubs around town. The group made me feel very welcome and they spoke about what they were going to put on next, in the spring. They were going to do *Easter Parade*, which was right up Mr O'Malley's street.

I left work that day feeling happy, feeling as though a new

door was opening up for me, even if it wasn't exactly the stage door to the Abbey Theatre. I was glad to be getting involved in something new for the new year, and excited about putting on a play with the group, even if I was very nervous about going out on stage. But I put that nervous feeling to the back of my mind. The show wouldn't be for months.

I bumped into Maeve by chance on O'Connell Street as I was walking up to Anthony's flat. She, just like me, was full of chat and cheer. 'Daniel, what a surprise,' she exclaimed, and I kissed her on the cheek. 'How've you been?' I asked. 'Great,' she replied, smiling broadly as she slipped her arm into mine. 'Come on, we're going for a drink. It's been too long.' We turned on our heel and headed towards the Gresham Hotel. I knew there was no point protesting that I had to be somewhere else. Maeve wasn't the kind of lady who took no for an answer.

When she asked if I had any news, I fought with all my might not to tell her about myself and Anthony. In a way I wanted to, wanted to shout about this new, disorienting, unbelievable love from the rooftops, and tell everybody including Maeve. On the other hand though it was still too fragile, this thing that I had with Anthony, to share it with anybody, and I had this terrible feeling it would fall apart if I put it out there into reality. And I was still too confused, too knocked sideways by the whole thing, to put it into words, to explain exactly what it was. I suppose part of me also wanted to keep it to myself, to keep this new life secret so that we could taste its delights in private. So instead I told Maeve I'd just joined the drama group at work. She put her glass down when I told her that. Put it down and studied me as if she was calculating something, going over something in her mind. 'I didn't know you were interested in acting,' she said. 'Well, I've sort of always wanted to do it but never really had the nerve to try it out,' I responded. 'I mean, I don't even know how this will go, but I thought new year, new start.' 'Good,' cheered Maeve. 'That's the attitude.'

She kept looking at me strangely, intensely, all through that drink, even when the talk turned to other things. I knew there was something on her mind, but couldn't tell what. 'Daniel, will you come and have dinner with me at my house tomorrow evening?' she asked as I was leaving. 'Of course,' I said, 'what time?' 'Around six?' she proposed. 'I'll be there,' I said, knowing I wasn't being asked around for a social meal, knowing there was more to it than that.

I left the hotel and jumped on the back of the number eleven bus that would take me to Anthony's. As it trundled through streets that were quiet after the evening rush, I thought about Maeve and thought about Anthony. Little did I know how the theatre would bring the three of us together, what it would do to all three of us.

6

February 1998

I GOT BACK FROM THE CANARIES with a tan and a newfound energy. I felt better able to cope with things, to get on with life. I decided there I'd invite Gerard for a drink or maybe dinner. I wanted to see if he could be trusted, to see what he knew about me, about Anthony, about that night. Besides sussing him out though, I wanted to see him again, if only to figure out why the hell I wanted to see him. Time to take control of this situation.

I went back to the library a few times to look for him. I spent most of a morning sitting at a desk behind an obese woman who consumed books as fast as she did food, sure he'd come through the door at any minute, with his pens and his notebooks, all fired up and ready for a day's work. He didn't come though and I sat there looking through a bunch of books on Irish history, feeling irritable and impatient. Eventually I gave up around lunchtime and went to get something to eat, feeling disappointed but telling myself I'd see him on my next visit.

I left it maybe a week and then one afternoon I returned, thinking maybe he'd changed his schedule and was working in the library in the afternoons. Again, he was nowhere to be seen. I resisted an urge to go up to the librarian and ask if he'd seen him, ask when he thought he'd be back. I didn't want to seem like a stalker, even though that's exactly what I felt like. Instead I took out a book of black-and-white photos of Dublin in the early fifties, and sat leafing through the pages, thinking the places looked like I remembered them, but somehow seemed different. After a while, I noticed I'd begun to look for myself and Anthony in the photos, searching for traces of our existence in that city, at that time, some proof that we'd really been there, that we really had lived those months together in Dublin. I closed the book after some time, not wanting to go too deep into it, refusing to spend another day with half remembrances. At six, when he still hadn't shown up, I left and went for dinner (on my own again).

As it turned out, the next time I saw him wasn't in the library but in the early hours of a Thursday morning. I'd been for a drink in The George. Don't ask me what drove me there. Let's just say it was the alcohol and keep it that way. Anyways, when I came outside it was heading for one o'clock and it was snowing. Not heavily, not like in New York. More like somebody was busy emptying a bag of white feathers on the ground. I was waiting for a cab when I spotted him. Saw him walking slowly on the other side of the road. He was drunk, I could tell that from how he dragged his feet, the way he seemed wrapped up in his own world. For a split second I thought about running after him, but instead I stood there staring at him.

I watched him turn into a laneway. For a moment I thought it was the laneway for the sauna but then I realised it wasn't. I asked myself what he was doing down there, though I guess I already knew. I wondered if I should go and follow him, to see what he was up to, to make sure he was okay, and slowly I began walking after him.

The laneway led into a dark, enclosed space. It smelled of

piss and garbage and I could sense the furtive fumblings as soon as I set foot in it. At first I couldn't see him though and thought maybe he'd just walked through to take a shortcut. I doubted it though and took a good look around. There were a few dark shadows in a corner, almost hidden by a container piled high with refuse sacks. Slowly, quietly, I walked over. And there he was, going down on some guy twice his age, his eyes closed, shut tight. A fat guy stood next to them, jerking himself off.

I walked away and grabbed the first cab I could find, feeling angry and depressed, feeling confused. I wondered if this was how Gerard made his money, or if it was just how he got his kicks. I took a pill when I got in, tried to forget about the whole night, and fell into a deep sleep.

I found myself in town the next morning. I had a few things to do: go to the dentist, buy a notebook, maybe catch a film. I got off the DART at Pearse Street and walked up to the Dental Hospital. Nothing major to report. Just a check-up and a cleaning. I still have all my own teeth, which would probably be unheard of here for someone my age. Americans do have good teeth, I'll give them that. I was on my way over to St Stephen's Green Centre, to a bookshop that sells the notebooks I like to write in, when I thought I'd take a look in the library. I didn't really think Gerard would be there, not after the tricks he'd got up to the night before, but I don't know, I just had this feeling and I knew I had to go there.

And what do you know? As soon as I passed through the ironwork gate, I saw him. Saw him sitting on a bench next to the door, smoking and staring off into space. This was my chance, my chance to talk to him, to begin to find out who he was and what he wanted. This was my opportunity to see if he could be trusted. Again and again I'd planned what I'd say in my head if I met him. How I'd walk right up to him, say hi casually enough, and then after some chit-chat say I'd been thinking about what he'd asked me and that maybe I could be of some help to him after all. That I'd said I was American just because I'd spent most of my life there and that I'd gotten mad at him because I just wasn't used to people coming up to me in a bar and asking me to spill the beans on somebody for a book. But that I'd thought about it and his project sounded very interesting and that I would help him if I could. I'd rehearsed all of this over and over, but instead of walking up to him, I stood there, suddenly frozen and tongue-tied, wondering if it was a good idea at all, thinking I was only asking for trouble. I was thinking about turning around when he looked over at me, when he stared at me as if to say 'What the fuck are you looking at, old man? What the fuck do you want?' He took a long drag from his cigarette and hoped I'd disappear.

'It's now or never,' I told myself, refusing to be intimidated by his bad attitude. 'Hi, how you doin'?' I said cheerfully as I took a cigarette from my pack and lit up. 'Grand,' he responded, with about as much energy as a doped-up snail, moving away from me and huddling into himself against the cold. 'Can I sit down?' I asked. 'Yeah,' he replied, not even looking at me. 'Cold this morning, isn't it?' I began, stalling, trying to buy time to figure out just how to approach the situation. 'I suppose,' he murmured, giving me a sideways look. He didn't seem to recognise me, looked more as though he might be trying to place me amidst all the guys he'd fucked and sucked down laneways, and for a second I felt hurt by this lack of recognition, I felt wounded. But he was clever, there was something sly about him, and I guessed he could have just been putting it on, feigning ignorance now that I'd cornered him and not the other way around.

'So how's the book coming along?' I inquired. 'The book?'

He looked directly at me and I saw the dark rings under his eyes. 'What book?' 'Aren't you writing a novel about some New Yorker that moved here?' I asked. He sat staring at me. 'Do I know you from somewhere?' he demanded aggressively. 'Sure,' I replied, 'I met you a few months ago in The George and you said you wanted to talk to people who knew Dublin after the war. Said you were writing a book about some guy called Mac or Jimmy or something like that.' I pretended not to remember who he was writing his book about, still pretending I'd never heard of Fitzer.

'Fitzer,' he stated. 'What?' I asked, like I wasn't all that interested anyway. 'The book. It's about Fitzer,' he repeated. 'Oh right,' I said. 'Don't know him, but I've been thinking, maybe I can help you after all.' 'Oh yeah?' He seemed more interested now, brightening a little. 'Yeah, I know I said I was from the States and all, but well, I've lived there for so long I kind of think of myself as a New Yorker. I mean I don't even feel Irish anymore. Anyway, I did live in Dublin for a while in the early fifties. I don't know if I can help you, but if there's anything you want to know about the city back then, well, I guess I'd be happy to do what I can.' 'Really? That would be great,' he chirped, suddenly in good spirits. 'Sure,' I contrived, 'I mean I don't know really if I'll be any use, but if you want to meet up for a chat, I'd be glad to.' 'That'd be great,' he said, 'if you really don't mind.' 'No, not at all, we can have dinner or go for a drink.' 'I'd love to,' he responded, flirting a little, even if he wasn't aware of it.

'When do you think you'd be free to meet?' he asked. 'I'm free pretty much most evenings during the week, but weekends are out,' I replied, lying, because I didn't want to seem like a lonely old loser. 'How about next Thursday? Would that suit you?' he proposed. 'Sure,' I enthused, 'Thursday at eight, say? And you choose the restaurant. You probably know better then me the good places to eat in the city.' 'All right, I'll think of somewhere,' he agreed. 'Is there any kind of food you don't like?' 'No, I'll eat just about anything, so long as it ain't Irish.' He laughed at that. 'No bacon and cabbage for you then. Damn, and I know a place where the spuds are like balls of flour,' he said, mimicking a country woman's accent.

'Give me your number and I'll give you a call in the next few days,' I suggested, but as soon as I said it I knew I'd been looking at him too intensely, my eyes betraying too much. I could sense a slight shift in his body then and I saw his own eyes flicker as he tried to figure out what I wanted. 'You stupid fool,' I thought to myself. 'Or I could give you mine,' I said, 'that might make more sense.' 'Yeah,' he agreed, relaxing a bit, but not fully. 'If you give me your number I'll give you a call and let you know where to meet me on Thursday.' 'Okay.' I scrawled my number in my notebook, tore out the page and handed it to him. 'Thanks,' he muttered.

I stood up and from the corner of my eye I saw him look me over, but I couldn't figure out exactly what he was thinking. I only knew I was under inspection. 'What are you doing in the library anyway?' he quizzed me. 'Oh, just researching some family history,' I lied again. 'You know how us Yanks are obsessed with our Irish roots.' I gave him an ironic smile and he smiled too. 'See you next week,' I said, turning into the library.

'Sorry, I don't remember your name.' I heard a clear, steady voice behind me a moment later in the entrance hall of the library. 'Fuck,' I thought and felt myself panic. 'It's Anthony.' I put the truth to one side again. 'Anthony,' I said as I turned around. 'Nice to meet you again, Anthony. I'm Gerard,' he said and put out his hand to shake mine. I took his hand and our eyes met again. He held me in his gaze a moment too long before allowing me to scurry upstairs to the reading room.

So it was a Thursday night in late February. He'd had a few drinks and was in a good mood. I'd had a shot of whiskey myself, just to steady the nerves. We met in a restaurant called Odessa, down a narrow street off George's Street. The place looked nice, but it was full of people trying too hard, full of the kind of assholes you can find in any restaurant in SoHo any night of the week, pushing their tortellini around a plate and bullshitting about Italian neo-realism. Give me a break! They could do with a dose of realism. But well, I know how to handle those kinds of people. Just don't look at them and soon enough they'll disappear up their own asses. And Gerard, he might have looked like some of them, with his faded jeans, his worn to shit satchel and his mod leather jacket, but there was something different about him. He interested me from the moment he walked in, fifteen minutes late, and sat down opposite me.

'Sorry I'm late,' he apologised, though I knew he wasn't all that sorry, otherwise he would have been on time. 'That's all right,' I said, 'I haven't been here for long.' 'Do you want to get some wine?' he asked, picking up the list. 'Sure,' I agreed, 'I could have some wine.' 'What's your poison then, guv'nor,' he asked in an over-the-top Cockney accent, 'red or white?' 'Red,' I replied, 'if that's all right with you.' 'Sure is,' he said in a Californian drawl and looked around for a waitress. He knocked back a glass before I'd taken two sips of mine, and as soon as we'd ordered the food, he a bruschetta and tortellini, me a soup and rare steak, he dashed off to the bathroom, looking slightly uncoordinated as he walked down the stairs.

When he came back he seemed like somebody else. He seemed more focused, more together, more serious. He reached into his bag and took out a notebook, asking did I mind if he wrote a few things down. I told him I didn't. He hit me with a few questions: what Dublin looked like when I lived there, what the fashions were like, if the trams were still running, where gay men hung out, if we had codes we used to recognise other guys like us, if there were places to cruise. I could hear his mind ticking over as he looked at me, his eyes probing, questioning, trying to put things into place. I could see him homing in on certain details and I looked at him as he mulled them over and his mind took flight. I watched him watching me, watched him scribbling furiously in his notebook when I said something he thought was useful. I searched every question for an ulterior motive, for a double edge, for a hidden meaning, but couldn't be all that sure I found any. Still, I knew I had to be careful. I watched him listening to me and I felt a bit like I was under a microscope. I was terrified he'd ask me something about Anthony and me, about that night, drop a hint about us, but he didn't. And as I began to relax in his company, I began to feel privileged, to feel a bit special, a bit interesting. And I don't know, I also felt a real admiration for this gutsy kid who was spending a Thursday evening listening to an old queen rattle on about the past and writing a book about another old queen.

He did ask me two things that were a bit strange though, when he was on his second bottle of wine and his eyes had turned to liquid around the edges. He asked if gays in Ireland had a lot of self-hatred back then. I told him I didn't know. And then he asked if love, true love, was possible between men at that time, and the way he looked at me was like he was staring into my soul, as if knew everything there was to know about me. I felt so uncomfortable then, all I wanted was to leave the restaurant. 'Who knows,' I deflected the question, 'who knows.' I changed the topic as smoothly as I could, and after a while asked the waitress for the bill.

I left Gerard on George's Street. He looked as though he was thinking about something until finally he decided. 'I'm going to head over to The George for a dance,' he said, his eyes lighting up with possibilities wider than the music, 'do you want to come?' I laughed. 'No, I don't want to cramp your style. You don't want to be dragging this old carcass with you.' 'Oh, come on,' he chided, 'you're only as young as the man you feel.' 'And this old queen ain't gonna be feelin' no man tonight,' I said. 'Are you sure you won't come?' he asked again. I could tell he didn't mind me going, but I knew he'd probably prefer to be on his own. Hell, I would. Much more chance of picking up. Having an old man hanging off your arm in a fag bar has only ever attracted other old fags who think they might be in with a chance, and bitchy little queens saying, 'Well, isn't Miss Thang gonna inherit a big old fortune when Sugar Daddy dies.' And still I wanted to go with him, have a dance with him, continue the chat. For a moment I regretted that I wasn't forty years younger, when I could have had a real chance with him. But what does that matter.

I let him go on his own. I watched him walk away, now moving like a puppet from all the alcohol he'd put away. 'Gerard,' I called after him. He turned around. 'Be careful,' I said, but he just smiled, waved me away, and walked off into the night.

February 1951

'SO, DANIEL, WHAT DID YOU think of the play?' Maeve wanted to know. I was sitting at the window of her first floor parlour, looking out at the winter trees in the square when she joined me, carrying a tray with tea. Amazing was the word that came into my head, but I was too self-conscious to use such a dramatic word back then. 'I really liked it,' I said. 'I mean, I didn't understand everything, even though I read it a few times, but I think it's really good.' Not exactly the words of a young literary critic, but then I found it difficult to express exactly how I felt about Federico García Lorca's *Blood Wedding*. I only knew that it had knocked me sideways, that it had had an enormous impact on me, and that its emotions were bigger than anything I'd ever known.

Maeve had given me the play that Saturday evening I'd called up to her house for dinner. Given it to me, asked me to read it, said I might like it but told me nothing more about it. I'd been a bit surprised, to be honest. I mean, there I was, expecting something momentous to happen, expecting her to drop a bombshell or tell me something that would change my life, and all we did was have dinner, chat about what was going on in our lives, and when I was leaving she gave me a tattered copy of the play. But things never were that simple, that transparent, not with Maeve.

Ay, what can I say about *Blood Wedding* after all this time? What can I say about that first time I read it, when I stayed up into the early hours of the morning, unable to put it down, blown away by it and unable to move from where I was sitting for a long time after I'd finished it. Let me summon all my strength and at least try to be objective about it, at least try to just tell you the story.

Blood Wedding, well, it's not a comedy. I guess you gathered that much from the title. It's a tragedy, like Shakespeare's great works, like the Ancient Greek dramas of Sophocles. It's a tragedy about a young woman about to marry a man she doesn't love. It's about how she flees her own wedding with the man she really loves, the sweetheart society separated her from, the young married man she has continued to meet in secret, a sworn enemy of her husband-to-be's family. And the knife fight between the two young men that follows, the lover and the spurned bridegroom. It's about fate and death. There, I've said it. It's about fate and death. To me it will always be about fate and death and how we all lost against our worlds in the end.

But what did I know about fate and death and tragedy that night in February when I first read *Blood Wedding*? I was a couple of weeks shy of my twenty-first birthday. I was in love for the first time. I was walking on air, doing cartwheels in my head, and so naive I thought that nothing bad would ever happen to the people I loved. It was life I lived for then, life I loved back then. And so while I loved that play from the first moment I read it, while I fell under the spell of its language, its dances, its symbolism and ever-encroaching darkness, I didn't really understand it. What I mean is that to me it was drama, a great drama, but not real life. It wasn't reality. It was just a play. Yes, it was one of the most memorable things I'd ever read, but still it was just a play.

'So would you consider taking the part of The Bridegroom?' Maeve asked after she had listened to my uncouth musings on the play for some time. 'What?' I blurted out, not sure exactly what she was asking me. 'Would you take the part of The Bridegroom,' she repeated, 'if somebody were to put on the play?' 'Maeve, what are you talking about?' I asked, still confused. 'I'm going to put on an amateur production of *Blood Wedding* this summer, Daniel,' she replied, 'and I want you to be a part of it. I want you to be in it.' 'Me?' I was incredulous. 'What do I know about acting? I've only been in the drama society a few weeks and I don't think I'll do very well there. I mean, I don't know the first thing about acting.' 'That's nonsense, Daniel. With acting you either have it or you don't. You can have all the training you want, but if you don't have that spark, that raw talent, there's no point, it's meaningless,' Maeve said. 'And what makes you think I have any talent, any spark?' 'Oh, I don't know. It's just a feeling I have. I've watched you. I've watched how you move, how you interact with people. And I've listened to how you speak. You have a strong voice that would be good on stage.'

I didn't know exactly how to react to her compliments. I mean of course I was flattered, but the whole situation was so bizarre, her asking me to be in a play and talking about me as if I were an actor, I was lost for words. 'I've been looking for a Bridegroom for a few weeks,' Maeve went on, 'and then when you said you'd joined the drama group, something clicked and I knew you'd be right for the part.' I laughed nervously. 'Oh, yeah. I'm a right Laurence Olivier.' 'Oh, Daniel, come on. You'll be great. And we have more than four months before the play goes on. You can learn a hell of a lot in that time. Besides, it's not as if it's going to be on in the West End. It will just be in a small theatre on Parnell Square.'

Maeve was excited by her project. I could see that by how flushed she got when talking about it. 'This is something I really want to do, and I'd love if you'd be part of it, Daniel.' Her eyes were imploring, encouraging, and it was then I began to think about taking her up on her offer.

As it turned out, I was going to the theatre with Anthony that evening and I had to meet him at the Gate at half seven, so I apologised to Maeve, said I had to meet somebody, but that I'd have a think about what she'd asked me. 'Are you meeting anybody nice?' she asked as she walked me to the front door, a glint in her eye and a smile on her face. 'Maybe,' I replied, half-wanting to tell her about Anthony, but still feeling too funny to talk about this mad new thing we had started. 'Telephone me when you've made your decision,' she said, lifting her cheek as always for me to kiss it. 'And please, Daniel, do think seriously about it.' 'I will,' I promised, and headed off through the evening streets and down to the theatre.

Anthony was waiting at the bar for me, cool as a cucumber, sipping a drink, and looking like the man about town that he was. I was so excited about what Maeve had asked me, and so happy to see him, so horny to see him, I wanted to walk right up to him and kiss him. But I didn't. You didn't normally do things like that in Dublin back then. From what I've seen, you still wouldn't do them now. Instead I stood there, grinning like an idiot, staring at Anthony, thinking how lucky I was, thinking how much my life had changed since a year ago, thinking of all the possibilities that were opening up for me. 'What are you smiling at?' Anthony asked. 'You look like the cat that got the cream.' 'Nothing,' I answered. 'I'm just happy to be here.' I didn't want to tell him anything about Maeve and *Blood Wedding* yet, not until I'd decided for definite whether I was going to do it. 'Well, I'll have whatever you're having,' he said. I finished my pint and

Anthony ordered two whiskeys, which we lowered back before we went into the auditorium.

The play that night wasn't great. Not one of Hilton and Micheál's better choices, but that didn't matter to me. Sitting in the theatre, watching the actors move around the stage, inhabiting their characters and making us, the audience, believe completely in what they were creating, I knew I'd say yes to *Blood Wedding*. I knew I'd cross the invisible line between the actors and the audience, that I wanted to create a world, a story, and not just watch one. I knew I'd step on stage and into that other, powerful, make-believe world, just as I'd promised myself when I was a kid. And when I saw myself on stage I was graceful and handsome. And when I heard myself speak, it wasn't my own voice that I heard, but the voice of Laurence Olivier or Orson Welles. And when I saw myself move, I was like a matador about to kill a bull with a thrust of his knife, mad with jealousy and out to take revenge on the man who'd run off with his lady.

Oh, like any aspiring actor I saw myself taking a bow with the rest of the cast after the play had finished, sure the audience was applauding for all the performances in general, but especially for mine. Okay, so these thoughts were intercut with images of me forgetting my lines and standing on stage like an idiot. And I did imagine getting pelted with rotten fruit and veg because my performance was the worst the audience had ever seen and I was a living disgrace to theatre, but I tried not to think about these things too much. I wanted to be on stage, I wanted to play The Bridegroom in *Blood Wedding*, and though I still had no idea how I was going to change from being a spectator to an actor, by the time the lights went up on the play Anthony and I were watching, I had all the blind confidence that leap of faith required.

My decision to be in the play gave me confidence with

Anthony that night, more confidence than I'd ever had with him. Now I was a leader, an actor, a somebody, and not just a bumpkin riding on his coattails. Of course I was jumping the gun. I mean Maeve had only just asked me to be in the play, and I really didn't know anything about acting, but her faith in me gave me faith in myself. 'Let's go for a drink,' I said to Anthony as we left the theatre. I felt like celebrating my decision, my new life treading the boards, my new life of greasepaint and the bright lights of the theatre, even though I wasn't quite ready to share the news with him. I wanted Maeve to be the first to know that I was going to be in the play, in her production. I'd call her the next morning, arrange to meet her and tell her I'd do it, yes, I'd do it, Jesus, I'd do it. But for now I was full of a nervous energy, and all I wanted to do was be with Anthony, have a drink with Anthony, dance and shout and sing with Anthony, and fall into bed with him when we'd taken all we could from our night in the city.

We went on a pub crawl and as the hours passed and we had more and more to drink, crawl from one pub to another is exactly what we did. Oh, we owned the city that night. We moved from The Oval on Abbey Street, to Mulligan's on Poolbeg Street, to The Stag's Head off Dame Street, to McDaids, The Bailey and Davy Byrnes. We were both giddy with excitement, with love, with possibility. It was one of those nights when two people meet on the same level, when they take everything they can from the world for their own private party, and celebrate and drink and live together, and forget about their worries. They say fuck it to everything else and get carried along on their emotions, the drink, and the ecstasy of that moment when two lives come together against the world. We had a drink with friends, we chatted with strangers and smiled at one another and laughed together, and if the time and place had allowed it, we would have kissed and danced and thrown our arms up and declared that this was life, this was happiness, and nobody could ever be more in love than the two of us. It was a page in our story, a night in our lives that neither of us wanted to end. We were triumphant that night, we thought we would always be triumphant in this life.

'I never expected this,' Anthony said to me as we stood by the corner of the bar in Davy Byrnes when I came back from the Gents. 'I never expected to feel this happy with someone.' I could see his eyes were moist. Okay, so we were loaded. In a couple of short hours, we'd drunk enough Jameson to sink a ship, but that didn't matter. No, scratch that, it did. It made everything more intense, it magnified everything and allowed us to release all those mad emotions we'd both been feeling for one another. It allowed us to say all those things that until then we'd been keeping to ourselves for fear of seeming like idiots, for fear of being rejected. And don't sneer at us because we couldn't talk about any of this without alcohol. We were two young Irish men having a relationship in 1951. How else were we to express ourselves, to open ourselves up like that? 'I never expected this either,' I said. 'My life has changed so much in the last few months. A year ago, I never would have thought any of this was possible and now I'm with you.' 'I know. It's strange, isn't it,' agreed Anthony. 'I mean, to think that we could have a future together, that we could make a life together. To think that we could be happy together. I never thought I would be, you know that, Daniel. I never thought I'd have this.'

He started to cry then, silently, uncontrollably, and all the while he was looking at me, as if he saw further inside me, saw much more of me, than anyone else ever had. Any barriers I'd kept to protect myself, to be careful for myself, fell away then and all I felt was love for him. All I wanted was to love him forever, to hold him, to comfort him, to say that everything was going to be great and we'd be together forever. I felt myself crying too, tears and tears, and I knew something deeper, something so huge I couldn't exactly comprehend it, had begun between us. I wanted to hold him so much then but the bar was crowded and I felt self-conscious. Instead I held his gaze, held it steady and, more sure of anything I'd ever said before, I said through our tears, 'I love you, Anthony. I love you so much.' 'I love you too, Daniel,' he responded, and ran his hand along mine for a moment and smiled at me. And that was the first time we mentioned that word, love.

We pulled ourselves together after a while, two puppies drunk on whiskey and love. 'Will we go for another drink?' Anthony proposed as Davy Byrnes closed up for the night. 'Yes,' I said. 'I want this night to go on forever.' 'Okay,' he said. 'I know a place where we can get one.' I don't know how long it took us to get to the place Anthony was talking about, only that the walk there didn't seem real. We were like two aliens dropped on earth, walking through a deserted city, under-standing nothing but what we shared, staring at the city as if it were the first time we'd seen it. We kept away from the main streets. We walked past corner shops closed up for the night, and sleeping houses, and every few minutes we stopped off in a laneway to kiss one another, to hold one another, to feel again the power of what was between us, before it became too much and we'd stumble on a bit more.

Eventually we reached a row of old houses up near Holles Street. Most of them looked a bit shabby and I imagined if there were people still living in any of them, they were sure to be asleep by now. Anthony checked the number on each house and looked a bit puzzled until he decided on one, a house with a wine coloured hall door that looked a bit shabbier than the rest. 'This is it,' he said, as he pushed open the gate and skipped down the steps to the basement.

He rapped on the door as if he were tapping out a secret code, but nobody appeared for a few minutes. I was about to ask if we should give up the ghost of another drink and just go home to his place, when the door was opened by the most effeminate-looking man I'd seen up until that point in my short life. He was about forty, incredibly skinny, and his long dark locks were swept back from his face and twisted into a kind of bun at the nape of his neck. He wore a well-cut suit, a silk blouse, and there was a brightly coloured scarf around his neck. 'Man, woman or what?' I thought. 'Anthony, darling, it's been an eternity,' he said, offering not one but two cheeks to be air-kissed by Anthony. 'And what delicacy have you brought with you?' he inquired, turning to me and holding out a hand, full of rings, to be kissed. 'Peter,' he said by way of an introduction, 'but you can call me Petra.' Shocked, I bent and kissed the hand, feeling like a fool or like a bit player in some pantomime. Petra took a good look at me. 'Actually, you can call me anytime, sweetheart,' he flirted, smiling like he'd eat me up right there and then. My face turned red. 'I'm Daniel,' I introduced myself, 'nice to meet you.' '*Enchanté, mon amour, enchanté*,' Petra said dramatically. 'Now let's get inside. It's freezing out here.' Anthony followed, laughing, while I kept close to him, already wary of what was inside.

'Now, what will you girls have to drink?' Petra wanted to know as he led us to a kind of Art Nouveau bar in the corner of the room. 'John, pull yourself together or I'll have to spank you,' he shouted at a man who looked a bit the worse for wear and was trying to put a painting back on the wall. 'I'll have a whiskey,' said Anthony. 'And you, sweetheart?' Petra asked me in honeyed tones. 'I'll have the same, please,' I replied, staring wide-eyed around the room. 'Good, two whiskeys it is then,' Petra said as he picked up a bottle of Jameson behind the bar, poured, and handed us two cut glass tumblers. 'And just a little top-up for Mama,' he smiled, pouring a bit more of the stuff into his own glass.

'So, where did you meet this devil?' Petra quizzed me, his eyes moving from me to Anthony, and back again. 'We met at a party,' I replied, feeling terribly young and shy. 'Yes, we met at some ambassador's party just before Christmas,' said Anthony. 'It was a dreadful party, but, well, I met Daniel there, so everything turned out perfectly in the end.' He looked at me and smiled, and I returned the exact same smile. We both knew what the other was thinking, how safe and happy we were in the love that had started that night in December. I guess we must have been looking at one another longer and more lovingly than we thought because Petra coughed, said weren't we quite the two young lovebirds in a way that was catty but also generous and warm, before he excused himself and went to talk to a woman in an evening gown.

As he walked away I looked around the big room, at the man playing some old jazz tune on the piano, at the people dancing, at the men in conversation, and the two couples kissing: one in a corner and one on a velvet couch. Looking around that room and with Anthony by my side, I felt free, I felt free to do anything. I felt liberated and all I wanted was to drink and dance. 'Let's dance,' I proposed, taking Anthony's hand, and the two of us moved into the centre of the room, dancing wildly, frenetically, as if we were in some nineteen twenties film. 'I love you,' Anthony said as we danced. 'I love you too,' I responded, and twirled him around like a marionette.

Just before dawn, a student Anthony knew from the university tapped a spoon against his glass and said he wanted to make a toast. 'We are gathered here tonight to declare this sacred, secular space a new Republic,' he bellowed with great ceremony. 'This underground nation, ruled over by Queen Petra, will henceforth be known as Subterraniana, and all who enter must pledge to uphold a way of life completely opposed to the law of the land in our mouldy Irish nation. Now please lift your glasses in a toast to Petra and Subterraniana.' There was laughter and howls of approval and everybody lifted their glass. 'To our nights beneath the nation,' Anthony whispered in my ear, before he emptied his glass in one go.

Deathly hung over, but full of excitement, I telephoned Maeve early the following morning and arranged to meet her that afternoon. Running late, I raced along to the Shelbourne Hotel, and as I did I imagined myself as The Bridegroom in *Blood Wedding*, galloping on horseback after his wife and her sweetheart, out to get revenge. I was still full of energy from the night before, still loved up and still half-drunk from the amount of whiskey we'd put away. What can I say? I was loving the drama of my own life, and Lorca's drama and the thought that I would be involved in that too only added to my high, made my heart beat like mad. I was euphoric in a manic kind of way as I skipped up the steps to the Shelbourne Hotel. Maeve was inside waiting for me, reading the paper and smoking a cigarette in a silver holder, dressed in black and looking like the most sophisticated woman Dublin had ever seen. I was so excited about telling her I'd do the play, I rushed right up to her, and before she knew it I was on top of her. 'Daniel!' she said, startled for once. 'I'm going to do it. I want to do it. I want to be The Bridegroom,' I said, barely able to catch my breath. She let out a squeal of delight, jumped up and kissed me. 'Oh, Daniel, that's great news,' she exclaimed. 'Now sit down before you have a heart attack.'

'I really want to do it, Maeve. I've been thinking about it a lot since yesterday. I mean, I know I'm not an actor. I know I don't know anything about the theatre, not really, but I really want to do it. I just hope I don't let you down.' My mind was racing, my hands were shaking, and I couldn't get the words out fast enough. There was so much I wanted to ask her: about the play, about Lorca, about how many nights it would be on for, about how I would become The Bridegroom, about how I would learn my lines and how I would deal with the stage fright that I was sure would paralyse me before the play. 'Daniel, don't worry,' Maeve reassured me. 'I think you'll be great. Don't worry about learning your lines or anything else for the moment.'

'And what about the rehearsals, when are they going to start?' I asked. 'Oh, we won't begin the rehearsals until April,' Maeve replied. I was a little bit disappointed. I mean, there I was, all fired up and ready to go, and Maeve was telling me it would be more than a month before we'd even start the rehearsals. She must have seen the disappointment in my face. 'Don't worry, Daniel, it's not that far away,' she said. 'And once you've met the rest of the cast, it will start to make sense.' 'And will we be rehearsing every day?' I wondered, naïve as hell. 'Oh good God, no,' she laughed. 'We're not putting a play on in the Abbey, God forbid. We'll just rehearse one evening a week for the first while, and then when it gets closer to the time we'll work a few more evenings and during the weekend.'

'And who's going to play The Bride?' I quizzed her. I realised I'd been so caught up in my own role, I hadn't even thought who else would be in the play. 'Oh, she's a great girl,' said Maeve. 'She's from over by the Pepper Cannister Church. She's done a few shows in different societies and she has real talent.' 'And who are you going to play,' I asked, 'The Mother?' 'How dare you,' she hissed in mock disbelief. 'I'm not nearly old enough to play her. I was first up to play The Bride, only I thought I'd give somebody else a chance.' She laughed. 'Directing this play will be quite enough for me, thank you very much, young man.' I smiled. 'Fitzer's going to help me with it,' she said. 'Fitzer?' I asked, thinking I'd heard the name somewhere before. 'Yes, Fitzer,' she said. 'You remember...' 'Ah, yeah. Of course,' I said, recalling the man she'd told me about, the one who'd fought with her husband in Spain. 'He knows a lot more about Spain than I do,' Maeve said. 'Incidentally, he's dying to meet you.' 'Really?' I asked, unable to believe that somebody as involved in the theatre, and with such an interesting life as Fitzer, would want to meet me. 'Yes, of course,' Maeve said. 'I've told him a lot about you. He thinks you'll make the perfect Bridegroom. In fact, he says he thinks he'd marry you himself if he wasn't already taken.' I tried to laugh my blushes away.

Lady about town that she was, Maeve said that she was sorry to dash off but she had a dinner date with somebody, a gentleman she wouldn't reveal anything about. There was still so much I wanted to ask her, had to ask her, about the play, but there was no time. As we stood on the steps and the concierge flagged down a taxi for her, I asked her one more question, just out of curiosity, just so I'd know. 'Who's going to play Leonardo?' I inquired, thinking of The Bride's true sweetheart who sweeps her away. 'Leonardo,' she said. 'I hadn't quite decided until this afternoon. But now I know. Leonardo will be played by a young man who auditioned for me last week. You'll be great together, perfect opposites,' she said. 'What's his name?' I asked, putting different faces and gestures on my sworn enemy of the play. 'Anthony,' she replied casually as she stepped into the cab. I felt my heart pounding but told myself there was no way what I was thinking could be true. No way. 'Anthony Stafford,' she said, rolling down the window.

'Anthony, Anthony,' I thought, but I was too surprised to say anything. 'See you soon, Daniel,' I heard Maeve say and then the car sped off, leaving me standing on the kerb.

7

March 1998

ALTERNATIVE MISS IRELAND, can you imagine? Roll up, roll up, for one of the most surreal beauty pageants ever known to man. A night of song and dance routines, where gay men and a few women compete for the coveted crown of AMI. I mean, I've been to a lot of drag shows in my day. I've been to Wigstock and seen the Pride parade in New York City, and spent more than a night in Trannyshack in San Francisco. I've been in clubs with Candy Darling and Divine, and done drugs with the best of them. Oh, I'm not trying to show off or pretend I was Bianca Jagger riding through Studio 54 on a white horse. All I'm trying to say is that the Alternative Miss Ireland pageant Gerard took me to was one of the strangest experiences of my life. Oh, and okay, it was also one of the most fun. Did I just say fun? I must be going soft or senile in my old age. Fuck it! I enjoyed myself. It was a blast.

I'd never heard of the thing before and even if I had, there was no way I would have gone on my own. I mean, give me a break! It's all down to Gerard that I ended up there, Gerard and his idea that nothing is impossible, that everything can be done. Gerard calling me up the day before the big event, saying somebody's dropped out and there's a spare seat at the table he has with some AIDS charity, and would I like to come. And me replying, 'No, I don't think so,' trying to crawl back into my shell like a too shy turtle, and Gerard saying, 'Why not?' And me saying, 'I'm too old for all that. It's a night for young people.' That old chestnut. And Gerard telling me, 'I don't accept that. Get over yourself.' Saying, 'You give me one good reason why you won't come to the best night on the Irish gay calendar and I'll leave you alone.' I just say, 'I really don't think so, Gerard. I wouldn't feel comfortable there and I have a lot on at the moment,' but I know none of my excuses are good enough. 'Okay,' he gives up finally, 'I'm not going to twist your arm, but if you change your mind, meet me tomorrow outside the Red Box on Harcourt Street at half-seven. I'll keep the ticket for you just in case.' 'Okay,' I say, just glad he's going to stop harassing me.

I won't go, I know I won't go. I mean, why the hell does he think I'd want to go to an Irish drag show? It may be the highlight of his year, but not mine. Still though, I have to admit I'm pleased he thought of me, that perhaps I'm not just a pawn in his game with the past, his link with that decade. But I wonder if he just wants to get me drunk, to loosen my tongue and get me to open up about my past. He's all sweetness and light, but I'm sure he's well able to get what he wants. And even if he is just writing a book on Fitzer, like he said he was, like I do actually believe he is, then surely he must have heard about me and Anthony by now. Surely somebody must have told him about the most sensational story of the summer of 1951. 'Well, he won't hear it from me, that's for sure,' I promise myself. But still, I can't quite believe he's cunning enough to try and manipulate me into telling my story. After dinner that night my instinct told me that he was just a nice guy, maybe a bit messed up, but a nice guy anyway. Maybe I've just been letting my paranoia get the better of me. My old friend, paranoia.

Something keeps bringing me back to Gerard. Maybe it's that night all those years ago, or the truth I know about life that he's only just finding out. Or maybe I just want to be with him, or need to be with him. Fuck, I haven't needed anybody in years. Oh, I don't know. Maybe he gives me hope or somehow helps me deal with the past. Funny, isn't it. He should put me on edge, scare the shit out of me with all his investigations into lost years and sometimes when I think about him, or even that night we had dinner, sometimes I just feel so at ease.

It was my birthday that Sunday of Alternative Miss Ireland. I've gotten used to spending my birthdays alone and I never, never celebrate them. I mean, what is there to celebrate; another year in the march towards the grave, another year without him, another year that could have been but wasn't.

Sitting at home on Sunday afternoon, trying to read but unable to concentrate, I began thinking of going to meet Gerard, began thinking why not, what the hell, what have I got to lose. Well, a hell of a lot as it happened: my sanity, my grasp on the past, the sorry story of my life. But I don't know, it touched me that he'd asked me, and I badly wanted to see him again, to see him laughing and enjoying himself. I wanted to forget my life for a night, even if Gerard only wanted me to remember. I decided I'd go to this Alternative Miss Ireland, whatever it was.

I arrived at the Red Box, a nightclub where Harcourt Street train station used to be, at seven-fifteen, just in case Gerard was early, just in case I missed him. There was a real carnival atmosphere around the place. A lot of people were dressed up: guys in drag, guys in sailor suits, guys in leather and girls in rubber. I wondered if it was Halloween for a minute, if I'd lost track of time again and it was really an evening in late October and not the middle of March. It wasn't, of course it wasn't, but I was so busy feeling disoriented by the spectacle around me, I didn't even notice Gerard come up to me and say, 'Anthony, you made it. I didn't think you were coming.' Well, I didn't notice him because I was disoriented, but also because I didn't recognise him. Gerard was standing before me, dressed as Faye Dunaway dressed as Bonnie Parker, with his very own Clyde Barrow in tow.

He stood there, proud as hell in a 1920s ladies' suit, with a beret on his head and a pistol in his hand, grinning as if this were the most natural thing in the world. I've never really been into drag queens myself, but I have to admit Gerard looked foxy as a woman. Like some kind of dame of cold, perfectly calculated sexuality. 'Not a woman to be messed with,' I thought to myself. 'Anthony, this is my friend John, but you can call him Clyde,' Gerard said, introducing me to his sidekick. 'I've got to remember my name is Anthony tonight,' I steeled myself. 'Pleased to meet you, partner,' John smiled, and put out the hand that wasn't holding a pistol to shake mine. 'Bonnie here didn't think you'd make it.' 'Good to meet you,' I replied, shaking his hand and wondering what Gerard had told him about me.

'We'd better go in,' said Gerard. 'They'll be waiting for us.' 'Are you two in the pageant?' I asked as we walked towards the door of the club. 'No,' said Gerard, 'not this year. But you gotta make an effort with the glad rags, Anthony. I mean, there's a depression going on.' We all laughed at that. Gerard gave our names at the door and as we walked up the stairs I found myself watching him as he moved, swaying gently from side to side. He reminded me of somebody.

We took our seats at a table with nine other people, all of whom were involved in the same AIDS charity as Gerard. I felt a bit self-conscious around them at first, though of course I didn't show that, and probably came across as cold, cocky, arrogant. I scanned the lot of them to see if they knew me, to see what they might ask me, to see how I would have to handle them, and after a few minutes I decided they seemed like a nice enough bunch of people. Some of them were good fun, a couple of them were the real earnest kind you find in every charity, and there was even a woman in her forties from New York among them. It was nice to hear that broad, open accent again. It helped me to relax.

It was funny sitting with these people from an AIDS charity when I'd lost so many friends and people I knew to the virus. I guess they all saw me as a survivor, a miraculous being who had emerged from the wreckage of those years unharmed. How could they have known I'd faced my worst trial before that plague swept a city away, that AIDS was nothing to me after what had happened, that I knew if I'd survived that night and the days, weeks and months that followed, I could survive anything. AIDS wasn't my disease, my Achilles Heel. For some reason it left me alone. It couldn't harm me. Anyway, enough about that. I was here to enjoy myself, to enjoy the show.

And what a show it was. There were three parts to it: Daywear, Swimwear and Eveningwear, and the whole thing was hosted by a drag queen called Panti. I'd seen a couple of her shows around town and I had to admit she was good; perfect make-up, a real dry wit and classy as hell. Some of the contestants were really good, some downright awful: there was a guy done up like Nefertiti, another one who looked like a Gothic princess, and a girl called Tampy Lilette, a kind of homage to Tammy Wynette. I looked around the place; at Bonnie and Clyde who were drinking champagne and popped off to the toilet every now and then to do a line or two of coke, at the punk couple at the next table, at a guy in a gold dress who'd sprayed his hair the colour of his outfit. I looked at the happy, drunk, manic crowd, dressed in strange and beautiful costumes, and I gave myself over to the joy of this room full of queers and non-conformists, these clubbers and creatures of the night. I allowed myself to relax.

In the intermission, a guy with pigtails and dressed like a schoolgirl came out on stage, twirling a long ribbon like an Olympic gymnast, and the crowd went wild; whistling, cheering and applauding like crazy. Like everybody else, I threw myself into the mad energy of the place, thinking I hadn't been to something like this, hadn't felt this wild, creative kind of energy in years. I went to the bar and bought a couple of bottles of champagne. 'Fuck it,' I thought, 'this is a night to celebrate, a night to remember.' It was the first birthday I enjoyed in years, even if I kept the fact that I was one year older entirely to myself.

It must have been about five in the morning when I was awoken by his call. I tried letting the phone ring out, but as soon as it stopped, the ringing started again. Whoever it was was persistent, and I began to think it might be something important, somebody calling from New York who'd forgotten about the time difference. 'Eh... hello,' I said, picking up the receiver, barely opening my eyes. 'Anthony, it's me. I'm really sorry. I'm really sorry. I didn't know who to call,' sobbed a voice on the other end of the line. The speech was slurred and it took me a moment to figure out it was Gerard. 'Gerard,' I said, 'what's wrong, what's happened?' I could feel my heart thumping, could feel my hands shaking, and my brain began to do somersaults imagining what had happened to him.

I'd left him at the club with his friends, taken a taxi when I was getting too close to being the wrong side of tipsy. He'd been on great form when I left, dancing and laughing and trying out all kinds of poses in his Bonnie get-up. Okay, so he was high as a kite from the coke and the booze, and there was a moment when I thought there was something too manic about his mood, that he just had too much energy and was sailing dangerously close to the edge of who knows what. But still, he was with friends and I was sure this wasn't the first time he'd dabbled in drugs and besides, he was a fully grown adult and he looked happy, he looked like he was more full of joy than anyone I'd ever seen. And I wanted him to be happy; for him, for me. I wanted to believe that he could be happy. But here he was three hours later, crying on the end of the phone.

'Gerard,' I said again. 'What's wrong? Where the hell are you?' 'I don't know,' he said. 'Somewhere around Rathmines. I don't know. Rathgar or something, I don't know. Jesus, I don't even know where I am. I've made such a mess of things.' He began sobbing again. 'What's happened? Are you hurt?' I panicked for a minute. His voice was serious, concerned for my concern then. 'No, it's not that. Nobody's ever attacked me and nobody ever will. I just let some guy fuck me up a laneway and he didn't use a condom and he just walked away, that's all.' I heard him crying, bawling like a baby, and I felt my heart break a little. 'But don't worry about me,' he said in a voice suddenly scary for its steady, measured tones. 'It's my own fault. I'm sorry for calling. I'm such a stupid fool.'

I knew then I had to take control of the situation. I've been around enough messy queens to know the biggest danger to them is themselves. That if Gerard walked away then, he could wind up under a bus or at the bottom of the canal. I had to keep him talking, keep him as together as he could be in that state. I was terrified at that moment. Everything came rushing back to me, but I kept my voice steady and managed to make what I said precise and authoritative.

'Listen, Gerard,' I said, 'listen very carefully. I want you to look around for a main road. Can you see one?' 'Yes, there's one at the end of this street,' he slurred. 'Okay,' I went on, 'now walk towards it. Are you walking?' 'Yes,' he said. 'Okay, when you get there I want you to take the first cab you see and come to my place. Let me give you the address.' I could sense a slight fear in his breathing and then there was a giddy laugh. 'Oh look, I'm really not into that. What do you take me for?' he asked. I was angry at his insinuation. 'Look, Gerard,' I snapped, 'I don't want to sleep with you. I'm trying to help you, so stop being a stupid little queen.' There was silence on the other end of the line for a moment, and I could tell I'd hurt his pride, but that was the least of my worries. 'I'm sorry,' he apologised. 'What's the address? There's a taxi coming now.' I gave him the address, told him to pass it on to the driver, and listened as he did so. 'Thanks, Anthony,' he said before he hung up. 'Thanks a million.'

He arrived about twenty minutes later. I'd made up the spare room for him, left some sweatpants and a T-shirt on the bed, and run a bath for him. I knew he'd need that, the comforts of home. I wondered where his parents were and if they knew how he spent his nights. I wondered if they worried about him. I think I would. As soon as I heard the taxi pull up outside, I went to the front door. I thanked the taxi driver for getting him here safely, and imagined him staring after us, a dishevelled Bonnie Parker and an old man walking up the garden path of a house by the sea.

Gerard sat in a chair by the window when he came out of the bathroom later, looking out at the sea. He seemed exhausted and broken, a bit like that morning I'd seen him in the library. I gave him a shot of whiskey to steady his nerves, then glass after glass of water, telling him he was going to have one hell of a hangover the next morning. His mood seemed to change every couple of minutes. He might be holding his head in his hands one moment and the next he'd be laughing, and then he'd turn suddenly silent and a terrified look would come over his face. I didn't want to press him, to push him to tell me what had happened. I knew he would tell me in his own time, when he felt ready. But I also knew I couldn't let him go in on himself, that that would be the worst thing to do. I had to keep things light.

I laughed out loud. 'What are you laughing at?' he asked, smiling. 'Sorry,' I said, 'I was just thinking of you getting out of that cab with your mascara running and your make-up all over the place. Sorry for laughing. It just looked so funny.' Gerard laughed too. 'I know,' he agreed. 'What would Faye Dunaway have thought of me?' We laughed for a few minutes, laughed and laughed and then Gerard said, serious now, 'Why do I always go too far, Anthony? Why do I always have to go too far?' and he began to tell me the story of what had happened.

It turned out he'd been on his way to an after-show party with his friends when he met some guy on the street. He told the others to go on, that he'd follow them, and stayed chatting with the guy. He said the guy was hot, Italian, apparently straight and, well, he turned him on. And though he didn't really trust him, though he hadn't planned to do anything with him, though there was no way he was going to do anything, ten minutes later he was down a laneway with the guy. And though he hadn't had unsafe sex for years, though there was no way he was going to let this guy fuck him down a laneway, being drunk and being high, being twenty-four and thinking he'd only ever win in this life, that was exactly what he did.

'He didn't even wait until I'd come,' Gerard murmured in a hurt, lost voice. 'He just fucked me and fucked off. Said I had a nice ass and left me with my cock in my hand. The fucking bastard. I'll bite his cock off if I see him again.' Gerard was angry now, furious. 'What if that cunt gave me HIV? What if I'm infected?' 'Did he come inside you?' I asked, trying to get the facts straight. 'No,' replied Gerard, 'I don't think so. I mean, I'm almost sure he didn't, but I don't know.' I watched him crying softly as he looked out at the sea. I would have reversed that night, turned back time and protected him if I could, but I knew I couldn't. 'Hey,' I said, 'now listen to me. If he didn't come inside you, you should be okay. Anyway, we'll get you tested in three months. Now stop thinking about it, okay?' 'Okay,' agreed Gerard, but I knew he'd have to live through his own hell.

Gerard had planned to stay for the night, but he ended up staying two. I knew it wouldn't be a good idea for him to go back to his flat on his own, with his head full of what had happened. I told him he could hang out at my place and stay another night if he wanted, and he seemed to relax when I said that. We went for a walk along the coast the next day, and though he was still agitated, I could see him letting the events of the previous night go, bit by bit. I wished I could have flung all that shit out to sea for him, let the enormous seagulls take it away, but I knew it was his own battle to fight, his and only his, battle with himself.

I cooked him dinner and as we ate, we both looked out the window at the evening that was growing stronger, growing lighter every day. We watched *The Apartment* on TV. Gerard said it was one of his favourite movies and as I watched him, watching it, I thought about how it felt to be taking care of somebody again, even if it was just for a day. I watched him and wondered why he had faith in me, why he thought I could protect him, help him. It's been so long since I've taken care of anyone, since anyone's needed me in that way. I've been so frightened of that for so long.

A card arrived from him this morning. A Modigliani print with a short note from him saying thanks, I'd been an angel. A card from Gerard, now back in the world of the living, now living his own life again. I read it over and over and then went out for a walk. Life's full of surprises.

March 1951

IT BOTHERED ME AND I wasn't sure why. But I had
to admit it bothered me. Maybe it was because I saw *Blood
Wedding* as my territory, my play, my project. It was something
I wanted to do for myself, something that was hugely
important for me. Of course I would have told Anthony later
that day that I was going to be in a play, in an actual play, an
amazing play by a Spanish playwright. And of course I wanted
him to be proud of me, knew he'd be proud of me, and sup-
portive, and help me learn my lines and get into the part, but
still, I wanted to be at the centre of this drama. And now I'd
have to share it with him and if the truth be told, I didn't want
to. Okay, so I was selfish and egocentric, but I was only
twenty, I'd just been asked to be in a play, and I wanted that
experience for myself. But now it was more about the two of
us than me. Now I wasn't so sure, so confident, of myself,
because I'd be sharing the stage with somebody a lot more
experienced, with somebody who knew a lot more about the
theatre, with a better actor than me. And that person was
Anthony, and already I could feel doubts surfacing in my
mind, already I felt like a charlatan and a failure next to him.
Already I felt the drama slipping from my grasp.

But it wasn't just that. It wasn't just the fact that I saw the seed of a kind of competition between us being sown. It was also because I'd just found out something I didn't know about Anthony, because there was something he hadn't told me. Because he'd never mentioned anything about Lorca or *Blood Wedding* or Maeve, or auditioning for the play. Of course I hadn't said anything about it either, but I didn't want to think about that now. I could only see things from my point of view, and I began thinking that if I didn't know about Anthony doing the play, then perhaps there were other things I didn't know about him. I'd only known him for a couple of months after all, and despite the fact I loved him, that I was sure I loved him; was madly, uncontrollably, cut off your right arm in love with him, standing there outside the Shelbourne, I saw him for a moment as a stranger, as somebody with a whole different life that I really didn't have any idea about. And rightly or wrongly, I resented him for that, hated him a bit for that.

Besides feeling jealous, and selfish and suspicious though, there was something else which got to me about the whole situation, something I couldn't quite put my finger on. It was a feeling, a sensation, a kind of unease in the pit of my stomach. I don't know why, but for some reason I had a bad feeling about us doing the play together. The whole thing seemed too intense, too claustrophobic, too much. I wanted to run after Maeve and tell her I couldn't do it, I wouldn't do it, I was no longer part of the equation. That I was sorry I hadn't told her earlier, but Anthony was my lover, and I just didn't feel right about doing the play with him, that I just thought it would be a bad idea. That I couldn't explain it, but it made me feel uneasy, it made me feel afraid.

But of course I didn't. Instead I walked home on my own, feeling downcast, feeling deflated, feeling as though the rug had been pulled from under me. I sat glumly through the afternoon, listening to Radio Luxembourg in my bedsit, smoking one cigarette after another. I was angry at Anthony and Maeve for what I saw as their conspiracy, furious that I wasn't in control and wasn't the centre of attention anymore. But I was also agitated about having these feelings, and I felt a bit guilty and ashamed for being so ungenerous, for not being kind and open and grown-up, for putting so many obstacles in the way when there really weren't any. 'Why can't we do the play together?' I asked myself. 'What can go wrong? Maybe it will be a good thing, maybe it will bring us even closer together. Just grow up and stop being so foolish,' I told myself. 'Theatre is about collaboration and if you can't even work together with the man you're in love with, then there's something wrong with you. I mean, look at Micheál MacLíammóir and Hilton Edwards,' I convinced myself. 'Where would they be now if they let petty jealousies and vague, terrible feelings get in the way?' No, I was being ridiculous, a drama queen before I'd even made my first appearance on the stage.

By eight o'clock I'd promised myself I'd do *Blood Wedding*, that we could and would do it together. I'd even begun to look forward to it, and felt a bit excited that we were about to embark on this new adventure together. 'Who knows,' I thought, 'maybe we'll turn out to be the new Hilton and Micheál.' There were still doubts of course, and I still had that feeling in my stomach that something wasn't right about the whole situation, but I put all of that to the back of my mind and focused only on the thought of me and Anthony on stage together, and all the great things that could come from this. I leapt up from the chair where I was sitting, ran from the house, and all the way along the canal to Anthony's flat to tell him I'd do it, we'd do it, we were going to be in *Blood Wedding* together.

All along the way, I began to see Anthony as Leonardo; passionate, wilful Leonardo. Leonardo who steals away from his wife at night to go and visit his sweetheart, my wife-to-be. Leonardo who flees with her on her wedding day, riding out into the summer's evening, leaving me seething and mad with rage. The man I hurtle after, the man I stab that night in the woods, the man who stabs me too, the enemy I die with. Funny how the mind works, isn't it? A few hours earlier, I couldn't handle the thought of Anthony playing Leonardo in Maeve's production of *Blood Wedding* and now he was the only one I could imagine taking the role. Now he was the only Leonardo I could imagine.

Anthony was there when I arrived. I knew he'd be in. He had an essay due the next morning and he was frantically working away at it. 'How's it going?' I asked. 'Oh, okay,' he said, but I could see he looked harassed and tired. 'My mother telephoned me earlier, asking why I wasn't coming to lunch, going on about family being the most important thing and me not doing my duty.' He sounded stressed and irritated. 'Jesus, they really fucking annoy me sometimes. Always trying to make me feel guilty. They wanted me to go to university, and when I say I can't come and see them because I have to get an essay finished, they start trying to make me feel guilty.' 'Don't worry about them,' I consoled, but I knew it bothered him, knew his parents made him angrier, put him more on edge, than anyone else could.

'I have some good news,' I announced, still coasting along on the newly found good feeling that we were going to do the play together. 'Oh yeah?' he said. 'Tell me.' 'Did Maeve call you today?' I asked. 'Maeve?' He looked blank for a moment. 'Maeve, how do you know Maeve?' he asked quizzically. 'She's a friend of mine,' I said, feeling a bit important for knowing this woman. 'Oh, really?' he said. 'I didn't know you knew her.

She did call me today, in any case. She said I got a part in a Spanish play she's going to put on this summer. It's called *Blood Wedding*. It's a Lorca play. I think it could be really good.' 'I know,' I said. 'What do you mean you know?' he asked. 'Has she talked to you about the play?'

'I'm going to be *in* the play,' I stated, and for a split second there was an arrogance in my tone. He looked surprised, as if he couldn't figure out exactly what I was saying. 'I'm going to be in the play,' I repeated. 'I'm going to play The Bridegroom. Maeve asked me to read the play a few weeks ago, and yesterday evening she asked me to be in it.' I was excited now. 'I wanted to wait until I'd told her I'd do it before I told you anything about it. And then today when I asked her who was playing Leonardo, she said it was you. I couldn't believe it at first, but it was you she was talking about all right.'

Anthony looked at me and I could tell he was trying to piece everything together in his mind. I suppose, like me, he'd thought of this as his own project and now there I was, saying I was friends with Maeve and I was going to be in the play with him. I saw a look of disdain, a look of 'I'm the actor here and not you', flicker across his face for a moment. A look of 'What are you doing in this part of my life, in my realm?' but he managed to keep it under control and I told myself not to think about it too much. After all, I understood where those feelings came from.

I smiled at him and tried to put my positive spin on things. 'Anthony, it's going to be great. Me and you on stage together, doing *Blood Wedding* together. It'll be great.' I was trying to encourage him, but I knew he was still having strong doubts. 'Come on,' I said, 'we'll be brilliant together. I mean, I know I don't know anything about acting, but you can help me with that, you can help me with the role. You know a lot more about acting than I do, you've done so many plays.' I wanted to reassure him that I wasn't trying to take his acting mantle from him, that I was no competition for him. I could see I was beginning to bring him around to my way of thinking, could see he was beginning to imagine how the whole experience could be, instead of focusing on the negative. He was silent for a few moments and then he let out a low whistle. 'So we're going to do *Blood Wedding* together?' he said. 'Me, you and Lorca, what a combination!' He stood up from his chair and lifted me over to his bed, where we made a frenzied, furious kind of love out of all of the day's energy.

As it turned out, *Blood Wedding* did bring Anthony and me even closer together. Lorca and his work was one of Anthony's interests, and Anthony was nothing if not intense about his interests. I learned so much about the man over the weeks that followed. I would listen to Anthony in the evenings as he told me about Lorca; about his beloved city of Granada, about his friendships with Dalí and Buñuel, about his trips to New York and Cuba, about his travelling theatre company that brought the theatre to the people of Spain, about how he'd had male lovers, and about his death in the early days of the Spanish Civil War, killed by what Anthony called Franco's fascist bastards. He talked about his plays: *Yerma* and *The House of Bernarda Alba*. He talked for hours about Lorca's poetry: *The Gypsy Ballads*, *Poet in New York*, and one wet Saturday night when we came home drunk, he read me 'Lament for Ignacio Sánchez Mejías', about the death of a famous Spanish matador in the bullring. The world outside disappeared that night; there was just Anthony reading Lorca's words and nothing else had any power against them.

I began reading more and more of Lorca's poems myself, became more and more intrigued by him and fascinated by Spain. I began to see him, to imagine the man, and when I was at work, making my way through a pile of mind-numbing files, I would hear his words, I would hear Anthony reciting his words, and everything would be transformed. On chilly mornings when I cycled to work, and on bland, brutal days, as grey as death, I would think of Spain and suddenly feel full of life again. It was all so romantic: poetry and tragedy, repressive mothers and punishing, backward communities, illicit love and untimely death and the gardens of the Alhambra Palace in Granada. Anthony and I took Lorca's gypsies and his deaths, his forbidden love and his images of Spain, and let them fill us up, let them open up our world and take us to emotional spaces we'd never been to and to real, physical places we thought we would visit together, one day.

That period was so beautiful, swimming around in his words, drowning sweetly in the weight of them, then flying high with his joy, tapping out the beat of his poems with our feet on the floor. But what did we know, what did we really know? To us it was all a game, a beautiful, intoxicating game. And being young and being foolish, we thought we could just take the best of him, the best of his words, his work, for our own private world. How could we know what we'd begun?

I took *Blood Wedding* with me wherever I went, and began learning my lines any free moment I had. I'd go over the lines I knew off by heart on my way to work, and then try and learn a few new ones at dinner hour, or in my bedsit in the evenings, or in Anthony's place if he was busy working away at his college stuff. Maeve might have said not to worry about learning them for the moment, but if Anthony and his prodigious knowledge of Lorca and his world was anything to go by, then I imagined the rest of the cast would be just as well up on things, and there was no way I wanted to be the country idiot amongst them. I suppose I wanted a head start, wanted to prove myself. And besides that I was just very eager to get going, to get the show up and running, to cross over into the world of the stage.

You have to understand; I was young, it was 1951 and I was living in Ireland. Another world, another life, another existence, had just opened up for me and I was ready as hell to leap into that world. There I'd been a year earlier, with a dull life in a country town that time had forgotten and now here I was with multiple lives: my new life of a different kind of love, my new life with Anthony, and my new life as The Bridegroom in *Blood Wedding*, riding through the scorched countryside of southern Spain. Through Anthony, through Lorca, through everything that Dublin had offered me in the few months I'd been living there, I imagined I could live many lives: creative, passionate, full to bursting lives, in places as far away as Spain and Argentina. All borders and barriers receded into the distance and I took a hold of my new lives with all the energy and imagination of any young man with a dream.

I decided to quit the drama group at work, even though I'd been given a part in their show and had learned a lot from the rehearsals and meetings I'd been to. But now that Maeve had asked me to be in *Blood Wedding*, now that I was going to be in a real play, a real tragedy, directed by Maeve, and acting alongside Anthony, the thought of rehearsing week after week for *Easter Parade* seemed somehow trivial. Okay, so I'd let all this Lorca stuff go to my head, and was quite pretentious about the whole thing, but well, that's who I was back then.

I can still remember the day I walked up to Mr O'Malley and told him I was leaving. 'What do you mean you're leaving?' I remember him demanding, disbelievingly. 'Well, I've been offered a part in a play a friend of mine is putting on,' I explained calmly, confidently, enjoying every moment of the situation. 'What do you mean you've been offered a part in a play?' he asked. 'Don't tell me you're leaving the drama group here for a two-minute part in some amateur production.' 'It's actually one of the main parts,' I said, 'and it's longer than two minutes.' 'A main part?' He was incredulous. 'But you've never even acted before.' I knew he was trying to put me down again and I was having none of it. 'Yes, a main part,' I confirmed, 'and the play is wonderful.' 'Oh really?' he said, arching his eyebrows. 'What play is it? Who's putting it on? When is it going to be on?' But I wasn't going to give the little worm anything. 'I'd love to stay and chat,' I smiled, 'but I have a read-through with the cast now.'

I left him staring after me but as I walked away I turned around and, casual as be damned, lifted my shoulders and said, 'Hey, that's showbiz.' I might have been meek and unsure of myself in some respects back then, but one thing I had, one thing I've always hung onto, was my pride. Eileen, who had also managed to wrangle a small part in Maeve's production, exploded in a fit of laughter when I told her what had happened.

In truth, I was petrified about meeting the cast that evening, afraid that I'd be revealed as an unsophisticated civil servant by a room full of cultured people. Anthony had a lot on that day so I arranged to meet him at Maeve's house, but walking up to Mountjoy Square after work, I couldn't help but wish he was with me. I needed his encouragement, his belief in me. I needed him to tell me, as he'd already done so many times, that it would just be an informal meeting, nothing major, nothing too intense. I was a bit early and so nervous about going into the house by the time I'd reached the square, I walked around it twice, trying to kill time with the most awful feeling in my stomach. Any arrogance I'd displayed with Mr O'Malley had disappeared like the smoke that was rising from the chimneys all around the square. But I steeled myself, told myself to stop being a fool and get myself inside. I took a deep breath, put my chest out and shoulders back, and knocked at Maeve's front door.

Anthony was already there, deep in conversation with a good-looking girl. 'He must have left one of his lectures early,' I thought to myself. The sight of him sitting there made me feel a bit relieved, but there was another sensation I had at the same time, one I didn't like at all. Watching him chatting to that girl, wearing a fawn-coloured blazer and white shirt, his movements casual and charming, I saw him for a moment as a stranger, as somebody I didn't know. Perhaps for the first time since we'd met, I saw him objectively, and that feeling made me shiver. He turned and saw me then, smiled at me, and I went over to talk to him.

We were talking together in low tones when Maeve came up to us. 'Daniel, Anthony, do you two know each other?' she asked. For a moment I thought her surprise was all an act, that she'd known all along that Anthony and I were having a relationship, and that the way she'd cast the play was all part of a game, the cool machinations of a theatre director. But as she stood there, I saw it was very possible she hadn't known anything about us. I felt uncomfortable and embarrassed and I also felt guilty because I'd kept Anthony a secret from her, and hadn't told Anthony anything about Maeve until a few weeks previously. 'Yes, we know each other,' I finally managed and, looking at Anthony, I couldn't help but laugh nervously like a teenager. Obviously Maeve knew then that we were lovers, that we weren't just friends. 'I see,' she said, looking intently at both of us. 'I see.' But whatever it was she saw, I couldn't see it. I only knew something was bothering her and the situation had thrown her off course a bit. 'Well, we'd better get started,' she said, and turned away from us to bring the group together.

We all arranged our chairs in a big circle and Maeve asked

everybody to introduce themselves and say which character they would be playing. I felt myself shrinking into my chair and felt my heart thumping in my chest; hoping, hoping, I would be the last person to speak. But then I heard her say, 'Daniel, would you like to begin,' pushing me already, trying to get me to lose my self-consciousness, challenging me and stretching everything I thought about myself. It was a precedent she was setting for the months that would follow. She was the director after all. This was her role.

But sitting there that first night, my palms felt sweaty, I heard the room turn very silent and I couldn't believe I'd let myself get into this, put myself in this situation. Oh, I snapped out of it after a few moments. I had to, what other choice was there, and feeling my face turn the colour of beetroot, but taking advantage of the adrenalin I could feel pumping through my blood, I spoke.

'I'm Daniel,' I began, 'and I'm going to play The Bridegroom. This is my first time acting, so I'm a bit nervous. Sorry.' I looked at Maeve quickly for approval, but her gaze had shifted to somebody else. I didn't dare look at Anthony because I didn't want to see him look at me, his face saying I'd never make it, I'd never be able to do this. Of course that was just in my head, but I still felt very insecure next to him.

One by one, everybody introduced themselves and said which part they were going to play. Anthony spoke clearly and knowledgeably, of course, but maybe he had a little bit too much to say, I thought to myself, as I watched Maeve skilfully, politely, cut him short and move onto the next person. Rosaleen, the beautiful, petite and very confident young woman from around Mount Street, was going to play The Bride. Raymond, the sun-tanned older man, was going to play her father. And Mary, one time bright young thing of the Irish theatre scene, was going to play my mother. She'd given up the theatre to raise her family, but still liked to keep her hand in.

Eileen was there, of course, all dolled up for this first meeting and looking as well as ever. She was going to play The Servant Woman, and though it was a small enough part, I knew she'd bring all of her boundless energy to it. A quiet girl called Elizabeth, with a dress sense I can only describe as eccentric, was down to play the part of Leonardo's wife, and an older woman called Maude, serious-looking but with a glint of mischief in her eyes, told us she was going to take the role of The Mother-In-Law, but would also play The Moon. Another older woman, Anne, who carried all of her life's experiences on her face, was going to be The Neighbour Woman as well as The Beggar Woman, the play's physical incarnation of death. There were other people with small and background roles who weren't there that night. Instead, we'd share their few lines between us and they would come to the later rehearsals.

As I looked around the group: at Anthony, at Maude, Raymond, Rosaleen and the rest, I wondered what had brought us together, what had brought us to Maeve's drawing room this mild Thursday evening. I imagined their lives and made up all kinds of stories as I sat there, each more dramatic than the last, drama queen that I was. I wondered what was different about us and what there was in us that was the same, what had attracted all of us to Lorca and his *Blood Wedding*, why each and every one of us had committed to giving up our free time to put on this play. And though it was just our first meeting, though we'd just introduced ourselves and hadn't even begun the read-through, already I could feel the energy and frisson in that room, all the dynamism of the collective dramatic experience.

There was one man who hadn't spoken yet though. He was a good-looking guy, classically handsome, with big features and dark hair. I guessed he was about forty, but a young kind of forty, though that still seemed ancient to me back then. He had a real presence about him; the kind of man people notice immediately when he walks into a room. 'Everybody, this is Fitzer,' Maeve announced. 'Fitzer has an enormous amount of experience in the theatre, both here and in New York, and he's going to help me produce the play.' He smiled a confident, warm smile and looked around the group. 'Hi, everybody,' he said. 'I'm very happy to be working with all of you and thank you very much for giving up your time this evening.'

'So this is the famous Fitzer,' I thought to myself. 'This is the Republican hero of the Spanish Civil War, the man who knew Maeve's husband there, the man who came to live in Ireland, who fell in love and settled down here.' I could already see Eileen swooning at his good looks, his gravelly voice and worldly air.

'Before we begin the read-through, I want to talk a bit about Lorca's life, his work and the origins of the play,' he began, and everybody was immediately captivated by the man himself as much as by what he was saying. He spoke about Lorca's Granada and, like a group of disciples, he led us up the hill to the Alhambra, where we all stood looking out over the old Moorish quarter, before he brought us back down and through the gypsy area of the city. He told us how *Blood Wedding* was based on real life events, where it had premiered, and what Spain had made of it at the time. He ended by telling us about Lorca's death, how he'd been murdered, executed, because he sympathised with the Republicans. You could have heard a pin drop as he spoke about his untimely, unceremonious, unjust death. I was fascinated by Fitzer, by his many lives, from the moment he spoke. Fascinated like everybody else in that room. Well, almost everybody, because all Anthony said about him later that night when we were back in his flat was that he thought Fitzer was a bit full of himself.

The read-through went fine that night. It was just our first meeting, so nothing major could have gone wrong. Some gave it more than they needed, and seemed as though they were on stage and not in Maeve's drawing room. Some of us, including me, were shy and awkward and unsure of ourselves. But the whole thing went all right and when we all had a drink afterwards, everybody seemed to be in good spirits. There was a lot of laughter in the pub, as well as anecdotes swapped and the odd name dropped. We told one another what we did, where we were from, and where we went on holiday. We traded scraps of information about Lorca and spoke about our individual and collective ideas for the play.

What I remember most about that first evening, though, was the feeling that I'd found a new kind of family, that all of us were in this together, that it was somehow a closed and magical world we were creating, separate from the reality outside Maeve's front door. I felt high, I felt full of hopes and energy and dreams and, unsure of myself and my ability as an actor though I might have been, I already felt a part of something very special.

I turned twenty-one a few days later. I didn't have one of those huge parties kids in Ireland seem to have now when they turn twenty-one, but Anthony had arranged to have a few friends around to his flat to celebrate the event. Late that night, as I swayed to an Ella Fitzgerald tune and looked around the room, at Anthony, at Maeve, at Eileen, and all the new friends I'd made since my last birthday, I couldn't help but feel that I'd become a man, a man with a life and a place he belonged to. But what did I know? I wasn't a man at all. I was still just a boy.

8

April 1998

GOOD FRIDAY! What the hell is good about it, I'd like to know. People taking a weird kind of pleasure in the crucifixion of the man they say is their Lord. Now that's what I call perverse, that's what I call sadistic! I mean, can you imagine stretching a man's death over twelve pictures? And can you imagine going to a church to re-enact that death once a year? That's just plain loony! I know not as many people follow the Stations of the Cross now as when I lived here, but still I saw a lot of people scurrying to the churches this morning and I couldn't help but feel oppressed. Oppressed by their piety, their idolatry, their screwed up way of seeing the world, their belief that pain equals goodness, their stubborn hypocrisies.

I remember all those Good Fridays when I was a kid, going to the Stations of the Cross and sticking to a diet of black tea and burnt toast with my mother. How we thought black tea and burnt toast could get us to heaven, I still can't quite figure out. But what did I know then? I was just a kid from a fucked up country.

It was wet today and I felt a bit restless. I turned on the radio and heard the news that the Good Friday Agreement had been signed. It seems as though there might be peace up the North at last. 'Good,' I thought, 'that's great news. Good for them.' But to be honest, I'd never really got involved in what they call 'the Troubles'. I was already so far away when the real killing began. I mean, I saw the explosions, the massacres and the hunger strikes on the news, but it all seemed as though it was happening in a foreign country, in a place I no longer had anything to do with it. Oh, friends would ask me about it over the years, and wonder how I could be so indifferent when my country was being racked by war, but from the moment I left – no, from the moment he left – that place was no longer my home. New York was my only home, Ireland just the place where I'd had the misfortune to be born. I left Ireland to the potato people in the Irish bars out in Queens and up in The Bronx.

'But they have their peace now and that's a good thing.' That's what I was thinking, or something like that, when Gerard phoned and asked me what I was up to for the day. 'Not much,' I said. 'This weather's bullshit and I'm not really in the mood to go into town. Are you gonna ask me if I want to go to the Stations of the Cross with you?' 'Yeah, right,' he shot back. 'I'd say I'd go up in flames if I darkened a church's door.' 'That makes two of us,' I said. 'And besides,' he went on, 'I don't have anything to wear and all my mantillas are in the wash.' I laughed.

'So, you wanna come out and visit me, kiddo?' I invited. 'We could have lunch or watch a movie.' 'Sure,' he said, mimicking my accent, 'that would be awesome.' I didn't sound like that, I knew I didn't, and for a moment I felt a bit pissed, before I laughed it off. 'I'll be out around two, is that okay?' he asked. 'I'm just doing a bit of writing at the moment.' 'Sure,' I said. 'How's the book coming along?' 'Oh, you know how it is,' he responded. 'Good one week, bad the next. This week has been good, though. I've got a lot done.' 'It's good to hear it's going so well,' I encouraged, trying not to sound too enthusiastic, too much like a bland, endlessly optimistic American. 'Touch wood,' Gerard said.

He arrived at a quarter past two. He was quiet at first, still going over what he'd written in his head, distracted, only half there. I tried talking to him about different things, but he didn't really engage with me, not until he'd snapped out of whatever he was thinking about.

'So, the book's going well?' I put the question to him again as we sat eating lunch in a café up in Dun Laoghaire. 'Yeah,' he said, looking at the rain outside and the people passing along the slippery street. 'I met a man last week who knew Fitzer from the theatre. His name's Sam Mirrelson.' Gerard looked at me to see if I recognised the name. I had met Sam once, years before, but I never really knew him. 'Oh, yeah?' I said. 'I don't know that guy.'

'He was really interesting,' Gerard went on. 'He gave me lots of information about the theatre in Dublin in the forties and fifties. You know, what theatres there were, what kind of plays they put on, that kind of stuff.' 'That's great,' I enthused, but really I felt a bit apprehensive. I mean, if Gerard had been talking to someone about the theatre in Dublin back then, there was a good chance he'd heard about *Blood Wedding*, about our *Blood Wedding*.

'I was really surprised at some of the plays they put on,' he continued. 'I mean, I thought it was all plays about Irish history and folklore, but there seem to have been a lot of English and European plays.' 'Oh yeah?' I said, feeling my heart skip a beat. 'Yeah, you know, political plays from England, and Sartre and Brecht.' I wondered if he was trying to get me to open up, if this was his way of getting me to talk, but when I looked at him I couldn't make out his expression. 'He hasn't said anything about Lorca. Perhaps he hasn't heard anything about *Blood Wedding* after all,' I thought.

'I was never really that interested in the theatre.' I tried to change the subject. 'I preferred going to the pictures.' 'Oh,' he said, 'pity. There was a lot of good stuff on.' 'Yeah, but it was never really my thing,' I lied.

'I'm sorry about calling you that night,' Gerard apologised when we were back in the house. His tone was serious and I could tell he was still upset about what had happened that night after Alternative Miss Ireland. 'Don't worry about it,' I said. 'Just try not to think about it.' 'I know,' he said, 'but it was such a stupid thing to do. I mean, letting that guy fuck me without a condom. What was I thinking?' 'Listen,' I said to him softly, 'we all do stupid things now and then.' 'Yeah,' he conceded, 'but I seem to do one stupid thing after another and I don't know why.'

'Have you ever had a boyfriend, Gerard?' I asked him after a while. 'No, not really,' he responded, 'though there was a guy I was with for a few years.' 'Oh yeah? Tell me about him,' I said. Gerard laughed nervously. 'There's not much to tell,' he said. 'He was forty and married. I was seventeen. He was a good friend of my dad's, a man I had a crush on from when I was a little kid. I was sure he wasn't gay, was sure it was all in my head, but then one day when I was seventeen, just after I'd finished the Leaving Cert, he gets me drunk, says he thinks he likes guys, asks me if I like guys too, and says maybe we should sleep together. And so we did, and we had sex for a few years.'

'And did you love him?' I probed. Gerard laughed again, a strange laugh. 'I don't know,' he replied. 'I thought it was just sex, just a game. I loved having sex with him and I loved the power I had over him. But I didn't think about love. I mean, I was seventeen. I was only interested in getting my rocks off. But I suppose I must have felt more for him than I admitted.'

His voice took on a cold, hollow kind of sound and all his words were measured. 'He dumped me one night,' Gerard continued. 'He told me he'd just been going through a phase, that he'd just been experimenting and that he was really straight.' 'Some chance,' I said. 'Yeah, I know,' Gerard concurred. 'That's what I told him. I tried to make him see that he was gay, that he was just like me, but he wasn't having any of it. One night after we'd been together up in the mountains, he said it had to stop, told me he didn't want to see me any more. Dropped me home, shook my hand and said he'd see me around.'

'And how did you take that?' I asked. 'Well, at first I couldn't believe it,' Gerard said slowly. 'I mean, we'd been seeing one another for quite a while, and out of the blue he says this. I mean, I knew it couldn't go on forever, but I always imagined I'd be the one to end it. And there I was, with his cum still all over me, being told it was over. I wasn't going to take it. I wasn't going to take that from him. And suddenly now that I'd been rejected, I wanted him even more. I wanted him more than ever. I missed him.' Gerard's face turned red and I felt myself wince a little.

'I called him, I called him to try and talk to him, but he didn't answer,' Gerard went on. 'I began thinking about him all the time, needing him all the time. I followed him to work, followed him to the shop, followed him when he went out with his wife and kids. He wouldn't talk to me though, pretended he didn't even see me. And then I got really desperate. I so badly wanted him again, so badly wanted him to want me, I wrote him a letter saying I'd spill the beans to his wife if he didn't meet me.'

'And did he meet you?' I wanted to know. 'Yeah, he took me out to Dollymount one night. We went to the dunes and fucked, fucked where we'd fucked loads of times. But I could see he was just doing it because he was scared, shit-scared. And afterwards, when I tried to get him to hold me, just to hold me, I knew there was nothing there, that there probably never was. Fucking cunt.' Gerard looked out the window. 'He dropped me home and that was that. I promised myself I'd never speak to him again, not that he cared. But I never did find out why he got rid of me like that and that bothered me for a long time. It gets to me even now. But who cares, it was all a long time ago.'

'And has there been anybody since then?' I asked. 'Yeah,' he said coolly, 'there's been lots of guys. None whose names I can remember though. It took me a long time to get over him, you know, to get over what happened, and I promised myself I'd never let myself get involved like that again. Oh, I still fucked around, had sex with loads of guys, but I never, never let myself fall for them. If I felt something I just killed it. I didn't want to be in love.' I knew what Gerard meant, knew exactly what he meant when he said that, even if his feeling came from someplace different to mine.

'Can I tell you something I've never told anybody?' he asked after a long, awkward silence. 'Sure,' I said, 'of course you can.' 'Don't ever tell anybody this, but I worked as a rent boy in London for a while,' he stated without emotion. 'Did you?' I asked, trying to sound more surprised than I really was. 'Yeah,' he said. 'I know this is going to sound funny, but it wasn't for the money, though I made lots of it. It was more that it gave me control. It gave me control over sex.' I said nothing, just sat there and listened. 'I used to love seeing the desire in their eyes,' Gerard went on, 'especially the straight guys, the married guys. I could smell the desire and the fear off them, and I loved having a bit of power over them. I loved that they'd do anything for me, risk it all to be with me. And I loved being able to walk away. It gave me a sense of freedom.' There was a calculated, almost cruel look in Gerard's eye, the same look I'd seen on his face that night in the sauna.

'Are you still doing it?' I asked, looking away uncomfortably. 'No,' he replied. 'I gave all that up when I came home last year. Maybe that's why I did come home, because I started to feel I needed something else. I started needing something more, even if I didn't want it, even if I tried to deny it at first. I started craving something more. And I've been trying to get away from whoring my ass ever since.' I looked back at him. 'Don't laugh at me, Anthony, but what I want now, what I want more than anything, is a relationship. I want somebody to love, somebody to love me. I've seen enough sex for a lifetime. I want something more now.'

'So, why don't you go out and get yourself a boyfriend?' I asked stupidly, knowing things are never that simple. 'Don't think I wouldn't love to, don't think I'm not trying,' he said. 'It's just any time I sleep with a guy I like, I just want to get out of there as fast as I can. I mean, I've never even spent the night with someone I like. And most of the time I go out, I just end up drunk, with some fucker I couldn't give a fuck about. Just like that guy up the laneway. Besides, I don't think I'd be able to have a relationship with someone. What do I know about love? What could I give to someone?' Suddenly he looked deflated, completely lost. 'Don't say that, Gerard,' I scolded without thinking. 'Fuck, Gerard, don't say things like that.'

And for the first time in years, in decades, I wanted to believe, had to believe, in love. Not for me, but for Gerard.

'Gerard?' I said to him, after a long silence. 'Yes,' he answered. 'You know how you asked me that night in the restaurant if love was possible between men back then, back when I lived in Dublin?' 'Yes,' he said. 'Well, I told you then I didn't know, but that was a lie. I do know. I'm sure of it. Love was possible between men in this city back then. Of course it was. I know that for a fact.'

And I promised myself then that one day soon, I would tell Gerard all about Anthony, all about Anthony and me.

April 1951

WE BEGAN THE ACTUAL rehearsals for the play the first Tuesday evening in April. April, and the light changed and sometimes the skies opened, and all the gardens of Dublin were full of flowers. Everybody was there that first evening and there was a real excitement in the air as we took those first steps towards putting the play on. None of us knew exactly what was before us, how exactly this thing would come to life, and that was part of the thrill. We were all about to step into the unknown, give up, or at least compromise on, our personal visions of *Blood Wedding* for the one we would arrive at together. And we were all about to put ourselves in Maeve's hands, the hands of the director, so not surprisingly we all felt vulnerable, felt exposed. We were all so giddy and light-headed, so full of inane chat, before Maeve clapped her hands and said she wanted to do some warm-up exercises.

She said she wanted each of us to imagine we were an animal, any animal. We were to imagine there was nobody else around and we were in whatever place this animal lived. 'Oh God,' I thought, 'is she serious?' I glanced around the room and saw a couple of other faces that looked just as confused, as unsure, as mine. There was a nervous giggle from someone, but Maeve helped us to focus, to concentrate on the exercise, and I tried to forget my fears and trust in her, telling myself she knew what she was doing.

The room was very silent for a few minutes. You could have heard a pin drop. All of a sudden though, when Maeve clapped her hands and said she wanted us to become the animals we'd imagined, to act exactly as they would, the room erupted in meows and roars, squeaks and squeals. I was a tiger hunting for prey in the jungle, Anthony was a horse galloping along the beach, Rosaleen was some kind of bird, and Eileen was a cat who sat licking her paws and flirting with everyone in the room. After a while of flying, racing, and swinging through that room, one by one we all began to laugh as we looked around us. We laughed and laughed at this out of control zoo that had taken over Maeve's front room, and as we laughed we felt a great tension disappear.

The first rehearsal went, I suppose, as most first rehearsals do. For all our faults, for all the mistakes we made and for everything we didn't yet know, we brought a raw, positive energy to it that night. I suppose the play meant something different to all of us, was important in a different way to each and every one of us, and because we all connected with the work in one way or another, I suppose we all wanted to do justice to it. Oh, I felt awkward and incompetent and like a piece of nothing a number of times in the room that night, but I don't know, I got the confidence, the belief in myself, from somewhere.

There was such an amount to learn though, and so much I hadn't thought about. I'd already learned my lines, even though we did this rehearsal reading from the script. And I tried to forget about myself and put myself in the place of The Bridegroom, whose wife has just run off on their wedding day. But there was so much more to think about. I had to start thinking about my voice. I didn't really know anything about projecting my voice so it would fill a theatre. And there was my posture, of course. I had to learn a lot about that, how to hold myself on stage and make my presence felt. And perhaps most importantly, most difficult, there was the slow process of learning how to become my character. Not just imagining I was him while I was in that room, but actually becoming him, inhabiting his skin: breathing, sweating, sighing and hating as he would.

I had a lot of work to do, but already I could feel myself learning, could feel myself opening up and becoming someone else. I knew it would be hard, of course it would, but the atmosphere in that room was thrilling, was electric and I… I was a part of it.

Spain seemed like a place that was very far away back then. Not like now, just a couple of hours from Ireland. Through *Blood Wedding*, and through Anthony and everything he told me about Lorca and his country, I learned a lot about Spain. And it was my images of Spain, my thoughts about Spain, all my romantic ideas and passion and sadness for that country, that I brought to those rehearsals, that I brought to my part as The Bridegroom. I imagined I was from a country I'd never been to, one I'd only read about and heard about. I became obsessed with Spain, but in time Maeve helped me see that I was focusing too much on the place, too much on what was on the outside and not enough on what was on the inside. She helped me understand something important; that though this play was set in the south of Spain, the story was a universal one. It could have been set in Russia or South Africa or Peru. 'Or,' as she said to me, 'this could be any town in Ireland, any town at all.'

And it was then I began, slowly, to make the connection between *Blood Wedding* and the country I came from, the town I came from. I found this hard to do at first. I mean, until that point *Blood Wedding* had meant Spain to me, in all its tragedy and glory. It had represented something exotic, something foreign, and now I was being forced to go backwards; to read the play into my town and my town into the play. I suppose *Blood Wedding* had been another way for me to escape from that bland little place, but Maeve wasn't that interested in escape. She wanted me to see the reality of the play, even if it made me uncomfortable, even if it meant journeying back to a life I wanted to forget, to a place and a time I thought I'd left behind.

And she was right, of course she was. If there was to be any real depth to my performance, then I would have to connect with the play on some kind of a personal level, would have to use my own individual experience to understand what was going on. I began to think more and more about the place where I'd grown up. I thought about all the guys I'd gone to school with who just wanted something normal, something like their fathers and grandfathers before them: a wife, children and a steady job. I'd always despised them a bit for their lack of ambition and originality, but now, instead of judging them, I had to try and understand them. I had to figure out what made them tick.

And when I looked beyond my own character and at the bigger picture of the whole play, I began to understand how it had everything to do with my town. After all, this was Ireland in 1951, not the most progressive of places by any standards.

There were still arranged marriages in my own town. Oh, people didn't call them that, but that's what they were. And there were lots and lots of couples terrified of using contraception because the church forbade it, and so you had women terrified of getting pregnant and spitting out babies year after year. There were gay men forced into the priesthood, or forced into loveless marriages, or whose only option was to go and live in England or the States.

There was incest, rape and child abuse in my town, but no one spoke about those things, not back then. There were husbands who cheated on their wives, husbands who beat up their wives, people who took their own lives. There was the man who tried to get me drunk and pick me up when I was sixteen. There were the explosions of violence on a Friday and Saturday night. And there were all those couples who repeated the same, stifling routines day after day, not quite sure if they were living or dead. There were so many repressions and restrictions in my town, in every town across the country, and nobody could breathe, not really, not freely. But one thing was always certain, almost everybody from where I came from would go to mass, take their seats in church every Sunday morning without fail. There was just no getting away from that.

Maeve brought all of this back to me, all of these truths that made me feel nauseous inside. I hated thinking about it. I hated thinking about that town and all its freaks and all their squalid lives, but I had to. I'd been so immersed in my new life in Dublin, I'd forgotten all about it, or thought I had, or hoped I had. But with *Blood Wedding* Maeve brought everything back to me, and I was forced out of the bubble I'd been so happily sharing with Anthony, and back into the harsher realities of the country in which I lived. I resented Maeve a little for dragging me back into that Ireland, for showing me everything that was impossible. I wanted to believe, had to believe, that anything was possible. But, well, all of this was essential for my character, for the play, and that was what was most important that April we began the rehearsals.

I went home that Easter. I went to the Stations of the Cross and to mass on Sunday with my family. I didn't really want to. I mean, I wouldn't have gone if I'd had anything to do with it, but it was just something you had to do back then. I know that sounds really cowardly, but they were different times. And besides, going to that church would give me the opportunity to observe the people of the town. It would help me with the character, help me with the play. Funny, isn't it? How I went back to the place I came from in order to get to Spain.

And it did help me. It helped me to see just how restrictive, how oppressive, life must be in every small town in the world. It helped me to understand that people don't always have options, or at least they can't or won't always take them. I could see how invisible forces pushed people into unhappy lives every day. How lives were lived according to the rules of the Church and the economics of the land. When I looked around the church that Good Friday, I could feel the fear in the air, the fear and the misguided devotion. I could see how people were being strangled, suffocated slowly; how their minds, their desires and their bodies were being taken away from them bit by bit.

And then, just as I was immersing myself in the realism of *Blood Wedding*, Maeve began talking about its surrealism. How it wasn't simply a story rooted in reality, how the characters moved like fate's puppets, how what was happening was bigger than the characters and how this was expressed in a more surreal and symbolic kind of way, outside of language. There I was, delving into the harsh realities of the piece, when Maeve went and put a new spin on things. She was going to keep me on my toes, that much I knew.

Rehearsals continued every Tuesday evening and, as the weeks progressed, that room in Maeve's house became a miniature world of its own. Maeve had a very clear vision of the play and of what she wanted from each of us. She had a style of working, method acting, that she used with us. As soon as we went into that room, we were to forget about ourselves and become the characters we were playing, even in the moments when we were not saying our lines. So in that room Mary was my mother, and she fawned over me for the duration of each evening as if I was her golden boy. Raymond was The Father of the Bride, eager to get a good marriage for his daughter. Anthony and Rosaleen were deeply in love, and looked at each other during those hours with such smouldering passion and such lingering looks of desire, I felt a stab of jealousy more than once.

And then there was Anthony and myself. In the real world we were lovers and spent practically every night together, but in the rehearsal room that meant nothing. There we were sworn enemies. There I would hate him as much as I could hate anybody. There I would race after him when he ran off with my bride and spat on my honour. There I would kill him. There we were the two young men who would take each other's lives with their knives. And it was good fun at first, pretending we were enemies, pretending that we would fight to the death, but there were one or two moments, just one or two, when I shivered at just how convincing we were.

Besides the dynamics between the characters that emerged as a result of the method acting, there were other dynamics that surfaced between the people in that room. There was the unspoken rivalry between Eileen and Rosaleen. Rosaleen had the bigger part, but Eileen was sure she could do a better job as The Bride. There was Maeve, who was constantly locked in battle with Raymond, trying to get him to understand what she was trying to do. There were Mary, Maude and Anne, all fawning over Fitzer and hanging on his every word, even though they must have known he wasn't interested in women.

Then there was Anthony. He started drinking more at the time, something I didn't pay that much attention to then. Because we were Irish, I suppose. Because we both drank a bit. Because, because. But he'd often turn up late smelling of whiskey, and this annoyed some people because they thought he wasn't taking it as seriously as them. But as soon as he became Leonardo he was so amazing, so convincing, most of them forgot they'd been angry with him in the first place.

As the rehearsals went on, I began to learn more and more about Lorca and the country he came from. Through Fitzer I learned more about the war there, about how the country had been torn apart for three years, how all the governments of the West had let the Spanish Republic down, and how men had come from all the corners of Europe to help defend that very same Republic. I learned how Germany and Italy had helped Franco, and how the Basque town of Guernica had become a fireball one day. I heard the story of how La Pasionaria, a female Communist leader, had spoken to the International Brigades in Barcelona when they were being disbanded, saying that history would remember them. I became fascinated by the whole conflict and by Fitzer, who'd gone and fought for his ideals. I told myself I would have done the same if I'd been old enough at the time. But who can say whether I would have or not. Maybe I was just another romantic, drawn to Spain and its tragedy.

It was through Fitzer that I became more aware of politics in Ireland, became more interested in the story of Noël Browne. You couldn't have avoided it at the time, it was all over the newspapers. Noël Browne was a doctor who became Minister for Health. He was the youngest minister in the government, as far as I remember. Anyway, he wanted to bring in a scheme, the Mother and Child Scheme, that would help with healthcare for mothers and their kids. Sounds like a good idea? Sounds like a humane and decent idea? Well, no, as it happens. Not in the eyes of the Church, who condemned the scheme and made a mess of the man's life because, as they saw it, it contravened Catholic teaching. In other words, they couldn't handle the idea that people wouldn't just be dependent on them. Couldn't handle the thought that they would have to give up a little bit of control over people's lives. Oh, I know what they were at. They knew if people were poor and dependent only on them, then they would be assured of their devotion.

It makes me sick to think about it, even now. How they treated Noël Browne like a dog. The Church, the papers, and many of the people. He was forced to resign. They said he was a Red, a Commie, a Bolshie; said the scheme he wanted to bring in was nothing but a free-for-all, that he was throwing the taxpayers' money away. They tore him to shreds, they hung him out to dry.

So, you see, Spain and its civil war weren't really that far away, in my mind anyway. 'At least they had the courage there to fight against injustice,' I remember thinking to myself one day, 'to speak out against inequalities and challenge the Catholic Church. And what do we do? Nothing. We let ourselves be walked over.'

I began to look at the country around me at the time, at the society we lived in and the government we had, and I began to question things more and more, not just in a personal way, but in a more political way. There were so many ways that play and those times forced me out of my dreams and into the world. It was then I began to really hate Ireland, then I understood why my father was so angry that this was the country he'd fought the War of Independence and Civil War for. It was in April of that year when I first thought about leaving Ireland, about the possibility of making a life someplace else, some place that wasn't so messed up.

I suppose I spent a lot of time with Fitzer those Tuesday evenings when the rehearsals were over. I didn't really think anything of it. I just enjoyed talking to him, learning things from him, listening to him talking about politics, which he had a real grasp of. I suppose I really admired him, wanted to be like him. His beliefs were so important to him, and though he was vocal about them, he didn't push them on anyone. And besides that, he was a gay man who'd been living with his partner for years, and people knew about it and they still respected him. And then there was his work. He was so passionate about the theatre and so involved in it. Oh, I admired and respected him all right. And yes, he was handsome and charming and intelligent, and I did feel a vague attraction for him, but it was nothing serious. Nothing serious at all. Try telling Anthony that though.

I'd seen him watching us a few times on those Tuesday evenings, with a serious look on his face. And then one night after rehearsal we were having a drink in my bedsit when I said something about the Civil War in Spain and he exploded. 'So suddenly you're an expert on the Spanish Civil War,' he snapped at me. 'What?' I said. 'Will you just shut up about Spain and the Civil War for a minute,' he commanded. 'Jesus, just give my head peace. It's over, you know.' I knew he'd been in a funny mood all night, irate and jittery, but I hadn't expected him to get so angry over something like this. 'What's wrong with you?' I asked, raising my voice. 'Nothing's wrong with me,' he threw back angrily. 'It's just all you go on about these days is the Civil War and Fitzer and politics. Jesus, you'd swear Fitzer was some kind of a god the way you go on about him, the way you hang around him.' And there it was, the real reason he was angry. It was because he was jealous, because somewhere in his head he thought there was something going on between Fitzer and me. Oh, he knew there wasn't, of course he did. But that's jealousy. It can do funny things to a mind, can do funny things to a man. And I, being young and as hot-tempered as Anthony, didn't know that at that point I should have just taken a step back, should have taken a deep breath, should have not got into an argument with him. But I did.

'What the fuck are you going on about?' I shouted at him. 'Oh, fuck off,' he shot back. 'Don't think I don't know you're in love with him.' 'In love with him? With Fitzer?' I asked. 'Yeah,' he spat at me. 'I've seen the way you smile at him. I've seen how he looks at you. And the two of you are always together.' I felt like I was under attack, being accused like this of something I wasn't guilty of, and I was furious. 'So what if I talk to him. So what if we talk about the war in Spain. So fucking what if we talk about politics. Anyway, what the fuck are you doing spying on me? You should cop yourself on.' 'Politics, Spain. You couldn't even find Spain on a map before you met me. Don't give me that bull about Spain. Don't try and pull the wool over my eyes. You just want to sleep with him, and that old misfit wants to sleep with you.' His voice was cold and steady as he said this, full of a hate I'd never seen in him before. 'Shut up,' I demanded. 'Shut your fat, stupid mouth. You know I love you and you know that Fitzer's with someone else.' 'Oh, don't be so naïve,' he sneered. 'Fitzer and his boyfriend sleep with other men. I know the boyfriend. He told me that. Guess you'll be next on his list. And as for me, well, you say you love me, but I don't know if I believe that.'

I laughed then. Laughed because suddenly all of this seemed ridiculous, seemed completely over the top, seemed incredibly stupid. 'Anthony, I am not interested in Fitzer,' I said through the laughter. 'Will you just listen to yourself.' But he wouldn't listen and my laughter only made him angrier.

'What the fuck are you laughing at, you little bogger?' he demanded. 'Have you two slept together? Are the two of you together? I knew it, I fucking knew it.' 'Anthony, get a grip on yourself,' I said, but I couldn't stop laughing. 'Me, me get a grip of myself?' he roared, and threw his glass against the wall in a rage. Suddenly he was standing over me, his face contorted with anger, someone I didn't recognise.

'Are you sleeping with Fitzer?' he shouted into my face. 'Tell me! Tell me how long it's been going on!' I could feel my heart beating as though it was about to explode and I suddenly felt scared, shit-scared, of this man who'd become a stranger. But I was still angry, so fucking angry, and I wanted him out of there. 'No,' I screamed right into his face. 'No we're not sleeping together. You're a fucking lunatic. You're mad. Now get the fuck out of here.' It was then his eyes turned, went wild, and he grabbed me by the throat and began to choke me. 'Never call me that. Never fucking call me that!' he roared at me. 'I'm not a lunatic.'

He held on for a few long moments before I saw the tears in his eyes, enormous tears, and he released his grip on me. He fell to the floor then and began sobbing, sobbing and sobbing as if the tears would never stop. He was inconsolable and as I listened to those tears, I felt my heart breaking. I actually felt it breaking and, despite all the anger and pain I felt, I went and lay down beside him. I lay down beside him and took him in my arms, held him as tight as I could. As we lay there, he kept repeating, 'I'm not mad. I'm not mad.' I knew then how afraid he was of losing me. I knew then I'd never love anyone that much again.

9

May 1998

GERARD WAS WORKING like crazy on his book. 'That's a good thing,' I thought. 'It might keep him occupied, keep him on the straight and narrow for a while.' He wanted to have a first draft finished by the end of July. A personal deadline more than anything. I'd called him and asked if he wanted to catch a movie or get something to eat, but he said all bets were off until then. 'I really need to get this finished. But if you're in town, call up and see me. It would be great to see you,' he said.

The flat was in an old Georgian house on Ely Place, off St Stephen's Green. Most of the houses around it were offices for insurance companies, solicitors, things like that, but this one was had been turned into flats years before, I guess back in the sixties. He met me at the front door, looking tired, but his smile was warm. We walked up flight after flight of uneven stairs, with torn carpet and the floorboards showing underneath. 'Man,' I thought, 'these landlords get away with a lot. Haven't they ever heard of maintenance? Just out to make some easy money.' But I didn't say anything to Gerard.

'Would you like a tea, a coffee?' he asked when we were inside the flat and I'd sat down in an armchair, trying to catch my breath. 'I'll have a coffee,' I replied, and he lit a flame beneath a steel coffee maker. 'So how've you been? Any news?' he chirped, sitting opposite me on a chair at the table he used for writing. 'Yeah, good,' I said. 'I don't have any real news, though. You know me, the quiet life.' He smiled. 'It must be nice out in Seapoint at this time of year. Do you ever go swimming out there?' 'No,' I said, 'I leave that for the real old-timers. You know, some of them swim there every day.' I shuddered. 'You wouldn't catch me swimming there.' 'Oh, that's a pity.' He sounded disappointed. 'I think if I lived by the sea, I'd go swimming every day. Well, in summer anyway. I'd love to live by the sea at this time of the year.' 'Well, if you ever get a free afternoon, come out and visit again,' I offered. 'Yeah, I might do that,' he replied, looking as though he was thinking it over.

'How's the book going?' I asked as he got up to pour out the coffee. 'Good, I think,' he responded. I looked around the flat: at the notebooks and books sitting in a neat pile, at the computer, at the pens, at the ashtray full of cigarette butts, at the half glass of water and the coffee cup. The early afternoon sun was strong and it warmed up the whole room. This was Gerard's space and I hoped he was safe here. 'Though it's hard to know whether to rewrite a lot of what I've written so far. I have so much information now,' he said. 'Maybe too much. And it's difficult to know what's true and what's not, you know.' He scratched his arm as he spoke. 'I've met a lot of people who knew Fitzer, but he was such a character, such an enigma, it's hard to separate the truth from the myths.' 'Oh, yeah?' I probed, but I knew he was right. Even when I knew Fitzer he had already lived several lives: growing up in New York; as a fighter with the International Brigades during the Spanish Civil War; as a politically active Socialist; as an actor in Dublin, and as half of one of the most openly gay couples in Ireland back then. Sometimes even when I spoke to Fitzer, he didn't seem real. I couldn't believe he was real. He was so larger than life and that life seemed so full, so extraordinary, so impossible.

'But you're writing a novel, right?' I said. 'It doesn't all have to be true.' 'No, I know,' he agreed. 'And some of those myths will make great stories, but I don't know. I suppose when I started this, I thought it would be easy to follow a life, to put everything in order. I thought it would be a lot easier to follow the events. You know: birth, childhood, career, love, death.' I looked at him closely. 'I thought it would be more simple. I mean, most of the biographies I've read, they seem to present things in such a clear way. You know, as if a life were really simple to follow.' 'Yeah, I know,' I sighed. 'I suppose that's something I've learned anyway,' he mused, looking at his coffee cup, trying to find the words to frame what he wanted to say. 'I suppose I've learned that lives are more complicated than I thought, that there's more than one truth to a life.' He looked at me then and I wondered exactly what he was thinking, if this was his way of telling me he knew more than I thought about my own life.

It was a sweltering Tuesday afternoon when he came out to see me. Sweltering by Irish standards anyway. He'd called me earlier that morning. Said he had cabin fever and needed an afternoon away from the book. 'Let's go for a swim,' he suggested. 'What?' I asked, incredulous. 'Let's go for a swim,' he repeated. 'It's a beautiful day. A perfect day for the sea. And don't give me any of that crap about not swimming there with the old folks.' He was really enthusiastic, and he sounded happier, more sassy than he'd been in a while. 'Look,' I said, 'it's not really my thing.' 'Well, it's your thing now,' he told me. 'I'm coming out and we're going in that water. Get those Speedos on!' And with that he hung up.

'He's a pushy little fucker,' I thought to myself, but I also felt a certain respect for him. He was gutsy and determined. When he'd decided on something, nobody could get him to see differently. 'But that has its downside as well,' I got to thinking. 'That might be why he ended up in laneways with strangers, because he wouldn't listen to anyone else, just followed whatever voices were in his head.' But anyway, I didn't want to think too much about all that. It was a bright, sunny day. The sky was cloudless and the water was still. I didn't want to think about anything dark, anything damaged that day.

But still, I didn't want to go into the sea. I don't know. It just made me nauseous thinking about it, thinking about being surrounded by all those old people. It made me feel claustrophobic. I mean, I wasn't one of them. Or I was and I didn't want to admit it. And I don't know, when I thought about going for a swim, I felt exposed. Oh, I don't mean in a physical sense. More, I don't know, like people could think whatever they wanted about me, like I was at their mercy. I guess I felt vulnerable. No, I felt scared. I felt like they could do whatever they wanted to me, like anything could happen. Oh, I know that sounds stupid, crazy, paranoid, neurotic. But what can I say? *C'est moi.*

Gerard arrived about one. He was full of energy and busy taking the day in his hands, taking control of the day. I knew he had black days. I'd seen them. I'd seen him look as though he was going to fall apart. I'd seen his mind curl in on itself and leave him paralysed and silent. Some days I could smell the fear off him. I knew that smell. Not necessarily the fear of anything in particular, just the fear of life itself. But he always pulled himself together, always managed to pull himself out of the shit in the end, always managed to survive. And that, more than anything, was what I liked about him. The fact that he could come to my house on a sunny afternoon like this, so full of positivity and life and warmth, you'd think he didn't have a care in the world. That day he was winning and that made me feel good. It made me feel great. So when I answered the door and he said, 'Hi. Are you ready? Let's go,' there was nothing for it but to go with him. 'Hold on just one sec,' I said and ran to put on the swim shorts I use for the pool. I grabbed a towel. Suddenly nothing else seemed to matter. We'd go for a swim together.

The water was freezing. It was my first time in the Irish Sea in almost fifty years and I'd forgotten how cold it was. We walked down the concrete steps that lead into the sea, Gerard going before me. I watched his long, lean body as he moved slowly along and down into the water. His shoulders were a bit hunched from the pressure he was under trying to get his book finished and his hair was a little messy, unkempt. He turned around and smiled then, smiled with the sun behind him, with his eyes shining, then dived into the water and swam out into the sea. I felt my heart dance a little at that moment. I think it was happiness, or something like it. I took the plunge, threw myself into the water, and began to swim.

Later, back in the house, after we'd had something to eat, I dozed off. I had a dream, a nightmare really. I was twenty-one again and at the beach with Anthony. It was a beautiful day but the sea was rough and choppy. I could hardly swim, but Anthony was a strong swimmer and he'd persuaded me to go into the water with him. When we had swum far out into the sea, I felt a spasm in my chest and I lost my breath. I tried to signal to Anthony to get him to help me. He saw me, he knew I was in danger, but he just laughed and began to swim back to the shore. I could feel myself drowning in the open sea. 'Anthony,' I heard myself shout again and again before I woke up.

I must have been asleep for a couple of hours. I looked at

my watch. It was six o'clock and the house was very silent. I looked around the room but Gerard wasn't there. 'Maybe he's sitting outside,' I thought, but when I looked out the window he wasn't in the front garden. I made my way to the kitchen, thinking he was probably there, but the door was shut and there wasn't a sound from inside. I opened the door and walked in and there he was, sitting at the table.

His face turned bright red and he looked startled to see me, that was the first thing I noticed. 'What's going on?' I began asking myself, smiling like an idiot who doesn't know what is happening but hopes a smile will make everything okay. And it was then I saw the quick movement of his hand and I saw something drop to the floor. I didn't know what it was until I recognised it as my notebook.

'Fuck,' I said in my head and the next thing I knew I was slamming my fist on the table. 'What the fuck do you think you're doing?' I shouted like a madman. 'Why the fuck were you reading that? Why were you snooping around?' 'I... I just picked it up. I didn't know what it was. I...' But he couldn't get the words out. He didn't know what he was saying, didn't know what to say. And I didn't want to hear it. In an instant everything went blank and all the feelings I'd had for him turned cold. I hated Gerard then, really hated him. 'Get out of here,' I heard a steely voice say. I couldn't look at him, I wouldn't look at him. 'Just get out.' He sat there stunned, unmoving, saying nothing, all colour drained from his face now. 'Get out of here now, you little whore. Get out, you fucking whore,' I heard myself bellow as I watched myself slip out of control. There was a long, terrible silence. 'Fuck you,' I heard somebody say. There was the sound of a glass smashing against the floor and then he was gone.

May 1951

ALL ANTHONY AND I COULD SEE that May was our future. We had so much to think about, to talk about. In July we would perform *Blood Wedding* to applause and ovations. Maybe afterwards we'd write a play of our own, a play about Spain. We'd move into a flat that overlooked the sea and on days when we felt this island, this Ireland, was just too small, we'd look out and see there was a wider world out there, a world that we belonged to. We talked about going to Granada in August. We'd climb the hill to the Alhambra in the scorching heat and look out over the city. And listen to the gypsies wailing in Sacromonte. And follow the ghost of Lorca through the Moorish streets.

But before *Blood Wedding*, before we moved in together, and before Granada, Anthony had his exams to think about. He was doing his finals that year and as April drifted by, he began to feel the heat. A lot was riding on these exams. He'd been dependent on his parents for years. They'd supported him through college and the flat he lived in belonged to his father. But for Anthony, this wasn't their way of helping him. This was their way of controlling him, of getting him to do exactly what they wanted. If he did well in his exams though, all of that would be over. He'd be able to find a good job, be able to make his own money, and he wouldn't need a penny from them anymore.

From the first night we met, I knew Anthony had an antagonistic relationship with his parents, but I didn't think that much about it in the beginning. I mean, yes, he seemed to really resent them, but I put a lot of that down to his rebellious nature. Nobody could tell Anthony what to do, and his parents were probably just over-controlling. He was their only child after all. But as I fell in love with him, I came to see there was more to it than that. He went to see them for lunch every Sunday without fail. Called it his penance. And on Saturday nights he would hold me so close, as close to him as two people could get. And the following morning, before he left, there would be a certain look, a hunted, frightened look, in his eyes.

I saw this look, I felt his grip, and what did I do? Nothing much, if I'm honest. I mean, I tried to talk to him about it, about them, to see what was wrong, what was going on, but besides lashing out now and then, he wouldn't talk to me about it. Said they didn't have anything to do with us, that they wouldn't come between us. Told me just to leave it. So I did, and though I tried to be there for him, to support him, to make it easier in whatever stupid way I could, what did I really do? Nothing, that's what I did. Sweet fuck all. Like Anthony I tried to pretend they weren't there and focused only on our future. Together we leaped into our future.

Though Anthony's exams were more important than anything else, he found it hard to sit down and study. He was intelligent all right, one of the most intelligent people I knew, but he never liked studying. Who does, really? All through April he would find all kinds of distractions to keep him away from that desk where all his books and notes sat neatly in a pile, unopened. There was *Blood Wedding*, there were the pubs that he began to spend more and more time in, there was the film he just had to see, the friend he had to meet, the new book from France that he had to read. And then there was the flat. He cleaned it so much in that month, I bet it was the cleanest flat in Dublin. There were so many moments of procrastination, his would he, wouldn't he, begin tonight. I suppose if he actually began studying it would make it all real. He wouldn't have been able to escape the fact that his exams were starting in a few short weeks and so much depended on them. He was terrified he'd fail, or that he wouldn't do well enough and that he would ruin everything: his future, our future. Sometimes he got so irritated, so anxious, so angry with himself, and I hated to see him like that.

I tried to help him. I saw how stressed he was and, though I knew nothing about university exams, I promised myself I'd help him any way I could. Early in May I began meeting him every evening after work, usually at the library on Earlsfort Terrace. I would walk up Grafton Street, past the couples gazing into the windows of Brown Thomas's and Weir's. Past the flower sellers and the horses and carriages at the top of the street. I would walk through St Stephen's Green, where the students were sprawled on the grass and the children were busy feeding the ducks. Moving through town on those evenings, going to meet Anthony, I felt as though I was walking on air.

I'd normally find him hanging around by the Drama Society's noticeboard, casually smoking a cigarette and chatting to a couple of people. I always felt like a bit of an intruder in this place. I mean, I wasn't a student. I was just a boring civil servant from the country, and I thought each and every one of these students knew it. Knew there was a fraud among them. And though I felt insecure, and resented them a bit, hated them a little for their privileges, they fascinated me. To me they were all intelligent and educated people who spent their days talking about difficult ideas and how they were going to change their world. And they had all the time in the world. To me they were free, freedom personified, and that liberty was intoxicating to be around. But what did I know then? I only saw that world from the outside. Anthony would always smile and call me over when he saw me, introduce me to his friends and make me feel as though I wasn't such an alien.

Every evening Anthony and I would walk along by the Green and down Leeson Street to his flat. We'd pass a couple of pubs along the way and sometimes it was a real struggle for us not to go in, get drunk and let another evening slip away. Well, I suppose it was Anthony's struggle really, but it became mine as well because as the days passed we even began to think as one. We both had to focus on the exams. They were all that mattered. They became our world, our reality, the air we breathed and the thoughts we thought. And so while other people passed along those grey streets soaked in the evening sunlight without a care in the world, we were always thinking about the upcoming exams. And sometimes Anthony would be focused and in control, on top of things, but some days the exams would come hurtling towards him like a freight train and I would see the panic and desperation in his face. All I could do then was tell him everything was going to be okay, that he was going to do brilliantly.

Anthony managed to settle into a routine and we began spending all of our evenings in his flat. Often the first thing we'd do was make a furious, rapid, amazing kind of love that would help to release all the tensions of the day. Then I'd normally make something to eat, we'd chat for a bit and Anthony would begin to psyche himself up for that evening's work.

He'd spend the rest of the night studying at his desk, with a gramophone record or Radio Luxembourg playing in the background. I'd read *Blood Wedding* again, or go over my lines in my head in an almost obsessive way, or read some of Lorca's poems slowly to myself. I devoured books by French and Spanish writers during those weeks: Voltaire's *Candide*, Sartre's *Nausea*, *Don Quixote*. When Anthony wanted to take a break, we'd go out on his balcony and smoke a cigarette, looking out at the world below us, a world that seemed somehow unreal against the small universe we had created for ourselves inside his flat. Or sometimes we'd talk about *Blood Wedding* or about our future, and once Anthony taught me to dance the Sevillanes, which he had learned from a Spanish dancer he knew. We always stayed up late, the caffeine from the endless cups of coffee we drank pushing us through the hours. And more than once we watched the dawn unfold over the city, listening, silent and exhausted, to the birds welcoming the new day.

Jesus, I still miss those times. Sure they were full of tension and pressure and anxiety, but I don't know. Everything became so vital, so raw, so immediate, because of that tension, that strain. And we were working towards something. We were taking our destiny in our hands and there were moments when it seemed as though we had made time stop. Times when it seemed like the two of us could do anything and go anywhere together. We thought we would forever be... undefeated.

For years afterwards, when I found myself at home in the evenings, I'd look up and expect to see Anthony there, poring over his books. But of course he never was.

Apart from me going to work and Anthony going to the library, we rarely left his flat during those few weeks leading up to the exams. One exception, though, was the rehearsals.

I remember walking up to Mountjoy Square that May, preparing to hate the man I loved, getting into character. I suppose that was another release for any tensions that built up between us in the flat. One evening a week we could hate each other more than anyone or anything. And of course we brought all our petty irritations and any anger and resentment that had emerged between us to that room. Oh, we became really good at hating one another in Maeve's front room. And like true enemies, we couldn't take our eyes off one another, each of us watching every move the other made. And though we were supposed to only be our characters, to think and behave and act as they would, behind our hatred and jealousy, there was also a great lust. We moved slowly, slowly, closer towards one another during those rehearsals, until we killed one another with knives, until we found ourselves, breathless, back at Anthony's flat, tearing each other's clothes off.

But ours wasn't the only relationship taking place behind the scenes of that play. Raymond and Mary had started having it off. Oh, they didn't announce it, of course they didn't. But we all knew by their body language, by the sexual frisson between them, that something was going on. I remember the first time I realised it, and how shocked I was. I mean, they were both married, and besides that, they were both in their late fifties. I'd thought that people gave up having sex by that age. I can laugh at that now. But back then I was young, and though I thought I was really radical and open-minded, there were still a lot of things I could only see in black and white.

Eileen was also having fun. She'd begun sleeping with a guy who was playing one of the woodcutters who appear in the play. He was a good-looking guy: stocky and rugged looking. Not my type, but well, I wasn't sleeping with him. Eileen was, and though I think he was in love with her, I knew for Eileen it was just sex, even if she never came right out and said it. Girls didn't back then.

There was also another passion afoot, but this one was unrequited. It took me a while to see it, but when I did, I couldn't understand how I'd missed it. Elizabeth, who was playing Leonardo's wife, felt a lot more than respect for Maeve. She never mentioned her feelings to anyone, and never mentioned them to Maeve, but by the way she looked at her, the way she watched her, I could see she was devoted to her. Maeve noticed it too, and dealt with the situation sensitively and with dignity. She nurtured the girl, was kind and respectful towards her, but she made it known, as subtly and carefully as she could, that she wasn't interested in women, even though she thought the world of Elizabeth.

Then there was all that wasn't said but filled the air. There was Maeve and Fitzer, in love with each other in a way, even though they would never be together. Pity, they would have made a great couple. And there was another of the woodcutters, a good-looking guy who said he had a girlfriend, but looked at me and Anthony with eyes full of desire. I'm sure if either of us had tried to seduce him, he wouldn't have thought twice about it. But we didn't. We felt sorry for him in a way, felt sorry that he couldn't express what we saw burning inside him, sometimes consuming him so completely. We did ask him once or twice if he wanted to come to one of the pubs with us, but we could see how terrified he became when we mentioned one of those names. I wonder where he is now.

Aside from all the affairs, friendships, rivalries and one or two tantrums, the rehearsals were going as they should. Our understanding of the play became deeper and we all became more skilled in our roles. One evening, it must have been late that May, we performed the whole of the play for the first time. I suppose that was the night when it all really came together, when all of us began to believe that we could make it work, that we could do a good job with *Blood Wedding*. That we wouldn't just be seen as a group of clumsy amateurs who didn't know what they were doing. The air was electric after that performance.

I remember another evening, before that one, when we all stood at the windows at the front of Maeve's house, staring at a religious procession passing down Gardiner Street. We stood there watching the spectacle, not quite knowing which was real and which was just a performance; that procession outside or our *Blood Wedding* inside. After a few minutes Maeve clapped her hands and helped us focus on the play again.

It was a sweltering May, one of the hottest I can remember. One clammy morning, when it was already bright outside, I reached for Anthony and found the bed was cold beside me. 'Anthony, Anthony,' I called, but there was no answer. I went to see where he was, and when I couldn't find him I felt my stomach lurch. It was only a few days before the exams were due to begin, and though he had put a lot of work in over the previous weeks, he'd suddenly started acting strangely. One minute he'd be happy, but happy in a manic kind of way, and the next he'd be completely depressed, as if a blackness had descended on him. And besides that he'd get really angry over nothing, over small, unimportant things. It got so bad I didn't know what he was going to do next. I was worried about him and that morning I was out of my mind with a mad kind of panic. I suddenly felt sure that he'd done something stupid, that the pressure had just become too much. I'd never imagined Anthony taking his own life, but at that moment I was certain this was exactly what he'd done. I threw open the door to the balcony and looked over, truly expecting to see his body down below.

He wasn't there, and though I breathed a sigh of relief, I was still desperate to find out where he'd gone. I thought about calling his parents, but I didn't have their telephone number. I considered calling a couple of his friends to ask if they'd seen him, but I decided to leave it a while, not wanting to wake them up, not wanting to worry them just yet. I thought about walking the streets to see if I could find him, but I wanted to be in the flat in case he came back. I made myself calm down and decided I would wait until a quarter past eight, the time I normally left for work, to do anything. I would wait until then and if he still hadn't appeared, then I could start to really panic.

It was an hour later and I was looking distractedly through the books on Anthony's shelves, still worried sick, still wondering where he was. I took one of them down, I think it was *Ulysses*, and I was flicking through it when something fell out. I picked it up and as I put it back in, I had a look at it absent-mindedly. I imagined it was some lecture note or maybe a letter Anthony used as a bookmark, but what I saw was something entirely different, something that made my mind do a quick somersault.

The piece of paper was a medical record, a record from a mental hospital in Dublin. It was a kind of certificate to say the patient had spent six months in the hospital, with the date of entry and release, a couple of years earlier, clearly printed on it. I looked at it carefully, not quite sure what I was seeing, but there it was, inescapable, Anthony's full name and date of birth. 'What is this? What is this?' I was thinking to myself, when I heard the front door of the flat slam and Anthony walk in. I put the piece of paper back and returned the book to the shelf. 'Good morning, beautiful,' Anthony said when he walked in and he came over to kiss me. He looked so happy that sunny morning, so happy and full of life, I couldn't believe what I'd just seen.

'Where were you?' I asked, so damn relieved he was safe, but still wanting to know where he'd been. 'Oh, sorry, I should have left a note, but I wanted to surprise you.' 'Surprise me?' I asked. 'Yeah,' he explained. 'I went to borrow the car from the old man. We're going down to Brittas Bay for the day. We've been stuck in this flat for long enough. It's time we took a break, got a bit of sun. Put the exams behind us for one day, what do you think?' What did I think? I thought going to the beach for the day would be like a dream. Getting away from the city, from the flat, from the exams, from all the tension and strain of those weeks, but I still knew I had to go to work, that I was already running late. 'I'd love to,' I said, 'but I have to go to work. I'm already late.' 'Don't worry about work,' Anthony said, and there was a mischievous look in his eye. 'I already called them and told them you wouldn't be coming in today. I said I lived in the flat next to yours and that you had food poisoning.' 'You did what?' I asked, already smiling at his audacity. 'So you want to spend the day with me, baby?' he proposed, grinning from ear to ear.

Of course I did, of course I'd go, and looking at Anthony standing there, so happy again, so okay again, I promised myself I'd forget all about that piece of paper I'd seen. I told myself that stupid piece of paper meant nothing.

An hour or so later, we had left Dublin and were zipping past green hills that seemed to float in the morning heat. Anthony was driving, I was sitting beside him, and we both felt the stress of the weeks before slip away as we moved further and further from the city. Okay, Dublin wasn't New York or Tokyo, it wasn't a crazily busy metropolis, but still, with the exams, the play and my work, there had been a lot going on for us, and we both really needed this break. We needed to escape those cobbled streets and that small flat for a day. As he drove, whistling an American song, I looked at Anthony. I looked at him, and he looked so happy, so carefree, I couldn't believe he was the same person that piece of paper claimed had been in an asylum. He could be highly strung and he had really black days and a ferocious temper, but he wasn't insane, he wasn't mad. That much I knew. And yet I began to remember how wild his eyes had looked that night he'd accused me of sleeping with Fitzer, how sometimes he'd get so angry when he spoke about his parents, and all of those moments of rage and sadness over the previous weeks.

But all of that still didn't make him mad, still didn't mean he'd actually spent six months in an asylum. It had to be some mistake, and even if it wasn't a mistake, even if it was true and he had been there, well, I still loved him, loved him more than anyone or anything. All that mattered was the future, and everything else belonged to the past. I smiled at him then and I felt everything else, everything that was going through my head, fall away.

The beach was practically empty when we got there. We walked for a bit, then found a spot in some dunes. It was hot out now and all we wanted was to get into the cool water of the sea. We both changed into our swimming trunks and a few moments later we were running towards the water. We waded into the still freezing sea and then dived beneath the water, one after the other, and swam out.

Afterwards we hungrily ate the sandwiches we'd brought with us, and drank a few cups of tea from the flask. We were so tired from the swim we said nothing as we sat there eating, the sun drying our bodies. When we'd finished, I moved over to Anthony, took his lips in mine, ran my hand along his neck and laid his body out along the golden sand. We made a slow, sweet kind of love then, with the sun on us, the sand beneath us, and the sound of the sea in the distance. He was so beautiful and that lovemaking, that expression of our love, was so perfect, I could have died there and then.

It seemed as though the countdown towards Anthony's exams had been going on forever, when all of a sudden they began. If I could, I would have gone and sat each and every one of those exams for him or with him, but the truth was Anthony was on his own now. He had four French exams the first week and four Spanish the second. I half expected him to throw it all up in the air at the last minute. Somewhere at the back of my mind, I suspected the pressure would become too much, that he'd fail to sit one or all of the exams, but my suspicions were proved wrong. During those two weeks, Anthony was more focused and dedicated than I'd ever seen him. He gave those exams everything he had, and after each one he looked more and more relieved, their end and our future closer and closer in sight. I felt so proud of him.

And then, suddenly, they were over. After weeks of studying and preparing, they were over. We were free, or we would be free if the exams had gone well, which I was sure they had.

The night he finished, Anthony went to McDaids with his friends from college. He had asked me along, and though I felt a little out of place because I wasn't a student and hadn't done any exams, I was happy, so happy, to celebrate with him. Besides, I knew a couple of his friends from parties we'd been to. Watching Anthony that night, I saw somebody who was full of life, somebody who had a great future ahead of them, somebody who was intelligent, funny, talented and handsome. Somebody who was free.

That Sunday Anthony went to his parents' house for lunch as usual. This lunch was special though. His parents said they wanted to celebrate the end of his finals, even though Anthony believed they only wanted to gloat and pat each other on the back because they'd raised a university-educated son. He wasn't looking forward to it, but the fact that soon, as soon as he got his results and found a job, he'd be free of them, made him walk a little taller than he normally did on Sunday. I remember waiting at the bus stop with him and he said, 'I wish you could come with me. That would wipe the smiles off their faces.' But I couldn't, I didn't, and instead we arranged to meet at six at my bedsit.

I waited there until eight and when he still hadn't shown up, I went out for a walk. I told myself nothing serious had happened. I thought maybe he'd had a reconciliation with his parents, as unlikely as that seemed, or that he'd met a friend from college and they'd decided to get drunk because university was over at last. Still, as I wandered along the canal and then on into town, past pubs, parks and picture houses where the couples were queuing up for the Sunday night show, I had a bad feeling about something. But I'd had bad feelings before and everything had always turned out okay in the end. Eventually I went home and tumbled into bed, exhausted.

On Monday evening, when I still hadn't heard anything, I went to his flat, feeling terribly sick, but he wasn't there. I called a few of his friends, but they hadn't seen him. I went home and tried to sleep, but couldn't. On Tuesday evening I went back to the flat, but he still wasn't there. When I met one of his neighbours in the corridor, I asked, desperate with worry now, if she'd seen Anthony. When she said she had, my first feeling was relief, relief that at least he was okay. It was a short-lived feeling though. She said she had seen him leaving the flat with lots of boxes and then drive off with a man she thought was his father. 'When, when did you see them?' I asked, frantic now. 'It was about ten o'clock this morning,' she said. 'His father said hello but Anthony didn't say anything. He looked as though he didn't even see me.'

I walked away from her in a daze, unable to believe what she'd just told me. Why had he left his flat without telling me? Where had he gone? What was he doing? I collapsed on a bench by the canal, just collapsed there and began to sob, to sob uncontrollably. I looked up at the people passing over the bridge, I looked at them and I couldn't imagine going back to that world without Anthony. I couldn't imagine that world would ever be a place I would belong to again. Eventually I dragged myself home, drank half a bottle of whiskey and cried myself to sleep.

The next afternoon, there was a call for me at work. When I picked up the receiver and said hello, there was no answer. I knew it was Anthony. I knew it was, but even though I said his name again and again, still there was no response and after a few moments the phone just went dead. That evening I managed to get the phone number for his parents' house from a friend of his. My hand was trembling as I dialled the number. After a few rings, a woman's voice answered. I asked for Anthony, but she said there was no Anthony there. I knew it was his mother, but when I persisted, said I had to talk to him, told her to put him on, she warned me that if I ever called again, she'd have the police onto me and hung up. I dialled the number again and again that evening, but she must have taken the phone off the hook.

It was a few days later when I heard it. I met one of Anthony's classmates on Nassau Street. The guy wasn't a friend of Anthony's, wasn't even somebody he liked, but when I saw him, I decided to ask him if he'd seen Anthony or heard anything from him. I would have tried anything just to have some news from him. I stopped him. 'Sorry,' I began, 'I'm a friend of Anthony Stafford's. I think you were in the same class.' The guy nodded. 'Anthony, yes I know him. We studied French together,' he confirmed. 'I just wondered if you'd seen him or heard anything from him,' I said, trying not to show my panic. 'No, I haven't seen him,' he replied, 'but I met a fella today who knows his family. He told me Anthony's getting married, getting married this July. Maybe he's got some girl in trouble.' He winked then and with that he walked away, as casual as you like, leaving me standing there, feeling like I'd just been hit by a train.

10
June 1998

I WAS WAITING IN THE restaurant for Gerard. It was a new place in Temple Bar, just behind the Irish Film Centre. I wanted to meet him somewhere bright, somewhere full of light, someplace there were no shadows. It was time to confront one another, it was time to tell Gerard the truth, and this seemed like the perfect place. But as I sat there waiting for him, I only felt cold, felt shivery, felt smothered by the anaesthetic atmosphere of the place. A waitress came up to me. 'Can I get you something to drink while you're waiting?' she asked. I could have done with a large whiskey, but I wanted to keep my head clear. 'I'll have a sparkling water,' I said, and she smiled a smile as soulless as the place and walked away.

For days, I'd been agonising over that evening in my house, asking myself again and again if he'd picked up that notebook because he knew something, because he'd known everything from the start, or if he'd just picked it up casually and was nosy enough to read on. Sleep refused to come on those nights, as my mind ran away with itself and I imagined a scenario where he'd sidled up to me from the beginning and manipulated me up to that moment. I was no longer sure if he was really writing a book, if the whole novel had been a charade. In truth I had no idea who he was, didn't know what he truly wanted, but one thing was for sure; I lay awake on those nights, haunted.

But I kept remembering how startled Gerard had been, how hurt and confused he'd looked when I confronted him. And though I wasn't sure, couldn't be sure, I had to believe he hadn't set me up, had to believe it was all just a coincidence, had to believe he hadn't come to hunt me down. More than anything, I needed to believe in him.

And so I tried to find him, searched the city by day and night for him. But he wouldn't answer his phone, wouldn't open the door of his flat to me, and when I walked into the restaurant where he worked he gave me such a look of pure hatred, I just turned and walked away. I thought about giving up a number of times, just packing up and going back to New York, but something stopped me. I was tired of running away. I didn't want to run away again. I didn't want to leave things like this. I wanted to, had to, make Gerard understand. Eventually he answered his phone and said he'd meet me. Said it without commitment or enthusiasm, said it like he was doing me a great favour. Still, he was going to see me and that was enough.

I was thinking about him, about what I was going to say to him, when he walked in. I smiled and when he saw me he began walking slowly towards me. He sat down opposite me. 'Hi, Daniel,' he said, and his smile was calculated and cold, cruel even. I felt the temperature in the room drop and I shivered again.

'Do you want something to drink?' I asked. 'No,' he refused point blank. 'I'm not drinking at the moment. And besides I don't have a lot of time. Can we just order?' He picked up a menu and quickly chose what he was going to eat. I fumbled with my menu and chose the first thing I saw.

'I guess I'll have the steak,' I said. 'I suppose you'll have it rare. Nice and bloody,' he hissed, and the conscious vindictiveness of that remark felt like an arrow piercing my heart. I looked at him, trying to gauge just how much he knew, but his eyes didn't meet mine. He was busy calling the waitress over.

'Look, Gerard, we need to talk,' I began awkwardly. 'Talk? It's a bit late for that, don't you think?' he replied. 'I've found out everything about you on my own. You got so angry that day, I knew you were hiding something, knew there was something you didn't want me to know. Only I didn't expect that. It seems there's no end to what you didn't tell me, Daniel. Isn't that right?' I'd never seen him like this before: so hard, so brittle, so dismissive. I knew he hated me for lying to him, for not telling him the truth, but I also felt a tremendous relief that he hadn't known about that night from the start, that he hadn't been after me from the start.

'Look,' I tried to reason with him, 'just let me explain. Let me tell you what really happened.' The food arrived then. The waitress obviously felt the tension because she got out of there as quickly as she could. 'No,' he said, 'I don't want to hear it. I just want to know why you've been hanging around with me, why you've been spending so much time with me. I just don't get it. I mean, was it all just a twisted game for you, knowing I was researching a friend of yours, and all the time able to keep your story hidden. Or maybe it made you feel clever. Maybe it gave you a thrill. Or maybe you just wanted to get me into bed. Thought I was easy, an easy lay as you say in the States.' He stopped then and studied my face for a moment.

'Gerard, none of those things are true,' I contradicted him. 'You mean a lot to me.' I caught his eye for a moment and there was a flicker of recognition and warmth, a flicker of the friend I knew, but he looked away, quickly looked out the window. There was a crowd of people out in the square, watching an open-air film. I think it was *Pulp Fiction* or *Reservoir Dogs*, something like that. I wished it would rain then, wished the heavens would open and they would all have to go home like drowned rats. 'Fools,' I thought to myself. 'Expecting something good of an Irish summer. When will they ever learn?'

Gerard began eating his food; looking like he'd eat and walk away and that would be the last I'd ever see of him. Somehow I'd hoped that maybe he'd come to let me speak, to let me explain why I'd lied, why I hadn't told him what I should have, but now I saw he'd just come to tell me exactly what he thought of me. The weight of his presence was unbearable.

As I watched him eating, I felt I had to say something, had to make him understand before it was too late. 'Gerard,' I said, 'I didn't want to lie to you. I wanted to tell you the truth. I was going to tell you the truth. You have to believe me. I wanted to tell you that day at my house. I really wanted to tell you, but the day was so perfect I didn't want to ruin it.' 'Um hmm,' he said, but didn't even look at me, just continued eating. I felt a flash of anger then. He was behaving so indifferently, as if nothing I said made any difference, as if all of this had been for nothing, as if meeting him and getting to know him meant nothing. I felt really aggravated, backed into a corner, and getting him to listen to me was the only thing that mattered.

'Gerard, listen to me,' I demanded, and when he still wouldn't look at me, I did something I shouldn't have. I grabbed his wrist and shouted at him. 'Just listen to me,' I erupted, harassed, and with that his fork fell and clattered on the floor. He looked shocked and a little frightened for a moment; before he reached down to pick it up. When he looked at me again, his face was cold and mean. 'Why,' he asked slowly, pronouncing every word, 'are you going to kill me too?' I felt as though I'd been punched then. I felt defeated and I wanted nothing more than to disappear from this life. But I also felt really mad, angrier than I'd felt in a while. I wanted to grab Gerard and throw him through the window, just get the vicious little bastard away from me. I tried to speak but no words came. I knew my heart must have been beating faster, but I only felt it slow down, as if it were about to stop completely.

'Funny, isn't it,' said Gerard, going for the jugular now. 'There I was writing about Fitzer and all this time there was a much juicier story right under my nose. But I was too stupid to see it, too stupid to put two and two together. Oh, I've found out all about you right enough. It wasn't really that difficult, not when I found out your real name.' He paused for breath and I sat there, white as a sheet, as he spat my past in my face. 'I just have one question for you before we finish this charming evening,' he continued, 'and I want you to answer me truthfully, if you even know what the truth is anymore. I want to know if you killed him, Daniel. I want to know if you killed Anthony.'

June 1951

'ANTHONY IS GETTING MARRIED. Anthony is getting married.' I said it over and over again in my head, but still it had no meaning. It didn't make any sense. It was crazy, bizarre, impossible. It just wasn't true. I remember laughing later that night I heard the news, laughing and laughing because it was so unbelievable, because it had to be a joke, couldn't be anything other than a joke. Only it wasn't. It was true.

He turned up in the end, turned up after more than a week of days and nights waiting for him. Knocked on my door late one night when I was dozing on the armchair; and when I saw him I thought he'd come back, thought everything that had happened had been nothing more than a bad dream and we were still together. My mind was only playing tricks on me though. What had happened was real enough. I saw that when I looked at Anthony's jaded face, a face that looked suddenly years older. I saw it in the dark circles under his eyes. In the way his whole body seemed to be shaking. In the way he looked at me from somewhere I couldn't reach. Before he even spoke, I knew I'd lost him.

'Can I come in?' he pleaded in a voice I didn't recognise. I didn't say anything, I couldn't say anything. I pulled back the door and he walked in. He fell into the armchair, exhausted, and sat staring at the wall. He looked so broken then, so twisted with despair, so entirely extinguished, I forgot about everything that had happened and all I wanted was to hold him. To make it all stop for him: the fear, the paralysis, the unbearable sadness. I went to put my arms around him because there was still a part of me that thought love could make everything better, could make everything okay again. But it couldn't. Just as I got close to him I heard a cold, empty voice say, 'No, don't touch me. Don't come near me.' I don't have to tell you how that felt, how in that moment I had the sensation that I'd been thrown across that room. 'Just don't,' he said, 'please.' I stood there staring at him, open-mouthed. 'Do you have any whiskey?' he asked. 'I think I need a whiskey.'

I poured two large whiskeys and sat opposite him. The curtains were still open and the moon was full in the navy pink sky. The weather would be good the next day, good for somebody. Anthony took a large gulp of the whiskey. 'We need to talk,' he began. 'Yes, we do,' I agreed, bracing myself for what was to come. He stared at the fireplace that hadn't been used in months, the ashes cold and without meaning that summer night. He stared at it for a long time and then, without even looking at me, he said, 'I can't see you anymore. We can't continue seeing each other.' The finality in his voice made me suddenly angry. 'And why is that?' I asked, my tone as cold as his. 'Because I don't love you,' he replied. 'Because I want to leave all this behind me. Because I don't want this life anymore.' 'And what life is that?' I wanted him to tell me. 'You know,' he said, 'you and me. We've just been fooling ourselves. What kind of a life would we have together? We couldn't live here together. What kind of a husband and wife would we make?' He laughed then, a manic kind of laugh that cut me to the bone. 'I had a great time, Daniel, but we weren't in love, not really. We can't be in love. I mean, what a fucking joke, me and you settling down together.' He laughed again.

I knew he was lying, knew this wasn't really him speaking, but the cruel finality of his words set me off in a rage. 'I never wanted to be your husband or your wife,' I spat at him. 'I only wanted to love you. And I don't believe you when you say you don't love me. I think you're a liar. But anyway, I hope you'll be very happy with your little bride.' He looked at me then and I saw the shock on his face. 'How do you know about that?' he asked. 'It doesn't really matter,' I answered. 'You're getting married, so I suppose that's that.' As he looked at me, he suddenly looked frightened, utterly terrified, and though I felt his pain, I couldn't stop my anger. 'So, do you love her?' I sneered. 'Do you love her more than me? Was whatever we had just a big joke to you? Look me straight in the eye and tell me you don't love me. Tell me!'

I must have been getting quite upset because I saw a flicker of emotion in his eyes then, a flicker of love, of affection, of pain at seeing me like this, but I took no notice. He tried to speak but I cut across him. 'Anyway, I don't fucking care anymore,' I shouted at him. 'The two of you can rot in hell for all I care. Now get out of here.' Even though I knew he hadn't left me of his own free will, that somebody had made him leave me, the fact that he'd come here to spin me a load of lies, to say it was all over instead of saying we'd find a way to be together, was just too much for me. I couldn't see past my anger and suddenly I just wanted him out. Suddenly I didn't want an explanation. I was so exhausted I didn't care anymore.

'Just get out,' I shouted, grabbing him, hauling him off the chair with more strength than I knew I had and pushing him out the door. I would hate myself for that afterwards, hate myself for all the hatred I felt for him, but at that moment I had to get him out. 'Get out!' I screamed, but he wouldn't go. He clung onto me, put his arms around me as I tried to force him out, and I knew then he was trying to cling on to whatever we'd had together, to the life we'd shared together. As we struggled he fell against the wall, slid down to the floor, and it was there, with his hands wrapped around his knees, that he broke down and began to wail. I can still hear that sound of him wailing sometimes. It was the most terrible sound I'd ever heard.

'I didn't want to leave you, Daniel. I couldn't leave you,' he moaned through his tears. 'They made me. They found out about us. They said they'd send me back there if I didn't stop seeing you, if I didn't settle down.' He couldn't look at me. He just sat there on the floor, trembling and crying and trying to make me see. I was down on my knees, trying to stop him from shaking, trying to get him to calm down, trying desperately to make his pain stop. He looked at me then, his eyes swollen from the tears he was crying. 'I can't go back there, Daniel. I can't go back. It would kill me,' he said and in a flash it came back to me, the piece of paper I'd seen that morning in his flat. I knew he was talking about the asylum, knew it was true he'd spent six months there, that his parents had put him there and that they'd put him back there if he kept seeing me. I felt sick, I felt we were trapped and, hold him as I might, I saw there would be no escape. I knew they were stronger than us.

'You were in a hospital, weren't you?' I asked when his tears had stopped, as we sat on the bed, drinking whiskey, Anthony laying in my arms, defeated. He nodded. 'They sent me there during my first year at university. They found out about me then. I was seeing somebody. His name was Peter. He was somebody I'd known from home, he was in the year above me at university. But they found out about it. Somebody from the town, some bastard who'd never liked me, told my father I was a queer, that I was having a relationship with Peter.' He took a gulp of his whiskey. 'My father was furious; his only son a homosexual. And my mother was even worse. She's so Catholic, the fucking hypocrite. She told me I'd go straight to hell. Told me I was filthy, disgusting, that I was a disgrace to the family.' I would have expected Anthony to cry when he was telling me all of this. Instead his voice was cold, hard, as if he could only talk about the experience as though it belonged to somebody else. As if he had filed it away because it had nearly destroyed him and now he only felt numb about it, had to turn numb in order to survive.

'Peter's family were just the same, maybe worse,' he went on. 'They had him pack his bags and sent him off to some relatives in England as soon as they found out. The bastards. He didn't turn up at college one morning and I knew then he was gone. They wouldn't talk to me, wouldn't give me his address or even let me know what city he was in. Told me if I tried to find them, I'd pay for it. Said I'd brought shame on their family and my own and said it would be a good idea if I disappeared as well.' 'The bastards. Who the hell did they think they were?' I said, feeling furious. 'They thought they were God. They really thought they had the right to ruin our lives because the way they saw it we had ruined theirs,' he said.

'Did you ever find Peter?' I asked. 'No,' he said, his voice heavy with regret. 'I tried for a while. I knew he was in London and I even went there to look for him, but it was useless. In the end I gave up. And that was when I fell apart. I started drinking a lot. I became violent. I even tried to kill myself. Put my head in the oven but they found me. Said I couldn't even do that right.'

'Was that when they sent you away?' I asked carefully, not wanting to trample on his past. 'Yeah, it was after that. They used that as an excuse. Said I was a danger to myself. But really they just wanted me cured. They actually thought they could cure me.' He laughed a sad, terrible laugh then. 'So they signed me in, had me taken away and left me to rot in that place for six months.' 'What did they do to you there?' I asked. I couldn't actually believe what I was hearing, couldn't believe that Anthony's parents had had him committed. 'Oh, Daniel, I still don't know if I can talk about that. It was horrible, so horrible. I didn't know if I'd ever get out. Didn't know if I'd ever be free again. And by the end of it, I thought I'd lost my mind. I didn't know who I was, I was frightened of everyone, of everything. They nearly took my mind, Daniel. Those bastards nearly took my mind. And all because they wanted to cure me.'

'Oh, Jesus, Anthony, why didn't you tell me any of this earlier?' I asked. 'Because I didn't want them to come between us. Because I wouldn't let them destroy things this time. Because I wanted all that to be in the past. And I suppose I didn't want you to think I was insane.' 'I know you're not insane, of course I know that,' I reassured him gently, and ran my fingers through his hair.

He looked up at me. 'You know, the funny thing is that they almost succeeded,' he went on. 'Those bastards in the hospital almost cured me. When I left that hospital I actually believed that I was sick, that there was something really wrong with me. I didn't even look at a man for ages. I started seeing girls again and I fought so hard to get rid of my feelings, to make them go away.' He paused for a minute. 'But I couldn't get rid of them. I started to sleep with men again, but I never got involved with them. I vowed I'd never let myself love a man again. For a long time I told myself this kind of love was wrong, was impossible. But then I met you. I met you, Daniel, and I began to feel hope again. I began to feel alive. I thought there was a chance of happiness.'

'But there is, there still is,' I pleaded. Anthony only shook his head sadly. 'No, my father saw us together one day and he began watching us, spying on us. He was watching us for weeks, Daniel, just waiting for my exams to finish to take me away.' I couldn't believe any parent could be so sly, so cunning, but I saw now that his mother and father were capable of anything. 'And then that Sunday I went for lunch, they gave me a choice. There's a girl from home, a girl who's at college with me, who's got herself pregnant, got herself in trouble with a tourist who's long gone,' Anthony said. 'Her parents are friends of mine and they've spoken, decided we're to marry. Either that or they'll put me away again, and God knows what will happen to her.' I looked horrified. I'd heard stories like this before, but had never expected one to come so close. 'And she, she's happy enough to marry you?' I was still puzzled. 'She has no other choice, Daniel, we have no other choice,' Anthony said with a bitter finality, looking at the ashes in the grate again.

We both fell asleep soon afterwards. We were so exhausted, so wasted by everything that had happened that night, we fell asleep right there, sitting on my bed. Just as dawn was breaking I woke up and saw that Anthony had gone, that he'd left me a second time. My heart ached, but in truth I'd known he wouldn't be there. I knew that night, no matter how much he loved me, no matter how much in love we were, it was all over. We knew we couldn't win against them. They'd already won. They'd made our love impossible.

The weeks that followed were a bit of a daze. It was midsummer in Dublin and the streets were painted with light well into the evening, but I only came to despise that city with its dirty river, its dank canals, its crooked houses and all her people full of relentless cheer, defying the past and the present with their keen knack of survival. I began to hate that city because it had told me a lie, had shown me everything that was possible, and then taken it all away from me. I had loved that city first and then when I met him, I had fallen in love with him in that same city. And now every corner I turned, every street I walked along, and every time I looked into the river, I only saw the reflection of our love, our love laid to waste. Oh, it was midsummer and everything was bright and everybody seemed happy, but all I wanted was to sit in darkness.

I started drinking heavily. Those first weeks without him I drank to make it all stop: my dreams, my twisted emotions, my faltering hope that I was wrong and all this was just a minor mishap in a miraculous relationship.

I retreated into the dark and gloomy bars on Parnell Street, on Marlborough Street, on Capel Street. Any bar where I knew I wouldn't see Anthony. Any bar that smelled of drink and misery and wasted lives. Sometimes the regulars would look at me funny, a stranger in their midst, but I didn't care. I was a stranger to myself anyway. I'd sit in those places, squandering my wages and whatever money I'd saved for the flat we'd planned to get together; avoiding eye contact, avoiding conversation and knocking back drink after drink. I even got barred from one of those pubs for starting a fight with a man who said I should take it easy, that I'd run myself into the ground if I continued drinking like this. I didn't care if I did.

I never went to the bars around Grafton Street that I used to go to, first on my own and then with Anthony. I started to hate those places with their cheap magic and their camp characters. I saw all of the men there as liars, as fools; pretending there was a place they belonged to, pretending that men could love one another in Dublin, in Ireland. To me they just went there to avoid the reality of the city, of the nation. They went there because they couldn't deal with the grim reality of their own lives, the inescapable fact that they would never be able to love as they wanted. More than I despised them though, I hated myself because I had been one of them. I too had thought I had a future, a real future, with Anthony. I had let my dreams lull me into a false sense of security, of hope, and now reality had me in its grip. It was choking me.

I stayed away from those bars, but that didn't stop me having sex with men. Oh no, I went at it like a maniac. I became a familiar face in the public toilets all over the city. Don't believe what they tell you about sex not having been invented in Ireland back then. I was there, I know. I know how easy it was. All you had to do was stand at a urinal for long enough, look at someone the right way, and you'd have it on a plate. And that was exactly what I did, night after night. I fucked strangers I didn't give a fuck about, I was with guys whose names I didn't even want to know, and I didn't enjoy any of it, hated all of it really. But I became addicted to those empty, unemotional exchanges, with the smell of shit and piss all around me. Those encounters that had nothing to do with love, that were as far from love as you could get. You see, I'd had enough of love. I no longer believed in love.

Most of those guys I've forgotten, forgot about them as soon as I walked away, but there is one face I cannot forget. It was a damp Monday night and I went into one of the pissoirs that had been put up along the Liffey for the Eucharistic Congress in the thirties, the one at the end of Capel Street. I thought I might get lucky, whatever that meant. There was a guy already in there and as soon as I went in our eyes connected and he gave me the nod. Wordlessly, we walked to a laneway over where Temple Bar is now. We were against the wall, in the shadows, when I saw how cold his eyes were, saw they were full of hate. He gave a low whistle then and a friend of his came around the corner. I needn't tell you what happened next.

I was punched, kicked, spat on, and called every configuration of faggot for what seemed like forever. And you know what? As I lay there curled up on the ground, my nose bleeding and my ribs aching, all I could think was that I deserved it. And for some reason I couldn't help laughing, couldn't stop myself laughing. When they'd finished with me I went to a bar where I cleaned myself up. After I'd had a drink, I went straight to the public toilets on O'Connell Street; to be with the first stranger I didn't care about.

So I suppose it's pretty clear I used drink and sex to forget, to try and help me forget. And I suppose you know it didn't work. Of course it didn't. It never does. I was only fooling myself if I thought I could make it all go away. Sure, the alcohol and that flesh that made my skin crawl would numb me for a while, but in the end all they ever did was sharpen the claws of my emotions, make bitter myths of my memories and leave me wasted and wretched, unable to forget.

The truth was I couldn't get Anthony out of my head. I couldn't let him go. I could still see him undressing, could still feel his hands on my body, could still see the clear blue of his eyes and his relaxed, happy smile. And all around the bedsit there was evidence of his existence and his exile: a scarf hanging on the back of a chair, a sweater I'd borrowed from him, a pair of underpants, a couple of long forgotten socks, a few books, a pen, a razor blade, a Bessie Smith record still on the gramophone player. I picked up the scarf and lifted it to my face. I could still smell his cologne off it. I wore his sweater for a few days at home, just to make me feel closer to him. I read his books again and played that record until I nearly wore it out. I ran his razor along my cheek. But still he was gone, still he would never return, and one day the pain was too much, was unbearable. I took all of his stuff, burned it on some waste ground near my house, and then I walked to the canal and threw his razor into the murky water.

But still I couldn't forget. More than ever, and in his absence, Anthony was everywhere. He was in my drunken dreams, in the darkness of my mornings. I would hear a voice on the street and, sure that it was him, I would turn around but he was never there. I would feel his hand caressing my neck as I worked away at my desk. I'd see somebody pass below my window and for a moment I'd think it was him, and lift my hand to rap against the glass, before the bitter fact that it wasn't hit me like a smack in the jaw. And when I was sitting on the bus, I'd think I saw him walking on the street and jump off to follow him. And when I cycled into work, I'd be certain that it was him I caught a glance of, cycling in the other direction. I saw him in bookshops and banks, walking by the river and going into the National Gallery. His ghost was all over that city. But he was never to be found.

I did see him one day though, really see him. I was walking along Abbey Street when the heavens opened. I took shelter in the doorway of the *Irish Independent* newspaper offices and as I stood there I saw a couple run by, a good-looking guy and a dark-haired girl, probably coming from the cinema. 'Another happy couple,' I thought bitterly, and it was only as they passed I realised it was Anthony and his fiancée. Anthony and his fiancée out for the afternoon. I stood there in the rain, staring after them until they'd disappeared into O'Connell Street. I thought about following them but I knew it was senseless. Instead I went to The Oval and drank myself stupid, chilled and numbed to the bone. I couldn't even cry anymore.

He was gone and though I thought about finding him, about taking him away, about escaping with him, I knew we would never make it. I knew they would find us somehow and when they did, they'd put him straight back in the asylum. I couldn't handle that, the thought of him wasting away in there, losing his mind day by day. I just couldn't do that to him. I loved him too much. And I knew that even if we ran away and they never found us, they already had Anthony in their clutches and wherever we were and whatever we did, he would always be ruled by fear. The fear that they were coming to get him, fear of the asylum. He would always be their prisoner, a prisoner of that terror, and that wasn't any way for him, for us, to live.

When Anthony left I knew I wouldn't be in *Blood Wedding*. Nothing seemed more ridiculous than the thought of taking part in some make-believe melodrama when reality had made a mess of my life. I didn't want to pretend to be somebody else, I couldn't pretend to be anybody else. I was lost in my own sadness, lost in myself. Anthony had told me he'd dropped out of the play and they'd found somebody to take his part, that I should still do it, that I couldn't let this ruin my life, ruin everything, but I knew if I went to those rehearsals all I would see was that he wasn't there. His absence in the collective illusion of that drama would have been as brutal a reality as his absence from my own life. I knew if I went there I would just break down, break down in front of everybody, and I didn't want that. I didn't want them to see me like that, though they might have been concerned and caring. I didn't even want to be around anybody I knew. I only wanted to be alone, to be alone or amongst strangers.

I didn't phone Maeve. I didn't call up to her. I didn't write to her. I just told Eileen to let her know I wasn't coming back, and when she tried to encourage me, said it might take my mind off things, I closed the discussion by walking away. Of course I felt the odd pang of guilt about leaving the production, especially seeing as they were rehearsing twice a week now the opening night was getting closer. And of course I knew the whole thing might fall apart without me and Anthony, but in truth I didn't care that much. All I cared about was the fact that I'd lost him. So I kept away from Eileen, kept away from Mountjoy Square, kept away from Maeve and Bewley's, and any place I might see any of those people from that production. I hoped I never saw any of them again. But my hopes came to nothing.

It was a Thursday evening and I was in Arnotts. I don't know what I'd gone in to buy, but anyway I was walking through the store when I saw Maeve at one of the perfume counters. I felt my heart race and before she had a chance to see me, I fled through the nearest exit. I turned down Henry Street and I was walking towards O'Connell Street, Nelson's Pillar rising up before me, when I felt an arm curl around mine. I turned around and there she was; Maeve. 'Daniel! It's so good to see you,' she exclaimed. 'Let's go and have a drink somewhere.' My heart was thumping, I felt myself begin to panic and I thought about turning and running, just running away. 'I can't,' I replied. 'I have to meet somebody and I'm already late.' I tried to walk away but she tightened her grip on my arm. 'Nonsense,' she said. 'Of course you have time for a drink with me.' And with that she led me over to the Gresham Hotel, her arm wrapped around mine.

'I'm really sorry I can't do the play,' I blurted out as soon as we sat down. 'I just can't do it.' 'Don't worry about that now,' she said. 'How have you been keeping?' The question seemed so absurd to me I snapped. 'Fantastic,' I replied sarcastically, 'Anthony's left and he's getting married next month, so I've been out celebrating his good fortune.' She looked concerned. She'd never seen me like this, so angry and bitter, but her concern only made me angrier. I didn't want her concern, I didn't want her sympathy, I didn't want her to care about me. And I didn't want to be sitting there with her, feeling so weak and exposed. She'd swooped down on me like a black crow, trapped me, and now I was terrified I'd break down there and then in front of her and never be able to go on.

I looked straight at her and did everything I could to stop myself from crying. I knew if I started then I'd never stop. 'Have you seen him?' I asked. 'Have you seen Anthony?' 'Yes,' she said after a moment of consideration. 'He called up to see me a few weeks ago.' I wanted to ask if he was okay, ask how he looked and what he was wearing. I wanted to know he was all right, but I didn't say anything. 'He loves you very much, you know that. He's very worried about you,' she went on. I couldn't look at her then, just couldn't look at her. What she was saying was true, I knew that. I knew Anthony better than I'd known anyone else and I knew being away from me, having to leave me and get married, would be killing him. But what point was there in Maeve telling me that he loved me, that he was thinking about me? It didn't bring us any closer together. We were still apart. And it only made the fact that it was over more monstrous, more unbearable. 'A damn lot of good that's going to do me, knowing that he's worried about me,' I shot at her. 'It doesn't change anything, does it?'

Maeve took a sip of her whiskey. 'Listen, Daniel,' she said, 'love has never been easy in this country. It never was and never will be, especially not for men like Anthony and you. But you have to try and hold onto that love. You can't let it turn to hatred. It will destroy you.' 'What would you know about it?' I demanded angrily, unable to see past my own pain. As I said it, I realised how stupid I was being, but it was too late. The words were already out and Maeve was suddenly angrier than I'd ever known her to be. I'd hit a nerve and she wasn't going to let me away with what I'd said.

'Listen, Daniel, I know a lot more about loss than I hope you'll ever have the misfortune to know,' she said, her voice like steel that cut right through me. 'I know what that loss, that grief, can do to somebody. I lost my father in the Civil War, I lost my husband in Spain. And there's something you don't know. I was carrying James's child when he went off to Spain, and when I heard the news I miscarried. I lost my child as well as everything else. So you drink your grief away, drink and go with strangers if that makes the pain any easier, but don't you dare tell me I don't know anything about loss.'

I felt so ashamed sitting there, more ashamed than I'd ever felt. 'Maeve, I'm sorry. I'm so sorry,' I apologised as soon as she'd finished. She sat there, unmoving, and her eyes were glistening with tears. I took her hand in mine. 'I'm sorry,' I repeated. She smiled then, smiled through the pain of her own memories. 'Let's just forget it, shall we?' she said. 'Let's have another quick drink and then I have to be off.' We had another whiskey, spoke for a short while about happier things, and then Maeve got up to leave. As she was walking towards the door, she turned and said, 'We're rehearsing this Saturday if you change your mind about the play. We'd all be delighted to see you there. We have somebody who's willing to step in, but if you come we'll think about giving you your part back.' She smiled as she walked away.

And sitting there, I began to think about going back to *Blood Wedding*, about doing the play, about joining the world of the theatre again. At first it seemed impossible and I told myself I wouldn't do it, but slowly I came around to the idea. By the end of that night, drunk though I was, I promised

myself I'd be in the play. I promised myself I'd play The Bridegroom. I promised myself I'd go on that stage. Whatever else
they'd taken from us, they wouldn't take our *Blood Wedding*.

11

July 1998

IT WAS A STILL, SILENT EVENING as Gerard and I made our way over to the theatre. I'd seen the poster for the play one day when I was walking down Pearse Street, on some hoardings around an old cinema. Suddenly there it was, an image of a horse lying in a pool of its own blood, and above it, printed in bold lettering: *Blood Wedding by Federico García Lorca.*

I stood there for a long time, thinking I might be seeing things, but I wasn't. It was real enough. The play was going to be on for a week at the end of July, on in a theatre in town, part of a festival to celebrate the centenary of Lorca's birth. I knew then I'd go to it, that I'd ask Gerard to come with me. Sure I felt terrified and panicked and wondered if the world was playing a big joke on me. Sure I knew it would take all the strength I could find to go and see that play, to sit through that tragedy again, but it was something I knew I had to do. I'd come this far and I knew running away now would be much worse than facing my final demons.

I'd told Gerard everything that night. After I'd convinced him to come to my house, pleaded with him to come with me because I couldn't, or wouldn't, talk about it there in that restaurant. We sat by the window in the sitting room, the night suspended in the sky, and I told him everything. Told him everything because it was time, because I knew, despite everything he'd said, he still believed in me, would believe me. Because I didn't want to lose him, couldn't lose him. Because he'd brought me home in a way; forced me back into that night and helped me stop lying and trying to forget. But besides telling him about that night, I wanted to tell him about Anthony and everything we'd shared before those dark, summer days laid us to waste. I wanted to tell him about the love we'd had, we'd shared. I wanted Gerard to believe in love, had to make him believe in it. And maybe then, unlike me, for all the years I've lived since that summer, he wouldn't spend all his midnights with strangers or in saunas. Maybe, just maybe, I could show him something else.

But there was so much to explain and he was so full of hate and anger and fear, I didn't know where to begin. I started slowly, as best I could. Gerard was looking out the window, only grudgingly half-listening, but after a while I saw him turn in my direction, move into what I was saying. He listened to everything as the half-light night fell over the sea. He listened to me talk, listened to me sigh, listened to me rage and cry, as I moved closer and closer to that night.

And sometimes I sailed on my words, and sometimes I galloped through my story, so eager was I to let him know, to make him understand. And then suddenly we were there, at that night. We were at that night and there was no escaping it, no running away this time. And with my hands shaking and my voice as tiny as a child's, I told Gerard what I thought I'd left on this island all those years ago, what I've never told anybody in the New World, in New York. I told him exactly what happened, looking away, looking anywhere but at him. And when I did look at him I could see the shock, the incomprehension on his face. I could see he wasn't sure what I was saying was real. He got up, got up and walked out of the house.

I watched him leaving, feeling my heart sink, thinking he was gone, this time for good, but when he left the garden he went to the wall where the sea and the road separate. I watched him as he stood there for a long time, staring out at the sea, and then I went out to him. I walked quietly up to him and when I called him, when he turned, I saw the tears streaming down his face. I took him inside, without saying anything, and we drank a bottle of whiskey as we awaited the new day.

The lights went down in the small theatre as we waited for the drama to begin. At first I felt nothing, I felt completely numb. I watched the actors move around the stage but that was all they seemed to me, actors on stage. I'd expected to feel so much, expected to be overwhelmed by the whole experience, but I just felt cold, felt as though this performance had nothing to do with me or my past. I looked around, looked at Gerard and at the audience, and as I did I heard The Mother speak, 'My dead men choked with weeds, silent, turning to dust. Two men like two beautiful flowers.' And listening to those words I suddenly found myself back in the heart of that tragedy, and all the bitter years I've lived since collapsed around me.

I was taken in again, riveted by the story. I watched the unhappy bride and Leonardo move around one another the morning of the wedding, speaking to one another from the abyss that has been put between them. I listened to Leonardo speak the words: 'You think that time heals and walls hide things, but it isn't true, it isn't true! When things get that deep inside you there isn't anybody can change them', and I knew how right he was. And though I knew, knew better than anyone, how it would all end, like a fool I found myself hoping they'd find a way, any way, to be together.

But I also found myself feeling sorry for The Bridegroom, The Bridegroom I'd played all those years ago, who would be cheated of his love, of his life, his wife, his future. Just as The Bride and Leonardo should never have been torn apart, so he should never have been so cheated. Oh, I could see the true tragedy of that play as if it were my own, and all the years I've lived without him. I could see how none of these three characters were right and none were wrong, not really. How they were all the sacrificial lambs of a society dominated by greed, by tradition. And how they were all fate's innocent handmaidens. How none of them could have cheated their fate.

It was during the wedding scene of the second act when I began to feel claustrophobic. The theatre became flooded with the sound of guitars, of poetry, of loud voices, and all the background characters began slowly, slowly circling the stage in white masks. I felt nauseous, I felt myself begin to panic, I felt drops of sweat break out on my forehead. I wanted to leave, I had to leave. I knew what was coming next and suddenly I couldn't bear it. I looked around for an escape route, to see if there was any way I could get out of there, but there wasn't. There was no way I could get out without disrupting the whole performance. I held my hands tightly together to stop them from shaking and I took a deep breath.

When I looked back at the stage, The Mother was speaking. 'The hour of blood has come again,' she said, and as she spoke I felt a chill run right through me.

July 1951

THE SKY WAS A HEAVY, leaden grey and all the summer roses were gasping for air that first night of *Blood Wedding*. It hadn't rained for weeks and the air was heavy and oppressive. We'd had a dress rehearsal the previous evening when somebody had let it slip that Anthony was getting married the following morning, the same day the play was to open. Married off as soon as was humanly possible by his twisted parents.

I felt so lonely, so forlorn and forgotten when I heard that. So alone I needed to be held by somebody, needed to be taken care of by somebody, needed to feel I had some feelings left. We had a drink at a pub on Parnell Street after the dress rehearsal and it was there, watching Fitzer, I decided I'd sleep with him, decided I'd take whatever cold comfort he could give to me.

It wasn't hard to seduce him, not really. We'd been spending more and more time together and there were moments when it was obvious to both of us there was a growing sexual attraction there. Fitzer's boyfriend was away in France for a few weeks, so I knew his house was free and if I wanted him, I could have him. The rest of the group didn't stay for long, knowing the next day was the big one, the first performance of the play before the public, and as they drifted away, one by one, I moved closer to my prey and he moved closer to me. We were both waiting for something to happen, we both felt nervous and light-headed at this vague possibility that had become a definite reality.

And so we were left alone in the pub, feeling exhausted but full of energy and so horny we might have done it there and then. I asked Fitzer if he wanted another drink, of course he said he did, and when I sat back down next to him, I let my leg rest against his. I let my leg rest against his, my heart beating like mad at my audacity, my forwardness, my indifference to the consequences. We moved in closer and closer to one other as we spoke about nothing in particular. I knew he wanted me as much as I wanted him and so after a while I asked him if we could have a drink back at his house.

We had sex a few times that night and it felt great. Felt great just to know I was wanted, desired, needed. Felt great to lay this older man down on the bed and make love to him. He held me that night when we slept and for a few hours I felt safe and not so alone. For a few hours I forgot all about Anthony in the escape of his embrace, in the arms of this man who would let me go just as easily as he'd given in to my flirtations.

The next morning when I cycled back to my flat, the memory of the night before still fresh on my body, I thought about Anthony. Feeling mean and spiteful, knowing none of this had been Anthony's choice: to leave me, to get married, I still hoped I'd somehow made him suffer a bit by sleeping with Fitzer. I thought of him seeing me leave Fitzer's house in Ranelagh that morning, thought of him spying that last, lingering kiss before Fitzer opened the door and let me go. Oh, I knew he'd be suffering already, stuffed into his straitjacket of a wedding suit as he went through those funeral rites of a wedding ceremony, but his suffering didn't erase mine. His suffering didn't wipe mine out. And though I felt sure he wanted me as desperately as I wanted him, admit it to myself though I wouldn't, couldn't, a new emotion had been born in me over the previous days, a new emotion that tasted delicious on my skin that morning I cycled home. Oh, none of it was his fault, just as none of it was mine, but that emotion made me feel alive again. That emotion, revenge.

I pushed open the heavy wooden door of the theatre, going over my opening lines in my head. Backstage the atmosphere was frenzied. We weren't at all sure that we were ready to do this, ready to put on the play before a real-life, breathing, coughing, watching, punishing public, but there was no longer time for doubts. We all knew we had to make that final leap of faith from rehearsal to real performance, even if it all still felt a bit rough around the edges, even if it all didn't seem real. We had to jump into the performance; not think, not consider, not wonder, just do it. And that was terrifying but thrilling. Though we were exhausted and frazzled, we were fuelled by a nervous tension and endless adrenalin.

Fitzer and I smiled at one another now and then, remembering the night before and knowing there was a good chance we'd end up together again, later on. The rest of the cast sat and stood, paced and pounded, putting the final touches to their performances. Affairs and friendships had begun quickly and expired just as rapidly, and all the old rivalries were still there, but despite everything that had gone on behind the scenes, we were all united that night. All committed to putting on a damn good show. One by one the members of the cast appeared in their costumes, and bit by bit that room took on the atmosphere of a village in the south of Spain, made all the more real by the unbearable heat in that small theatre.

Anthony's replacement was a drama student. His name

was Philip and he was a nice guy, but there was a part of me that hated him because he had taken Anthony's role. Oh, of course I knew it was wrong and he'd done us all a great favour by stepping in just a few weeks before opening night, but that didn't change the fact that there was somebody else where Anthony should have been. And besides, he was struggling with the part and there was no way he could play the role as well as Anthony. Still, there was no time to think of all that now, no time to think of anything but the rapidly approaching curtain up. And as the minutes disappeared, one after another, all I could think about was walking out on that stage.

I was all set to go on with Mary, my mother, in the opening scene, when I heard a commotion behind me and a squeal of delight. I looked around, wondering what was going on, and that was when I saw him. Anthony! Standing there in a tuxedo, looking at me with pained, imploring eyes.

I didn't know what was happening and just stood there, frozen to the spot. He quickly turned to Maeve and spoke to her in low, hushed tones. She went and spoke to Philip who, after a few moments, grudgingly nodded his assent. Maeve announced that Anthony would be playing Leonardo. Anthony would be playing Leonardo! Everything seemed to happen so quickly. There was no time to think, to understand. The audience was starting to get restless and the show had to go on. And though I felt a thrill of excitement to see him back, to see him there before me, I also felt confused, felt hurt, felt exhausted, and all I could do was give him a look of pure hatred before I walked out on stage.

Suddenly the play was on for real and I was The Bridegroom. I had to be him, nothing else mattered. Suddenly we were speaking and making the audience believe in another world, in the world of *Blood Wedding*. My mother lamented the death of her husband and one of her sons at the hands of the Felix family, of which Leonardo was a member, already terrified of losing me. I laughed at her worries. Why wouldn't I? I was young, I was happy, I was getting married. I didn't pay any attention to her when she said, 'Oh, is it right – how can it be – that a small thing like a knife or a pistol can finish off a man – a bull of a man?' Of course I didn't listen to the lamentations of an old woman. I left and went out to work in the vineyards. I exited stage left.

And there was Anthony, waiting to go on for his first scene. I wanted to go up to him and ask what had happened, demand to know how and why he'd made it back to me. And though I wanted to kiss him, to hold him, I decided I wouldn't. I couldn't. Not now. Not yet. Besides, we were The Bridegroom and Leonardo now. He was my bride's sweetheart, her true love, and though we hadn't met yet in the play, we knew we had to hate each other as we had in the rehearsals. We stood there for a few moments, staring at each other, and from the stage we heard the words 'My rose, asleep now lie, the horse is starting to cry. His poor hooves were bleeding, his long mane was frozen, and deep in his eyes stuck a silvery dagger.'

Soon afterwards he strode out on stage as Leonardo, lying about where he's been taking his horse, losing his temper when a girl comes to tell about the things I've bought for my wife-to-be. And all of Leonardo's frustrations, all his anger and bitterness and his inability to forget his sweetheart and see her be married to another man, were stretched across Anthony's face. More than anyone that night, he understood his character perfectly.

The scenes seemed to gallop by, one after the other. I went to meet my bride and her father with my mother and then when I looked on stage again, Leonardo was with my bride. It was the morning of the wedding and she stood there

in her petticoats. They both wound around each other in a
sensual dance of death, achingly expressing the love they
could not repress, the love that they could not bury. I felt my
heart beat faster as I watched them. I hated Leonardo right
enough but though his words hit me, The Bridegroom, like a
punch in the stomach, I felt myself, Daniel, knocked sideways
by them. I tried to stay in character, to think only as The
Bridegroom, but the words of that scene got me and for a
moment I didn't know who I was. And that was why it seemed
as though Anthony was speaking to me, was looking straight
at me, had ripped the skin and bone right off me and gone
straight to the heart when he said, 'To burn with desire and
keep quiet about it is the greatest punishment we can bring
on ourselves. What good was pride to me – and not seeing
you, and letting you lie awake night after night?' I felt my
heart stop, but I managed to snap out of it. He was Leonardo,
I was The Bridegroom and I would kill him.

Then it was the wedding party and my mother was
outside, cursing Leonardo and all of the Felix family for the
men they had taken from her. I remember those words she
spoke as clear as day, 'But it's not like that. It takes a long
time. That's why it's so terrible to see one's own blood spilled
out on the ground. A fountain that spurts for a minute, but
costs us years.' I felt her words catch in my throat, but what
did that matter? What did I, the happy bridegroom, think of
those words on this, my wedding day, the happiest day of my
life? Well, nothing really. I thought only of my future, of our
future, as the music struck up and the guests began to dance.
I had everything to live for, to dance for. But then I went to
look for my bride and she was gone, and Leonardo was gone.
'They've run away! They've run away! She and Leonardo. On
the horse. With their arms around each other, they rode off
like a shooting star!'

I watched the beginning of the next scene from the sidelines. I braced myself for the death, the two deaths that would take place: mine and Leonardo's. I was all fired up: sweating, raging, and cursing him in my head. I watched The Moon light up the stage and listened to the Beggar Woman. 'The coffins are ready, and white sheets wait on the floor of the bedroom.' And then I galloped on stage in pursuit of the runaway couple and when I stumbled on the beggar woman, she said she was cold, told me she could hear them, said she'd lead me to them. But I didn't know she was death. I didn't know or I wouldn't have gone. But I let her lead me to them.

And Leonardo and my wife were together. 'Because I tried to forget you and put a wall of stone between your house and mine... But I was riding a horse and the horse went straight to your door. And the silver pins of your wedding turned my red blood black.' My heart was pounding, my head was thumping, as I rode deeper and deeper into the countryside to find them. Faster and faster and the smell of blood was written across the stillness of the night. There was one last embrace between the two of them, with Leonardo saying, 'If they separate us, it will be because I am dead,' and The Bride saying, 'And I dead too.' But what did I care for their love that had destroyed my life, robbed me of my wife and insulted my honour? Faster and faster and I was upon them, and my knife was in my pocket, and I was ready to take my revenge. And then the stage was silent, empty. There were two terrible screams. Leonardo and I were dead.

Backstage I looked at Anthony. We were both shaking, both sweating, both overpowered by the emotions of the play and our own feelings. I could hear my breathing, my heart banging against my chest. I could see his eyes terrified and his body vital and powerful. As the last scene began on stage, I wanted to walk straight up to him. I wanted to kiss his lips, his neck, his ears, as he ran his hands along my spine and over my arse. We could have drunk from one another's bodies. We could have laid our passion down and dragged it along that floor and not stopped until every last bead of sweat had left us, and all the wild quiverings had stopped, and all of this soaring hunger had been satisfied. But I still couldn't. Not yet. Standing there, desperate for him, I wanted to make him pay a bit more before I gave myself so easily to him. He, it, everything that had happened, had almost driven me mad. So I wanted a little revenge, a small twist of the knife, before we fell into one another. Anthony was looking at me, staring at me, but I wouldn't give in just yet.

As he stood looking at me, I looked over at Fitzer. He looked at me, then at Anthony, and back to me. I didn't know what he was thinking, didn't really care. All I wanted was that look of confusion, despair and pain I saw on Anthony's face. That was what I wanted and when I saw it, I went to watch the last moments of the final scene. The scene of women: my mother, my bride and Leonardo's wife, all mourning their dead men. I watched them, those women left to survive, to carry on, to keep from going mad after their men have been taken away from them in a flash of knives. And as I watched their despair, I felt myself shiver even though it was sweltering in that theatre. I felt a deep shiver and I'm sure Anthony felt it too.

All of a sudden, the performance was over and we were walking out on stage, all of us together, smiling and shaking and lapping up the audience's applause. Later, backstage, Fitzer opened a couple of bottles of champagne, the corks flying across the room while all of us gathered around the foaming liquid with our glasses. 'To Federico and *Blood Wedding*,' Maeve said by way of a toast and we all lifted our glasses. 'To Federico and *Blood Wedding*,' we all repeated. 'And to Maeve,' Fitzer added happily. 'To Maeve,' we repeated, and two men who played woodcutters lifted her to their shoulders. We all cheered and clapped.

There was so much excitement and relief backstage that night. People milled around the place: taking off make-up, changing back into their regular clothes, talking about the night's performance, worrying that they had done little things wrong. We were all high as kites and there was no way we could go home and sleep now. We didn't have to, anyway. Maeve was having a party in her house, an opening-night party, and that was where we all headed. We tumbled out of the door of the theatre; speaking loudly, using gestures to go with every word, actors still caught up in the night's drama, unable yet to stop acting. I remember Maeve catching my eye as I left without Anthony and the concerned, worried kind of look on her face. But I thought nothing of it. I knew what I was doing. Everything would be fine.

Back at the party, we all seemed to get drunk very quickly. I don't know if it was the heat, the fact that nobody had eaten before the performance, or that final release of tension after the months of preparing for the play. Anthony had tried to speak to me in the hall, but I'd brushed him off, saying we could talk later. He looked desperate, looked terrified, but I couldn't bear to talk to him then. Later, later, I'd make it okay. Later we'd lie down together. But for now I just wanted him to see that I'd been okay without him, that I could be okay without him. Of course we'd sleep and love and live together; now that he'd come back, now that he'd come back. But my pride was burning inside me, my pride and that twisted thirst for a small revenge, a thirst as strong as that for the whiskey I drank, glass after glass, unable to stop.

I told him we'd talk later and left him sitting on the couch, beside Rosaleen. She was full of chat and I left him there. Left to get another whiskey, to flirt with Fitzer; feeling wild, feeling reckless, feeling like I owned that room. I knew this would drive Anthony mad, knew it would make his blood boil, and make him want me even more, make him want me so much he'd never let me go again, no matter what happened. I knew he was watching me throw myself at Fitzer, just as Fitzer knew what I was doing and kept looking at Anthony. He must have seen how on edge Anthony was, how exhausted and sick he looked, because he tried to make me stop, tried to get me to talk to Anthony, but that only made me more determined. Oh, I wasn't going to sleep with Fitzer or anything like that. I couldn't have done that, wouldn't have done that, to Anthony. I was madly, desperately in love with him, but suddenly so much in love with him I wanted to hurt him like he'd hurt me, or like they'd hurt me, us. I just wanted him to see what he'd given up, wanted him to know that it wouldn't be that easy to reclaim what he'd left behind, his lost treasure. I just wanted him to think that I was going to sleep with Fitzer in front of him, jut wanted him to think it. That was all.

A sing-song had broken out. Maeve was singing. 'Summertime, and the livin' is easy. Fish are jumpin' and the cotton is high.' Anthony was staring at us. 'Can you come with me for minute, Fitzer?' I asked. 'There's something I need to talk to you about.' 'Come with you? Where?' Fitzer wondered. He knew I was up to something, knew it. 'I don't think it's me you should be talking to in any case,' he said. 'Anthony's waiting for you.' 'He'll be okay,' I hissed. 'Just come with me for a minute.' We left the room and I led Fitzer up flight after flight of stairs, up to the small room at the top of the house, the room I'd fallen asleep in that night when everything had begun, after I'd kissed that man. I had a glass of whiskey in my hand, spilling everything I didn't drink on the way up. I didn't know exactly what I was doing, didn't know what I wanted to do, only that I wanted Anthony to burn with jealousy. Only that I wanted him to fight for me, really fight for me this time.

But when we got to that room, I just felt foolish, felt stupid and cruel. I felt so drunk I just let Fitzer help me to the bed. And suddenly, lying there, all I wanted was Anthony beside me, for Anthony to lay down and hold me. 'Are you okay?' Fitzer asked as he went to open the window. It still hadn't rained and it was stifling in the room. 'I'm okay,' I slurred, crying now. 'Will you go and get Anthony for me? Will you tell him I'm here?' I pleaded. 'Sure,' said Fitzer and he put his hand on the door knob.

Everything happened so quickly then, so quickly. When he opened the door there was a flash of a knife, Leonardo's knife, Anthony's knife. There was a slash as the blade cut Fitzer's arm. It was Anthony. Anthony, crazier than I'd ever seen him. He lashed out again at Fitzer but he managed to dodge him. I sat up in bed, wondering if this was really happening. Fitzer tried to get the knife out of his hand but it was no use. Anthony was wild, out of control, out of his mind, and he pinned Fitzer against the wall, put the knife up to his throat, and told him if he didn't get out he'd kill him. Fitzer left and hurried downstairs.

Anthony was on top of me then, standing over me, with the knife pressed to my throat. I was terrified, terrified as he ran the blade along my skin. 'Why didn't you wait for me? Why didn't you wait for me?' he demanded. 'I… I, Anthony, I don't know. I'm here now, you're here now. It's going to be okay.' I knew then how insane what I'd done was, knew it had pushed him over the edge. 'I was sitting there, sitting there with that girl and my parents, and all I could think about was you. All I could think about was getting back here.' 'It's okay, Anthony, we're together now,' I pleaded with him. 'Just drop that thing.' He was swaying with the drink and his eyes had turned hollow. 'It's too late,' he murmured. 'It's too late. I left it all for you, Daniel. I ran away from my wedding. They're probably searching for me now. It's too late.'

He took the blade from my throat then and went and stood by the window, looking down at the grey church on Gardiner Street and the trees that stretched out in the distance. 'There's no place for us to go now, no place for us to go,' he said. 'Look what they've done to us.' 'Anthony, please just listen,' I cried, trying to get him to calm down, trying to find a way out of this. 'Anthony, please,' I repeated and got up off the bed. He took another look out at the church. 'I loved you, Daniel. I really loved you,' he said, but as I began walking towards him I saw the glint of the blade as he put the knife to his own throat. There was a fountain of blood as he fell to the floor. The door opened and Maeve and Fitzer were there. There were two screams.

12

August 1998

I WAKE UP EARLY THAT MORNING. The morning we're going to his grave. I've slept well the night before. Funny that, how I've slept better than I have in all these years. I go to the window to let the sunlight in. I open the shutters and there it is below me, glistening like a jewel, Granada!

As the morning heat is rising Gerard and I take a taxi to where he died, to where they believe Lorca died that summer the Civil War broke out. When the soldiers of Granada revolted, joined Franco's uprising and rounded up any dissidents, anybody who didn't subscribe to their fat, fascist beliefs. That summer they took him to a lonely piece of land outside the village of Víznar and shot him. That summer they executed him for his Republican sympathies and then fired two shots up his ass for being a queer. Ay, the loneliness of your death, Federico!

For years I tried to forget you. Forget your *Blood Wedding*, forget that vision of his body soaked in blood. I tried to forget, did everything I could to forget, to keep myself from going under, to stop myself sinking into the darkness. But you and he always came back to me and I couldn't forget how I'd driven him to his death. How I'd made him feel so alone, so lost, he could only see one way out. I was left with his blood on my hands, left living but stained, left breathing but barely.

And your words, they came to infect me after he died. Wherever I went, whatever I did, I couldn't escape them. They were always going round and round inside my head. You wouldn't let me go. You wouldn't let me go. Neither of you. And when I opened a newspaper and saw one of your plays had come to New York City, I would only feel even more haunted by you, by him. And even when I'd pass a bar or a community hall where they were speaking Spanish, your Spanish, I would cross the street. The weight of that language was unbearable. It reminded me of everything I'd done, everything I'd lost, was so caught up with my guilt I couldn't separate them. Ay Federico, even in that city that you had visited, that man-made metropolis rising from the sea, even in New York City, I could feel your ghost and his following me through the streets.

This is where you died, Federico. You'd come home to Granada for a brief stay when the military revolt broke out in Spanish Morocco in July 1936. The following day the Falangists captured Seville. Then the soldiers in Granada joined this national movement and soon enough the city was in their hands. The executions began: teachers, lawyers, doctors, workers, anybody suspected of being a Red, a Bolshie, anybody who sympathised with the workers.

They were coming for you, coming for you. Any day, any hour, any minute, they'd drag you away to your death. And for years I asked myself if you could have escaped, if you should have escaped. Fled to France or Mexico. Before they came to your family's home and put you under house arrest. But you went to hide in the house of a friend of yours, a poet, some of whose family were Falangists. And there you stayed for days, in that house beside Falangist headquarters, playing folk songs on the piano. Did you see your death, did you know you were going to die? Is there any way you could have escaped your fate?

And if I hadn't pushed you over the edge, Anthony, if I hadn't taken Fitzer upstairs that night, or slept with him the night before that? Or if I had found you, if I'd come and found you and taken you away? Or never let you go, never let you go that night you came to see me in my flat? Or never let them get you in the first place? Or made you feel safe enough, loved enough, they wouldn't have been able to get to you, been able to take you away? Then would you still be living, would you still be alive?

And sometimes I thought if we had never let your black blood poetry into our lives, Federico, then everything would have been okay. For years I cursed your fate and your tragedy, your silver daggers bringing two young men to their knees. Oh, I knew the power of the theatre that night, that night he died, that same night the Abbey Theatre burned down in Dublin, and I've never trusted it since.

They came and put you in prison, took you to this lonely olive grove and shot you. And I put that knife to your throat, or just as good as. You both fell, two men who were lions. You both fell. And I was left with your poetry and his blood. Left to live all these years.

But now I'm tired of hating myself, tired of blaming myself, tired of feeling bitter and cheated, tired of all these years with death asking me to lie down and curl up inside it, ever since that night you left, when I put the knife to my own throat afterwards, dropping it only at the last minute, knowing I couldn't go through with it. I still have my life, what's left of it, and I'll live it for both of you. I came here to Granada, came here to this last city of the Moors to fall to the Catholic Kings, to your city of the gypsies, to let you go, to finally let both of you go. I came here to say sorry. I came here to this small monument where they say you fell, came here to say goodbye. To say goodbye to both of you, to you, Federico, and you, Anthony. My one and only love, Anthony. I came here to say goodbye.

I take the roses we've brought in my hand, and as I do a thorn pricks my finger and a few drops of my blood fall and mingle with your earth. And I still can't see any sense in your deaths, but I know I'll never understand them. I never, never will.

We stand there for a while, silent, before I let Gerard take my arm and slowly lead me away. 'I got the results of the HIV test,' he says as we walk away. 'I'm negative. I'm clean.'

August 1951

IT WAS A MORNING IN early August when I boarded the ship that would take me to America. There was a chill in the air, the first whisperings of the September to come. Maeve and Fitzer were there, come to say farewell. My family had said goodbye to me the day before when they came down to Cork; my mother uncomprehending, devastated, my father trying to keep it together. It was horrible saying goodbye to them, just horrible. That's all I can say about it. And parting with Maeve and Fitzer that morning; when they took me in their arms, one after the other, and said that they were sorry, so sorry, told me it wasn't my fault, told me that they'd be thinking of me every day.

I didn't know what I was doing, didn't know where I was going, not really, but now there was no other choice. Not after what I'd done, not after what I'd forced him to do. Not after the police had got involved, not after they and Anthony's family had forced me to leave. They said they'd have me put in prison. Oh, they knew it was suicide, knew Anthony had taken his own life, but they made me believe they could pin it on me. They made me believe that I was to blame, which I fully believed I was. And even if they couldn't have me put away for his death, I knew they could and would have me thrown in some asylum for being a queer. I wouldn't have that, I wouldn't. Oh, I was confused and wrecked and terrified but I wouldn't let them destroy me too.

The newspapers got word of the story soon after it happened and though they never said anything outright, their bland allusions were enough to see me condemned in the eyes of that pitiless public. And all you twisted bastards of that barren island came baying for my blood. You made of me the charming, queer, killer. You made of me the monster that you put outside yourselves to make yourselves feel safer, more good, more honest, more saintly. And Maeve was the demonic witch, the twisted queen lording over perverted parties. You tried to destroy her too, with your whispers and accusations, but she was stronger than that, had been through worse than that. She continued going to Bewley's night after night, despite you all, continued going there for years. Even in old age, when she was just an eccentric, elegant old lady to the young people working there, who looked to the future and not to the past.

And Fitzer, he nearly left, nearly went back to New York. He felt so guilty about what had happened, as if some of the blame was his, as if it had somehow been his fault. But in the end he stayed. He stayed with his partner; they stayed and continued to live together in Dublin. He stayed. And though he didn't work for years, you flocked to the theatre for his last show, a monologue he'd been working on for ages. You praised him and applauded him and laid your garlands at his feet, you smiling, island hypocrites.

It was time to go. The steam was rising from the ship, almost everybody had boarded, and it was time to go. I embraced them one last time and walked up the gangplank. When I was up on deck, I looked down and Fitzer had his arm around Maeve and Anthony had been buried in a lonely grave that I couldn't have brought myself to visit even if I'd been allowed. I looked down at them and waved. I looked at that island one more time and as the ship began to move out to sea, I turned away and promised myself I'd never come back. He was dead, he was gone, and Ireland had died within me. I looked out towards the New World.

And it was a warm August morning when you came to the airport with me, Gerard. After I'd packed up all my things and had them shipped back to the States. After I'd said goodbye to that house in Seapoint that looks out over the sea. There was nothing left to do but say our goodbyes, to get on that plane and come home. And I held you in my arms for a few long moments, my friend, before I walked away, walked away before I started crying. And when I turned back, just before I went through security, you smiled and traced your arms in the air and stamped your heels like the flamenco dancer we'd seen in that bar in Granada. I smiled at you and then walked through. I smiled until I cried, broke down and cried like an old fool.

I look out my window at a Manhattan day in early September. The city is full of life, of movement, of noise. I know I won't sink, I know I won't be afraid to think, not this September.

Skin Lane
Neil Bartlett

Shortlisted for the Costa Novel Award 2007

'A cunningly narrated story in a totally original milieu. A tale of the unexpected' Judges of the 2007 Costa Novel Award

'Neil Bartlett is a protean polymath of a creator, ceaselessly inventing new artistic worlds – and then conquering them. *Skin Lane* is a fiendishly taut little psycho-shocker that recalls Simenon at his most hardboiled and Highsmith at her creepiest. It made the hairs rise on the back of my neck and I still can't get them down again' Will Self

'*Skin Lane* is a hymn to a quiet man who leads a highly disciplined life and practices his trade – until one day passion drives him over the edge. The characters are masterfully drawn but the central focus of this book is London itself – a grey London of the past perfectly evoked in this hushed, confidant prose' Edmund White

'In his *Skin Lane* Neil Bartlett shows eerie skill in his evocation of a small, secret pocket of the City of London… masterly in its sinister progression' Francis King, *Spectator*

'Original, disturbing and… beautifully written, this is an always fascinating work' *Literary Review*

'Affectionately evoked… always apt and precise… *Skin Lane* grips with real force' *TLS*

'A potent fable about the destructive power of lust and an unsettling psychological study in the manner of Patricia Highsmith' *Daily Telegraph*

'A modern day fairy tale dripping with the tension of desire and repression that lingers long in the memory after the final page has been turned. The journey may not be comfortable but it is certainly compelling' *Attitude*

'Intense, erotic and highly theatrical, with a shocking climax and, as with all Bartlett's work, a complex take on our history' *Gay Times*

'With *Skin Lane*, Bartlett further demonstrates his skills as a creative polymath of the highest order' *Dazed & Confused*

'Charting the outer limits of desire and personal rejection with compassion, made all the more striking because of the unsparing clarity of Bartlett's vision, *Skin Lane* pulls off the triple whammy of being shocking, sexy and tenderly humane' *Metro*

'Claustrophobic and tense... Bartlett is an expert in the stories we tell ourselves and why we tell them' *Time Out*

'A beautiful book; well-proportioned with supple, sensuous text and an aching raw heart at its core' *Aesthetica*

'A haunting read... both merciful and poignant' *Yorkshire Post*

'Beautifully constructed and evocatively written' *What's On In London*

'A precise work of intensity' *Herald*